NATIC

RALPH COTTON

"One of the best Western writers today."
...Western Horseman

WOLF
VALLEY

Formerly ***Guns of Wolf Valley***

WESTERN CLASSICS

WOLF VALLEY

RALPH COTTON

He may be reached at **www.ralphcotton.com**
or **ralphcotton@yahoo.com**

Cover photo & inside wolves from **123RF.com**

Cover design & book layout by Laura Ashton
laura@gitflorida.com

Author's photo, p.283, by Shay Morton

ISBN: 978-1530303137

Printed in the United States of America

Some Reviews by Amazon Readers

by 'Jerry' – **Crazy Hypocrite**

Waco was not the first town in Texas to come under the control of an evil man like David Koresh.

by David Carlyle – **a Mildly Racy Story**

Cotton's story is about a bank robber, CC Ellis, and a corrupt priest, Jessup. The priest runs a town, likes to see people suffer, takes other men's wives, and is dishonest and greedy.

The story starts with a gunfight, then moves to two romances, more fighting, several struggles between Jessup and many of the other characters in the story, and a decision by CC to reform. Due to an unexpected event near the end of the five-star story, CC dumps his 'good guy' plan, and returns to his outlaw objective.

by Robert Gage – **best yet**

Cutting edge story, one of Ralph Cotton's best yet! If this isn't made into a film, Hollywood is missing a great story.

Millions Of Ralph Cotton Novels In Print Worldwide

For Mary Lynn ... *of course*

PART I

Chapter 1

Christian Ellis brought the big bay to a halt at the water's edge. He wasn't thirsty, nor was the horse, yet he stepped down from the brush-scarred bay with his canteen in hand and let the animal poke its muzzle into the creek. He sank the open canteen into the cold water as if letting it fill while he himself sipped moderately from his cupped hand and looked off across a slate gray sky. To the west a boiling darkness had spread the width of the horizon. A streak of lightning licked down from the storm's black belly like a snake giving warning before its strike. But right then the coming storm was his least concern, he thought, turning a wary eye to the wide dissolute land surrounding him.

Only moments earlier something across the creek had caused a covey of birds to rise from within the shelter of towering pine. He'd watched the hard batting of wings as the birds raced away on the wind. Since then a white-tailed doe and her fawn had broken cover and crossed the creek less than fifty yards ahead of him, exposing themselves to him in a way no creature of the wilds would do without good reason, storm or no storm. Ellis pushed back his broad-brimmed flop hat, raised his cupped hand and rubbed water around on his face while he guardedly searched the woods across the shallow creek. Someone was there; he had no doubt.

Indians ...? He didn't think so. No Indian would have

stirred up the wild life that way. *Then who ...?* He considered as he sipped a mouthful of water, spit it out in a stream and wiped his gloved hand across his lips. Whoever it was they had to know he'd seen them scare up the birds and the deer, he reminded himself. After all that, it would have only been good manners to show themselves to a fellow traveler.

Even as he considered the situation, from within the cover of the tree line he saw four horsemen ease their animals into sight and nudge them slowly toward him, riding abreast, spreading out as they crossed the shallow rippling creek. *Trappers,* he surmised, noting the ragged road clothes and dusty rawhides they wore, each of them with a stack of wolf pelts draped over his horse's rump. They carried their bedrolls and trappings piled high and tied behind their saddles. They carried themselves with a menacing air. Three of them carried rifles across their laps. All of them carried pistol butts in tied-down holsters. *Not good ...*

Standing up slowly, Ellis reached his right hand inside his faded black riding duster, took out a wadded bandanna, dried his mustache and eased the bandanna back inside his duster. Only this time, when his hand went inside the long frayed duster, he wrapped it around the bone-handled butt of the long-barreled Colt he carried in a shoulder harness under his left arm. From the west, thin raindrops blew in ahead of the storm and dotted his black duster sleeve. The wind strengthened.

A few steps ahead of the other three riders, a man with a dark beard called out without stopping his horse, "Hello the creekbank."

"Hello the *creek*," Ellis called out in reply. Then he stood silent with a trace of a polite smile on his face. Yet, as he'd spoken he'd swept his broad-brimmed flop hat from his head with his left hand in a gesture of courtesy and held it down in front of him, using it to hide the big Colt as he slipped it from beneath his duster. A single larger raindrop blew in, this one landing coolly on his bare cheek. Wind licked at his hair.

The bearded man did not see Ellis's big Colt, yet something in this stranger's bearing instinctively caused him to stop his horse fifteen feet away in the clear rippling water. The other riders drew to a halt behind him. "We've been watching you the past ten miles or so, mister," said the bearded man, without offering to introduce either himself or the other riders. As he spoke he looked Ellis up and down.

"I thought as much," Ellis said flatly. "Now what is it I can I do for you?" From the corner of his eye he caught a glimpse of lightning as it twisted in the distant blackness.

Jerking his head back toward the three men behind him, the bearded man said, "Me and the boys here take wolves for bounty. But we're also what you might call *gatekeepers* for these parts." Without taking his eyes off Ellis, he gestured a hand taking in all of the northern mountain line. "From here on up, there will be no law to protect you. You'll do as you're told if you want to feel welcome up here." He spoke above the growing whir of wind.

Ellis only stared in silence. From the blackness came the rumble of thunder. More thin raindrops slipped in and appeared silently on his duster sleeve.

"Yeah," said one of the other three men, the only one without a rifle across his lap. "We're what you might call the *welcoming party* up here." He spread a nasty grin, and his hand rested on his pistol butt.

"Shut up, Singer," the bearded man barked over his shoulder at him. "I'm the one doing the talking here." He leveled a harsh stare at Ellis, and added, "We kill off wolves, keep away bummers, undesirables, Injuns and whatnot. It costs us a lot of time and expense to do all that."

"I bet it does," Ellis commented quietly, keeping both his smile and his poise in place.

The bearded man cocked his head slightly to one side and asked, "Do you understand what I'm getting at, mister?"

"I believe I do," said Ellis, his eyes going from man to man, sizing them up, already knowing trouble was upon him. "I believe you're saying I owe you something for traveling through here."

"Call it a road tax if you will, for providing safe traveling for pilgrims such as yourself." The man grinned and added, "I can see you *do* understand the ways of the world clear enough."

"I understand all right," said Ellis. "Problem is, I allow no money for such expenses."

The man shrugged as if not realizing what Ellis meant. "We can sympathize with a man being short on cash, times being such as they are." He eyed Ellis's horse and said, "We just lost our pack mule two days ago. I always say, a good riding animal is just as good as legal tender when a man finds himself in a spot."

"Funny, I always say that myself," said Ellis. His smile remained as he continued to stand in silence, leaving the man unsure of what to say or do next.

Finally the man cleared his throat and said, "So, if you have no cash, we'll be obliged to take the animal off your hands."

"There he stands," said Ellis, giving a nod toward the big bay. "Take him whenever you're ready."

But in spite of his invitation, the riders made no move forward. Studying the resolve in Ellis's cold gray eyes, the bearded man said, as if it had just dawned on him, "You've got a gun cocked behind that hat, don't you?"

"You can count on it," said Ellis, his smile still showing beneath his broad dark mustache.

Tension set in upon the riders. The first sheet of rain blew in mildly, the hissing sound of it moving up the creek. Duster tails fluttered sidelong, as did the horses' manes. Not backing off, the bearded man said firmly, his hand tightening on his rifle stock, "Mister, there are no exceptions. Everybody pays."

"I don't," said Ellis. "Be advised of it and move on."

"You better do some quick counting," said the bearded man. "There's four of us. We are not men to argue with."

"Nor am I," said Ellis, still smiling. "Now either take that horse like you threatened to or ride away. I don't want to see or smell any of you on my trail again."

As the man's hand tightened on his rifle stock he asked, "Who are you, mister? I like to know who I kill."

"My name is Christian Clayton Ellis. Any other questions?"

Lightning twisted and curled, the body of the storm having drawn closer. "CC Ellis!" one of the riders said as if suddenly stricken with awe. His words were followed by a hard clap of thunder that caused the creekbed to tremble for a second. The other riders looked stunned at the realization.

"You're one of them long riders, ain't you?" said the man with the beard, his hand already coming up with the rifle, his thumb cocking it on the upswing.

"I am," Ellis said calmly. With his hat in his left hand he swung open his black duster as his right hand streaked forward with the big Colt.

"Hold it!" the bearded man shouted, trying too late to call off what he and his men had started. But Ellis had already triggered the first shot into action, the first bullet blasting through the bearded man's chest and sending fragments of his heart spraying through the back of his shirt.

Left to right Ellis's Colt rose and fell with each blast, the first two shots finding their targets easily, one lifting a man from his saddle as he let go of his reins. The next shot caused a horse to rear, its rider holding firmly on to the reins as he flew from the saddle, his horse raising high on its hind legs and splashing down onto its side in a high sheet of water. But as Ellis's third shot leveled and exploded toward the man carrying only a tied-down pistol, Ellis felt a burning pain stab his side, another along the side of his head as the man drew and got off two shots before slumping in pain himself. Blood spewed from a gaping wound in the man's right shoulder.

Ellis raised his Colt again with much effort, feeling the world began to wobble beneath his feet. He watched the young man spur his horse away along the center of the shallow creek. The man whose horse had fallen with him arose from the water and ran limping away behind the rider calling out, "Singer! Wait! Help me!" But the rider wasn't about to turn back for his wounded comrade. Nor was his wounded comrade about to look behind him. If he had, he would've seen his horse rise up, shake himself off, run in a wide circle around the creek and come loping along at a slow trot, following him.

Ellis managed to get off one more shot at the fleeing men, but he hadn't really aimed it. The shot was meant to keep them running, and it did. Then, as soon as the two were out of sight, Ellis allowed himself to slump to his knees, rain pelting him, his side and his head bleeding steadily. Pain racked him until he rolled into a ball on the wet gravelly creekbank, feeling the world turning dark around him. *Of all times and places in this world for a man to get shot*, he thought to himself, catching a glimpse of the high desolate land with the storm moving in above him, *why did it have to be here and now?* He had business....

Young Dillard Mosely and his yellow hound, Tic, moved with caution across the creek, loose wolf pelts that had fallen from the horses' backs bobbed and floated past them. When Dillard eased onto the flat sandy bank in a crouch, the hound went off a few feet and raised a paw and sniffed curiously toward one of the two bodies that lay bobbing gently in the shallow water. "Mister?" Dillard inquired softly, seeing no sign of life from the man lying in a ball with his pistol clutched to his bloody stomach. He looked all around, first at the two bodies lying in the rippling water, then at the three horses standing a few yards away, their reins hanging loose, Ellis's big bay standing off by itself, away from the other two. "Holy moly!" the boy whispered breathlessly, feeling rain run down the back of his neck. He looked at the hound, who had ventured over with his neck stretched out only inches from the gaping exit wound on one of the dead men's back. "Tic! Get away from there!" he said. The hound backed away grudgingly but continued to probe the air surrounding the dead, rain dripping steadily from his drooping ears.

Dillard heard a low moan come from the man on the bank, and the sound startled him so badly it sent him scurrying backward, causing him to slip on the wet ground and fall solidly on his behind. Noting the boy's action, the hound looped through the water and stopped beside him. "Stay back, Tic!" Dillard whispered, regaining his courage and curiosity. He stood up in a crouch and wiped a hand across the wet seat of his trousers. From beside him he picked up a short stick, ventured forward with it and poked the man carefully in his ribs.

"Get out of here, kid," Ellis managed to say in a strained raspy voice, thinking that at any moment the two men might return, see his condition and come to finish him off. Blood filled his eyes and ran freely down his face.

"You—you're alive!" Dillard stammered, his heart pounding furiously in his chest. The stick flew from his hand; he jumped back a foot. Tic growled low and took a defensive stand beside him. "Don't—don't you want help, mister?" he asked.

"No … get *away!*" Ellis said with much effort, unable to explain himself. Pain held him locked in its grasp, yet he wiped a hand across his bloody eyes and forced himself to look off in the direction the two fleeing men had taken.

Seeing him search along the creek, Dillard said, "Don't worry, mister. They're gone."

But the boy's words didn't satisfy Ellis. He struggled against his pain and pushed himself up onto his knees, feeling warm blood oozing between his fingers as he pressed his left hand to his wounded side. Rain ran down him in bloody streaks. "I said ... get away from me!" he growled, managing to jiggle the Colt in his right hand, trying to frighten the boy.

It worked, he told himself, his gun slumping as he watched both the boy and the dog scurry backward a few feet, turn and run splashing across the shallow creek. *And stay away ...* He was unsure if he had actually said the words or only thought them. He felt the world turn dark around him once again, this time as he began trying to drag himself to the cover of a large boulder lying half sunken in the ground.

From the other side of the creek, Dillard Mosely stopped only long enough to look back and see the man crawling, dragging himself with his gun hand, the gun still in it. As Dillard watched, he saw the man stop, stretched out on the wet ground. The man appeared to go limp, the gun relaxing on the ground in front of him. "Come on, Tic! Hurry!" Dillard said, turning, then running as fast as he could along the wet slippery path toward the house sitting up on the hillside a hundred yards away.

Inside the house Callie Mosely heard her son calling out to her as she ran down off the porch with the rifle in her hands, a blanket thrown over her head. Before she'd reached the path leading down toward the creek, she saw Dillard and the hound run into sight through the falling rain. "Dillard, up here!" she called out, looking past him along the trail for any sign of someone chasing him.

"Mother!" the young boy shouted loudly, running even faster at the sight of her coming toward him, the hound running on ahead of him now, barking loudly. "Hurry, Mother! He killed them all! He killed them all! I saw the whole thing from across the creek!"

"Good heavens, Dillard!" said Callie Mosely, stooping, catching her son into her arms as if he might otherwise race straight past her. "Didn't I tell you to get home before the storm? What on earth are you talking about?"

"A gunfight, Mother!" Dillard gasped, ignoring her question. "A real, honest-to-God gunfight!" His heart pounded wildly in his chest. "There's dead men lying everywhere! Hurry! Come see!"

"A gunfight?" Callie had heard the gunshots through the coming storm only moments ago and had wiped flour from her hands on a towel and taken her husband's rifle down from above the hearth. "Who? Where?" she asked, keeping one hand on her son's wet shoulder to settle him down as she stood and once again gazed warily along the path behind him. At her feet the dripping hound barked loudly, caught up in the excitement. "Quiet, Tic!" she demanded, slapping a hand at the hound's rump.

"At the creek, Mother!" Dillard said, gulping hard to get his words and mind settled enough to make sense. "Some of Falon's wolf hunters shot it out with another man on the creekbank!"

"They killed some poor traveler?" Callie asked.

"No, ma'am!" said Dillard. "He shot all four of them … killed two of them, and the other two hightailed it away!"

Hiking her dress, she started down the path with the rifle raised in both hands. "Now, Dillard, I'm sure you're mistaken!"

"No, ma'am!" Dillard exclaimed, rushing a bit ahead of his mother, the hound circling him, barking loudly. "He shot them, all four! You'll see! Hurry! He's bleeding something awful!"

"You mean"—Callie hesitated in her tracks for a moment—"you mean he is still alive?"

Dillard ran back, grabbed her hand and pulled her forward. "Hurry, Mother, please! I think he is! I heard him groan! He spoke to me!"

Spoke to him …? Callie wanted to stall for a second, yet she hurried on at her son's insistence, saying in a chastising tone of voice, "Dillard James Mosely, did you get close to Frank Falon's men?"

"No, Mother! I didn't!" he said, pulling her along. But as she began to once again hasten her steps, he said, "I did get close to the stranger though, just for a minute! Just long enough to make sure he's alive! That was all right, wasn't it?" He hurried her along through the pelting rain, his small damp hand gripping hers.

"Dillard Mosely!" she said without answering him as they splashed along the path, "what*ever* am I going to do with you?"

Chapter 2

"Wait, please!" Kirby Falon had pleaded with Willie Singer, watching him disappear out of the creek, up along the bracken and overgrowth toward the north trail. Lightning glittered, followed by a hard clap of thunder.

"Go to hell, Kirby!" Willie Singer said to himself, not even looking back at the wounded man. Kirby Falon limped along trying to catch up to him on foot. As far as Willie Singer was concerned he didn't owe Kirby a thing, even if Kirby was Frank Falon's brother. Kirby should never have allowed himself to get felled from his horse that way. Willie Singer kicked his horse into a run along the wet slippery trail and didn't dare slow it to a halt until he was well over a mile from the spot where he had left the others lying dead or wounded.

When Singer finally did stop, it was not to allow Kirby Falon to catch up to him, but rather to attend to the wound in his upper right shoulder. Yet, as he stepped down in the splashing mud and stripped a wet bandanna from around his neck and pressed it to the wound in his shoulder, he heard the sound of hoofbeats coming along the trail behind him and cursed under his breath. In the melee he had lost his pistol, the only firearm he carried. Wiping a hand across his wet face, he looked around wildly and found a heavy five-foot-long length of downfall spruce lying on the ground. He snatched it up with his good hand, hurried into the cover of brush along the trail, and waited with it drawn back one-handed, ready for action, as the hoofbeats grew louder and closer.

Now …! Singer shouted to himself, stepping out into the trail. He unleashed a long, hard swing at just the right second and felt the large tree limb connect solidly with the rider's chest. The force of the one-handed blow lifted the rider from his saddle and seemed to hold him suspended in air for a second, just long enough for Singer to see his mistake. "Oh my God!" he shouted, catching the stunned look on Kirby Falon's face before Kirby spilled onto the wet, hard ground, his head striking the rounded top of a sunken boulder.

The hapless young man didn't know what had hit him when he awakened slowly a few minutes later, his ribs feeling crushed, his breathing short and painful in his throbbing chest. "Who … who did this to me?" he asked in a shallow, groggy voice. One hand went to his ribs, his other to the egg-sized bump on the side of his head The world above him rolled back and forth as if he were lying on the deck of a floundering ship. As he blinked and concentrated on focusing his eyes on Willie Singer, he saw the pistol hanging loosely in Willie's hand. "What sumbitch did this to me?" he asked, his mind becoming clearer but the pain in his chest and his head causing him to wince with each word.

"You—you don't know?" Willie asked. The pistol in his hand lowered an inch, the tip of the barrel moving slightly away from Kirby.

"No, I don't," Kirby groaned, wincing as his hand felt around on the throbbing knot.

Willie Singer stared at him in contemplation for a moment, then replied warily, "Kirby, you mean you don't you remember anything at all about what happened to us back there?"

As Kirby's mind cleared a bit more, he recognized that it was his own pistol hanging in Singer's hand. He swallowed hard and said, "I almost didn't know who you are, let alone what happened to us."

Willie Singer had given as much thought as he could to the situation. "Damn it, Kirby," he said, "you don't remember me riding in and saving you from that crazy sumbitch who ambushed us?"

"Us? Who's *us?*" Kirby asked, reaching a hand up for Willie to help him to his feet.

"*Us* is you and me, and Dick and Elmer," said Willie, pulling Kirby to his feet and watching him stagger in place for a moment. "Are you going to be all right, Kirby? You're paler than a plucked goose!"

"I'm coming around some," said Kirby, struggling to maintain his balance, grabbing Willie's shoulder for support. "Tell me everything that's happened. Maybe it'll help me remember." Pain shot through his chest, causing him to suddenly bow forward and grasp his ribs.

"Jesus, Kirby!" said Willie Singer. "Let's get you settled down and look at you first." Looping an arm over Kirby's bowed back, Willie led him off alongside the trail into the shelter of some tall rocks. Keeping a cautious eye on the trail, Willie held a canteen for Kirby while the other man sipped, groaned and finally managed to let the pain in his head and chest settle down a little.

Eyeing the pistol shoved down in Willie Singer's holster, Kirby nodded at it and asked, "Ain't that my gun, Willie?"

"Why, yes, it is!" said Willie. "I'm glad to hear you recognize it. Looks like you've got some memory left after all. Has anything else come back to you?" He studied Kirby's eyes for any other sign of recognition, but he saw none.

Kirby sighed. "No, I can't remember a damn thing once we rode down off the hillside into the creek. I remember seeing a deer and her fawn, and that's about as much as I can recollect."

"Then you don't recall Dick and Elmer and you getting bested by some stranger on the creekbank?"

"Hunh?" Kirby looked puzzled. "Bested? All three of us, by one man?" He shook his head. "Hell no! I don't recall nothing like that." He gave Singer a suspicious stare. "Where were *you* while all this happened?"

"Where was *I?*" Singer said with indignation, making his story up as he went. "I'll tell you where *I* was. I was racing in there like a dart to save your hide, once I heard the shooting and saw what was going on! That's where *I* was."

Kirby gave a troubled frown, taxing his memory hard for any trace of what had happened. Noting the wound in Singer's shoulder, he nodded at it and said, "I reckon he got you too, huh?"

"Not as bad as he did the rest of yas," Singer said. "I killed him. I put two bullets in his chest, left him staring up in the rain." He eyed Kirby, judging how much if any of the story Kirby believed. "I don't mean to hold it over you, but lucky for you I came back from attending my personal bodily functions when I did. If I had been a minute later you'd be dead, along with Dick and Elmer."

Kirby appeared to consider things and he winced and once again probed the knot on his head with his fingertips. Finally he nodded again at his pistol in Singer's holster. "Where's your own gun, Willie?"

Willie gave him a curious look, then said, "It's bothering you that I'm wearing your gun, ain't it?"

"Yeah, sort of," Kirby admitted.

"This is the thanks I get after saving your life," Singer said, shaking his lowered head slowly. "The truth is, when you smacked into that low tree limb, you caused both of our horses to go down in the mud. I lost my pistol. Seeing the shape you was in, I took your gun … to protect us both, you might say."

"Protect us from who?" said Kirby. "I thought you killed the stranger?" He gave Singer a dubious look.

"Damn it," said Singer, realizing he had slipped up in his story, "I did kill him! But for all I knew there could have been more than just him. I couldn't take no chance!"

"Oh." Kirby dismissed the matter for a moment, thinking things over, then saying, "Frank is going to be madder than hell, one man doing us this much damage. We've lost all our pelts and everything."

"I know he's going to have a fit, Kirby," Singer said quietly. "That's why I think it's in both of our best interests to make sure we're careful telling him how this happened. I've got no problem since I did kill the man and save you ... but your brother might get harsh with you for you and the others letting yourselves get bested that way."

"Quit saying that word, *bested!*" Kirby snapped. "I don't like the sound of it! I can't even recall any of it. I don't know what the hell happened!"

"Then you best take my word on things and go along with me on it," said Singer. "I don't want your brother, Frank, blaming me for things. If you're smart, you don't either!"

"All right," said Kirby relenting, seeing the wisdom in Singer's words, "tell me everything that happened. Don't make me out to look like a fool."

"No, hell no, Kirby," said Singer. "Is that what you're worried about? If it is, you can forget it. You did the best you could, given the situation." He sank down onto a wet rock beside Kirby, with rain running freely from the brim of his hat. Overhead, thunder roared as the storm moved slowly across the sky. "Let me tell you everything just like it happened, and see if will help you get your memory back some."

For a day and a half Frank Falon had paced back and forth on the porch of the trade shack, the sour musty smell of damp wolf pelts hanging heavy in the air. During the night the storm had moved off across the plains, leaving the grasslands sodden and the single trail across it thick with mud. The wet ground out front of the trade shack lay strewn with empty whiskey bottles, broken glass and the shattered remnants of a card table Frank had upended over the porch rail in a fit of rage the night before. Cards and poker chips lay in the mud.

"Where the hell could they be, Tomblin?" Frank demanded of the man sitting in a wooden chair sipping coffee. "This waiting is making me crazy." His hand fell idly to the long-barreled Starr revolver holstered on his hip. He tapped his fingers on the gun butt and gazed out across the valley lands.

Ace Tomblin gave him a sidelong look and said in a flat tone, "They laid up out of the rain somewhere if they've got any sense." He sipped his coffee and added, "Why don't you settle down for a spell? All this blowing up ain't bringing them here any faster."

"Settle down, you say?" Frank gave a sweep of his arm taking in the surrounding piles of wolf hides and the pile of putrid bloated animal carcasses lying only a few yards from the shack. "How can anybody settle down in a mud hole like this?" He stared hard and cold at one of the trade shack attendants whose job it was to count and inspect the wolf pelts and pay the bounty on them. The payment was made in script that had to be then taken to Reverend Malcom Jessup's bank to be redeemed for cash. The old man stood over a large black caldron stirring a long stick around in a greasy boiling froth. Beside the caldron another old man stood ankle deep in mud, a bloody skinning knife in one hand, the hind leg of a wolf carcass in his other. "Look at these contemptible sons of a bitch," Frank murmured to Tomblin. "How much lower can a man sink than that?"

"They ain't complaining," Ace Tomblin said, knowing what would come next, having heard this conversation too many times to count. He eyed Frank Falon closely and added, "Sometimes a man is wise to see what he has and be satisfied with it."

But not seeming to hear Tomblin, Falon continued with what had become his litany. "How much different are we than these sorry, miserable wolf-boiling wretches? We're settling for crumbs off of Father Jessup's table just like them, ain't we?"

Tomblin sighed to himself and said flatly the same thing he'd said before at this point, "Frank, Jessup ain't our boss like he is to these men. He's just providing us what you call an agreement for services. Since when has he kept us from coming and going as we please?" Seeing Falon turn his gaze to him, Ace Tomblin answered himself, saying, "Never, that's when. I think we've got a good setup here, and we ought to be careful not to mess it up."

"Good setup, my ass!" Falon said, but first dropping his hand from his pistol butt, realizing that Ace Tomblin was not one of the men he could buffalo anytime he chose to. "We pay big for any services we provide Jessup … and pardon me if I don't call him *Father!* He gets his part of every dollar we squeeze out of these ragged settlers coming through here." He made a face of contempt and said, "*Gatekeepers!*" Then he spit as if attempting to get a bitter taste from his mouth. "That sounds no better than wolf boilers to me. I'm *sick of it!*" His voice had grown louder as he spoke.

"Easy, Frank. These fellows like to carry news back to Fath—I mean, *Jessup*," Ace Tomblin said, correcting himself. He gave a signal with his eyes, drawing Falon's attention to the wolf skinner who had looked up from his grizzly task and stared toward them.

Seeing the old man's eyes on him didn't cause Frank Falon to quiet down; instead he turned to them at their caldron and said, "What are you staring at, you gut-plucking turd! Yeah, you heard me right! I said I'm sick of this place and the people in it! Run and tell that to *Father* Jessup. See if he'll shake you down a handful of crumbs for it! You sorry, gut-sucking—"

"Frank! Come on, damn it!" Tomblin said, cutting him off. "These men ain't worth getting all this fired up over!" His voice lowered a notch and he added, "But make no mistake. Everything you just said will get back to Jessup before the week is out."

Frank snatched his Starr from its holster, cocking it. "Not if I kill these miserable bastards first!" he shouted. In the muddy yard the station attendants saw his gun barrel sweep back and forth over them and began trying to flee through the thick sucking mud. One man lost a boot to the deep mire, another slipped in his haste and turned a complete backward flip. The sight turned Frank's rage into laughter.

"Jesus, Frank!" said Tomblin, also seeing the comical sight as he rose up with his coffee cup in his hand. "You'll cause them to break their fool necks!"

"Good enough for them!" Frank let out a peal of laughter and began firing shots into the mud close to the fleeing men. One man slipped and slid under one of the hiding mules, sending the animal into a braying, kicking frenzy.

"*Yiii-hiii!*" Frank shouted, still firing, not really trying to hit anyone, but not really caring much if he did. "It's about damn time we found some sport in this place!"

"Hold up, Frank," said Ace Tomblin, suddenly turning serious again, "we've got two riders coming!"

"Yeah …?" Frank became more serious himself, turning his gaze out along the trail to the two tiny dots on the horizon. "Where's Lewis? He's supposed to be keeping watch." No sooner had Frank spoken than a rifle shot sounded from amid a rocky hillside two hundred yards out.

"There he is, Frank," said Tomblin, gesturing toward the sound of the rifle shot. "He's doing his job."

"Right …" said Falon, reaching out his palm to Ace Tomblin as Tomblin stepped up close beside him. Tomblin had picked up the pair of binoculars from beside his chair; he put them in Falon's hand and continued to sip his coffee, squinting toward the two distant riders. In the mud the two attendants took advantage of the lull in gunfire and helped each other up out of the mud and to the shelter of a rickety shack. One grabbed the hysterical mule and settled it long enough for the man beneath it to crawl out and run crouched and slipping across the ground.

Inside the shack, two other men stood watching with fearful expressions on their faces. The youngest of them wiped mud from his cheeks and lips. Spitting to cleanse his mouth he said in a guarded tone of voice to the ragged old man beside him, "I've had all I can take here, Soupbone. I'm getting out of this place. This is too much like that hell Father Jessup keeps railing about."

"Watch your mouth, Randall," the old man said almost in a whisper. "This ain't the Father's doings. It's these saddle tramps!"

"They work for him," the young man said. "That's enough for me. He allows them to get by with this sort of thing.... He's no fool. Father knows this keeps us beaten down. He knows it reminds us that he's got us where he wants us, and that there's not a damn thing we can do about it."

Soupbone turned his tired red-rimmed eyes to the other three wolf skinners standing behind them. "Fellows, Randall's just worn-out. There's no need in anybody telling the Father what he said, now is there?"

The three only stared in silence. Soupbone searched their eyes for any sign of who might be the one relaying this sort of thing to Father Jessup of late.

"I'm too fed up to care anymore," said Randall. "Whoever tells Father what I said might as well tell him that too. Far as I'm concerned I'd as soon be dead as go on living this way. If it wasn't for Father having my wife under his thumb I'd be in Oregon right now, living like a free man ought to live."

"Hush, boy!" said Soupbone. "You've said too much already! She ain't your wife no more. She's Father Jessup's. She's the one you best be thinking about, and keep quiet!" He turned to the others and added in an apologetic tone, "I believe he might have the fever.... You can't hold this agin him. He don't know what he's saying. Look how he's sweating!" He ran a hand across Randall's forehead and slung sweat to the ground. The others only stared.

A hundred yards out along the trail, hearing the first gunshots, Willie Singer turned in his saddle and said to Kirby Falon, "It sounds like he's in one of his moods already this morning. Let's be sure to keep our heads and stick to the story we came up with."

"You're right," said Kirby, having flinched at the first sound of gunfire. When the rifle shot went off fifty yards ahead of them, they both knew it was a warning shot from one of the men keeping watch from the hillside. "Far as I'm concerned, I'm going to say as little as I can get by with and let you do all the talking."

"Whoa now, hold on," said Singer. "That ain't what we agreed to. I'm not going to be the only one sticking my neck out! You're going to have to speak up and back me up. I want you as involved in this as I am. Otherwise, I'll turn my horse right here and let you face it alone!" He jerked on his reins as if he were about to turn around on the trail.

"All right then!" said Kirby. "I'm with you all the way, just like we agreed. I just got rattled there for a minute. I'm okay now."

"You better be," Willie Singer warned him, righting his horse on the trail beside him.

On the porch, gazing out through the binoculars, seeing the two as if they were no more than a few yards away, Frank Falon said to Ace Tomblin, "Yep, it's just the two of them, Kirby and Willie. No sign of the others." He studied the two a moment longer.

"What do you suppose has happened to Dick and Elmer?" Tomblin asked, also squinting toward the two riders.

Having seen Willie Singer threaten to turn his horse back on the trail, and having seen the worried look on his brother Kirby's face, Frank lowered the binoculars and said, "I don't know, but this ought to be good."

Chapter 3

Kirby Falon kept his mouth shut and nodded in agreement to everything Willie Singer had to say about what had happened to Elmer McGrew and Dick Gance. When Willie Singer had finished telling the story, he stood slumped, taking all of his effort and nerve to look Frank Falon in the eyes as Frank searched deeply for any sign of deceit. Singer breathed easier once he realized that Frank saw no such signs. Holding the reins to his horse, Singer took off his hat and shook his head slowly, saying, "Lord have mercy on poor Elmer and Dick … and bless their miserable souls."

Frank Falon only stared a moment longer at Willie Singer before turning to his brother, Kirby, and asking him, "Is that the whole of it, what he said?"

"He's telling the truth, Frank," said Kirby. "This man was like nothing I ever seen with gun. Lucky for me Willie came along when he did … or I'd be laying dead alongside Elmer and Dick."

Hearing Kirby helped Willie Singer breathe even easier. He offered a slight smile and said, "I just did what any of us would for one another, eh, Frank?"

But Frank gave him a skeptical look and didn't reply. Instead he said to Kirby, "Are you ready and able to ride?"

"Right now?" Kirby replied.

"Yes, right now," said Frank. "We've been waiting on

you. We've got traps that need running in the upper valley." Turning a dubious sidelong glance to Willie Singer he added, "Besides, I want to see this man's body all 'shot to pieces,' the way Willie said he left him."

"Well, yes, I reckon I can ride," said Kirby, rubbing his chin as if in speculation. "Water's up everywhere through. ... I need to get a rested horse, maybe something to eat first."

"Good," said Frank. He turned to the other six men gathered around him and said to Tomblin, who stood the closest to him, "We're pulling out of here as quick as we get these two remounted and fed. We could be gone a week, so take whatever coffee and grub is in the shack. If these hiders don't like it, they can come see me about it."

"All right," said Tomblin. He turned to the others and said, "You heard Frank. Let's get buckled up and ready to ride ... unless you all prefer lounging around here watching wolves boil!"

"I've *been* buckled up and ready ever since we got here," commented a young Montana gunman named Jim Heady. "The smell of this place keeps me about half sick to my guts."

Frank Falon heard Heady's words and swung around toward him with an angry look on his face. "Then shut your damn mouth and saddle up! You think any of us likes this shithole?" His voice was loud enough for the hiders to hear from where they stood, away from Falon's men. "Only some low-life bastard could stand being around this all the time!" He gave the hiders a dark look of contempt, and said in only a slightly lowered voice, "You bunch of stinking rotten sons a bitches!"

Tomblin gave a dark chuckle under his breath and waved the men off toward the horses, walking along between Jim Heady and an older gunman called Jaw Hughes, owing to the larger than normal lump of chewing tobacco he kept inside his left cheek. Jaw spit a large splattering of brown tobacco juice on the ground and said, as he wiped his hand across his mouth,

"Damn, Heady, what made him fly into you that way?"

"I don't know what the hell he's got up his shirt," said Heady, keeping his voice low. "I just wish he'd get it out." He gave Tomblin a look. "Do you see anything I've done wrong, Tomblin?"

"Forget about it," said Tomblin, as the three of them walked abreast through the mud to where the horses stood corralled. "He hates this place too. I reckon after a while he can't keep from hollering at somebody."

"Yeah, but damn," said Jaw, interceding on Heady's behalf, "he's been treating Jim here like a bastard child at a homecoming lately."

"I can speak for myself, Jaw," said Jim Heady, giving the man a cold stare.

Tomblin gave a nod toward the trade shack attendants as they ventured on about their work while the rest of Falon's men stepped inside the muddy corral and began gathering their horses. "You saw how he done these wretches a while ago. Be glad you ain't one of them."

"If I was one of them," said Jim Heady, "I'd not only shoot myself in the head, I'd do it three or four times, just to make certain!" He gave the attendants a glance and asked Tomblin, "What the hell's wrong with these fools anyway, allowing themselves to live this way?"

"They've got no choice." Tomblin stared straight ahead at the corral as he spoke. "They work for Father Jessup. Most of them are so deep in debt to him, they'll be boiling wolves the rest of their lives, or whatever else Jessup can come up with. They'll die broke and still be in debt to him."

"Hell," said Jim Heady, "I'd crawfish on his damned debt before I'd live this way."

"Not if you wanted to stay alive, you wouldn't," said Jaw. "These men are no more than slaves of Father Jessup. He owns them from tooth to toenail, and they all know it. There ain't a damn thing they can do about it either."

"I'd do something about it if I was them," said Jim Heady.

Jaw spit another stream, saying, "*Hmmph* ... just thank your stars you're not one of them," as they walked into the muddy corral.

Once the men were mounted and on their way, ten of them riding in twos along the muddy trail, Frank Falon turned to his brother beside him and said, just between the two of them, "You know I wouldn't kill you for lying to me the way I would Willie Singer, don't you?"

Kirby sat rigid in his saddle and stared straight ahead, replying calmly, "I know that, Frank. But this ain't no lie, none of it."

Frank grinned slightly. He turned a menacing gaze to his younger brother and said with persistence, "I might have to box your jaws and bust you upside your head a lick or two, but I wouldn't kill you for it."

"Damn it, Frank," said Kirby, "why are you going on like this? I told you the truth, as best I could!"

"I'm going on like this because it's a long, wet, muddy trail down to the valley lands. I'm going on like this because I know what a low, lying, miserable coward Willie Singer is. He never saved a pal in his life. And I wouldn't take kindly to be made a fool of over him, going off on some wild-goose chase. Do you understand me?"

"I understand, Frank," said Kirby, still staring straight ahead.

"All right then," said Frank, giving up for the moment but still convinced there was something wrong with the story his brother and Willie had told him. He looked back at Willie Singer, just in time to see the other man avert his eyes. Nodding to himself with resolve, Frank kicked his horse up into a quicker pace and led the men up off the trail onto a higher, dryer path.

They rode on throughout the day, avoiding broad puddles and muddy stretches of low spots that would have sunk their horses to their knees.

By afternoon they'd reached the swollen creek and followed it down onto the valley lands for another hour before stopping and looking out at the rushing muddy creek filled with tangles of driftwood, debris and brush the storm had washed down from the rocky hillsides. Sitting farther back from Frank and Kirby Falon, Ace Tomblin said in a hushed tone to the men who had bunched their horses up around him, "See? I told him there's not going to be any bodies laying around, after a storm that bad."

Splint Mullins, Arby Ryan, Lewis Barr, and Quentin Fuller gave one another looks. Then Fuller said to Ace Tomblin, "Hell, I would've gone off chasing my tail all day, so long as it got me out and away from that shack."

"Yeah," said Mullins, "me too. But I see what Ace is saying. It makes us all look bad, out here traipsing around … especially since we're looking for one man who killed two of us and sent more of our men running with their tails between their legs."

Before anyone else could comment, Frank Falon's voice boomed above the roar of the rushing creek, calling out, "Tomblin! Get up here!"

Ace Tomblin gave the others a quick glance, then nudged his horse forward and stopped at the creek's edge beside Falon. "What is it, Frank?" he asked, gazing out across the muddy frothing torrent.

"Willie says this is the spot where it happened." He shot Willie Singer a harsh stare. "Right, Willie?"

Sitting on the other side of Kirby, Willie shrugged a little and said, "Yep, it sure looks like the spot. But don't hold me to it." He looked to Kirby for support. "What do you say, Kirby?"

"I can't tell nothing," said Kirby, looking all around. "This creek is forty feet wider than it was." He raised his hat and scratched his head.

Speaking quietly to Tomblin, Frank said, "You don't suppose that could have been Sloane Mosely, do you?"

"Naw, I don't think so," said Tomblin. "Even if Kirby and Willie didn't recognize him, Dick and Elmer would have. They wouldn't have got themselves into a shootout with Mosely. They would have spotted him and rode wide of him. They weren't crazy enough to take him on." He considered for another second and said, "Willie for damned sure didn't kill Sloane Mosely."

"Yeah, that's what I'm thinking," said Frank. Gazing across the wide raging creek he said, "His house is over there. If this water wasn't up so bad we'd ride over and see if Sloane knows anything about what happened."

"Yeah," said Tomblin, relieved that the water was too high to permit such an undertaking right then. "It'll be another day or two I expect before this creek is back in its banks. We can always come back and talk to him then."

Frank nodded, then backed his horse a couple of steps and said aloud to all the men, "All right, let's spread out and get to looking downstream. As fast as this water's running, Dick's and Elmer's bodies could be anywhere ... so could the man who's killed them. Find them all three.... Let's go. We've got traps waiting to be run!"

For the next hour the riders worked their way along the sodden ground along the creek, but they found no sign of their two comrades or the stranger who killed them. At a point where the swollen creek took a turn around a tall rocky hillside, Frank Falon and Ace Tomblin stopped and watched three riders come into sight on the muddy trail ahead of them. "Looks like some of Jessup's *saints* have rode down out of Paradise." He spoke with sarcasm, then spit as if to wash a bitter taste from his mouth.

"Yeah," said Tomblin, ignoring Falon's contempt for the coming riders, "maybe they saw something downstream." He gave the men a short wave of his hand, then sat quietly beside Falon and watched the riders approach them. At the front of the three riders a large man with blond hair wearing a black flat-crowned hat turned his horse sideways to Falon and Tomblin and said in a no-nonsense tone, "Are you looking for a couple of your men, Falon?"

"That's right, Chapin," said Falon, neither man greeting the other with anything akin to courtesy. "Why? Have you seen them?"

"Two miles down," said the big man, "we found a hat and a wolf pelt floating among some rocks. I judged they might belong to some of your trappers."

"You didn't even make an *effort* to look around, see if somebody might need your help?" said Falon, a bit put off by Chapin.

"No," the big man said. "We don't attend to those not our own. Father instructs us not to."

"I should've known that without asking," Falon commented. Making little effort to hide his contempt, he said to Tomblin, "Hear that? Offering to help somebody is not *their way.*"

"If a man is not sanctified, what does it matter what becomes of him here on this mortal plane?" the big man cut in.

"Beats the hell out of me," said Falon, dismissing that portion of the conversation. "You didn't see anything else by any chance? Some sign of a stranger traveling through here?"

"No," said Chapin, his gaze piercing, his tone vindictive, "we saw only what I told you we saw. It wouldn't surprise me to hear that some of your men have come to a violent end. The likes of those kind most often do."

"Well," said Falon, settling himself a little rather than continuing in an air of outright hostility toward Father Jessup's followers, "my men don't concern themselves so much with spiritual sanctification as they do with more earthy pursuits, Chapin. But I'm obliged for your information." He lifted a nod toward a higher hill line in the distance. "Did you happen upon anybody else coming across Wolf Valley?"

"I told you already, we happened upon no one else," said Chapin, "neither down along the creek nor crossing Wolf Valley."

Falon gave him a crooked smile. "I thought maybe you might have seen Sloane Mosely along your way." He gave a nod back over his shoulder toward the far side of the creek. Falon relished the fact that Jessup and his followers could not abide having a man like Sloane Mosely in their midst, but that so far they had appeared powerless to do anything about him.

Chapin answered him in a straightforward tone. "We have seen Sloane Mosely only twice since early spring."

"I saw him myself back in the spring," said Falon. "Saw him one evening at dark riding that big silver stallion of his along the high ridges. Talk about *unsanctified*, whooo-ee!" Falon grinned, taunting Chapin. "Now there's one devil you boys ought to be casting out of Paradise, before he goes to corrupting your whole flock."

"Sloane Mosely does not come into Paradise, not even for supplies," said Chapin. "As long as he remains in his place, Father Jessup says we will tolerate him living up here."

With a smug grin Frank Falon said, "Now that's kind of you, tolerating Mosely that way, unsanctified sinner that he is."

"Sloan Mosely will face the Creator and answer for all he is and all he has done when the Great Day of Judgment arrives," said Chapin, sounding as if he was reading the words aloud from a book.

"Yeah, I bet he will," said Falon, "but meanwhile, it sure doesn't seem like anybody can unseat his sinful, sorry—"

"We best be getting on with it," Ace Tomblin said, cutting in before Frank Falon could say any more on the matter. "We're obliged for you telling us about our men, Chapin."

Brother Paul Chapin only nodded, backed his horse a step, turned it and rode away, the other two men flanking him. As soon as the three were out of hearing range, Ace Tomblin shook his head slowly and said, "Frank, I don't like these zealots any more than you do. But we've got to live and let live up here."

Frank Falon chuckled. "Sometimes I just can't help but poke a stick at them, Ace. Them and their religious malarkey." He spit and wiped a hand across his mouth. "It all rubs me the wrong way. As for Jessup, there's days I hate him. Other days I look at him and think he really is God! And that makes me hate him worse, for mixing me up that way." He rubbed his temples as if thinking about the man gave him a headache.

"These religious zealots are like a swarm of hornets if you ever get them too stirred up at you, Frank," Ace said. "I find it best to leave them be. I try not to even think about them."

"Then you can leave them be, Ace," said Falon. "Myself, I can't stand a hypocrite … and no matter how you slice it, Father Jessup is a fake and a hypocrite. He takes other men's possessions for his own and claims the Lord tells him to. He even takes their wives and children."

In spite of no one being close around them, Ace Tomblin shot a quick wary glance back and forth as if some of Father Jessup's followers might overhear them. "So?" He grinned. "You have to admire a man for being slick enough to get what he wants without firing a shot."

"There's times I do," said Falon. "But other times I say if you've got the guts to take something by force, take it. Don't do it and drag the Lord's name into it. Be bold enough to say you're the one who wants it done." He spit again. "See how he keeps me rattled all the time?"

"Yeah, but so what?" Tomblin shrugged, knowing it would do no good to continue the conversation. "It's no hide off our asses whose wives he takes. We've got a good thing up here."

"I'm sick of hearing you go on and on about how good we've got it up here, Ace!" Falon hissed, cutting him off. "If you care so damn much for Jessup, why don't you up and join his happy little flock?"

Tomblin gave him a confused look. "Damn, he does have your mind pulled apart, doesn't he!"

Without replying, Falon jerked his horse around and stopped for a moment before riding off along the creekbank. "Let's keep searching while we head toward the high valley pass. If we can't find them, we'll run our traps and search some more on our way back."

Tomblin nodded, saying quietly, "By then the water will be down. If you want me to, I'll cross over by myself and search around on the other side. It don't take every man we've got to do it."

"Yeah," said Falon, "that's how we'll do it." He stopped his horse as Willie Singer came riding slowly past him, searching along the raging creek. "Have no doubt about it. Ace," said Falon, giving Singer a cold, hard stare. "If you don't find those bodies, we'll all come back and keep searching until we *do*. I intend to see just exactly what happened out here if it means we have to search this creek a dozen times." He nailed his spurs to his horse's sides and raced away, leaving Singer with a worried look on his face.

Chapter 4

For several days CC Ellis had drifted in and out of consciousness, the wound in his lower side having drained his strength, the long, deep graze just above his left temple having addled his senses. But last night he had awakened in the dark room feeling stronger and more mentally alert than he had since the shooting. His head still throbbed, but as he lay awake in the darkness he managed to piece together his fragmented recollection of that day on the creekbank. Instinctively his eyes had gone to the chair beside the cot, where his shoulder harness lay wrapped around his empty holster. On the floor beside the chair sat his saddlebags. He eyed the saddlebags with relief. But then his eyes went back to the empty holster.

Being unarmed disturbed him, so at the sound of someone opening and closing the front door, he pushed himself up from the cot, stepped painfully over to the only window in the small room and peeped out, anxious to know more about his surroundings and his benefactors.

In the gray-black hour before daylight he stood with a hand pressed to the dressing on his side and watched the women lead a big silver gray from the barn and out across the muddy yard until both she and the horse faded into the darkness. Yet no sooner had she led the horse away than Ellis watched her return, moving with an air of secrecy, he thought, watching her look both ways guardedly before leading the horse back inside the barn quietly and quietly closing the wide barn door behind herself. *Peculiar...*

He waited, leaning against the window ledge until he saw her leave the barn moments later. She came out through a smaller door, carrying herself in the same manner, searching the darkness in both directions on her way back to the house. But CC noted that her eyes did not search her immediate surroundings. Her search was more concerned with whoever or whatever might be watching from a distance. *Very peculiar...* He smiled curiously to himself, still watching her closely as her hand reached out to open the front door to the house. Before she stepped inside the house, Ellis turned stiffly, limped back to the bed, eased himself down onto the hard rope-strung cot and pulled the quilt over himself. He heard muffled conversation between the woman and the boy, followed by the sound of their footsteps crossing the creaking floor to the room. As he heard a quiet knocking on the door, Ellis closed his eyes and feigned sleep.

"Mister ...?" Ellis heard the boy whisper as he stepped into the room, the woman close behind him holding up a lit lamp. "Mister?" Ellis heard him whisper again.

"It's all right, Dillard," the woman whispered to the boy. "Let's not disturb him. He'll awaken soon."

Ellis opened his eyes a sliver, enough to see the two start to back out of the room silently. "Wait," he said, "I'm awake."

"See, Mother, he is awake!" Dillard said, sounding excited at the prospect.

As he opened his eyes in the lamp glow, Ellis sensed relief as well as excitement from the boy. From the woman he sensed nothing, but that was as it should be, he told himself.

"Yes, Dillard, I see," the woman replied, both of them stepping back inside the room. She crossed the floor, set the lamp on a small bedside table and raised the wick. "There now, let's take a look at you in the light with your eyes open. I'm Callie Mosely. This is my son, Dillard."

"Mosely?" CC said.

"Yes, Mosely," Callie said. Thinking she saw a glint of recognition in his eyes, she said, "Perhaps you've heard of my husband, Sloane Mosely?"

But whatever recognition she thought she'd seen seemed to leave his eyes quickly. *Too quickly?* she wondered.

"No, ma'am, I have not heard of your husband, but I'll be pleased to make his acquaintance."

"And so you will, soon enough, Mr. Ellis," she said.

Ellis found himself stunned by the fact that she knew his name. He rubbed his eyes and looked closer at her. "How did you know my name, ma'am?" he asked.

"I told her!" the boy cut in eagerly. "I heard you say it on the creekbank! I was there, watching from a pine thicket!"

"Oh … I see," said Ellis. He paused for a second, looking at the woman, then said to the boy, "So you saw everything that happened.…" His words trailed.

"I—sure did!" Dillard exclaimed. "I saw how you shot it out with those wolf hunters and never even—"

"That's quite enough, Dillard," said the woman. "I'm sure Mr. Ellis doesn't feel like recounting the situation right now."

The boy fell silent.

Seeing the dejected look on the boy's face, Ellis said, "Young man, it appears I owe you my life. I'm much obliged to you."

His words raised the boy's downcast eyes from the floor. "You're welcome Mr. Ellis. It was my pleasure … me and Tic's, that is." His hand fell to the knobby head of the big yellow hound who had crept in and stood beside him.

"Then I'm obliged to you and Tic," Ellis said, offering a weak smile. Looking back at the woman, he asked, "What about my horse, ma'am? Is he all right?"

"Yes, your horse is fine, Mr. Ellis," Callie replied. "Dillard has been tending to him for you."

"Obliged again, young man," Ellis said with a nod to the boy.

"My husband will be glad to hear that you're conscious, Mr. Ellis," the woman said.

Looking from the boy and the dog, back to her, Ellis said, "How long have I been here, ma'am?"

"Almost a week," she replied.

Ellis rubbed the side of his head, feeling the healing scar left by the bullet graze. Fragments of memory drifted back and forth across his mind. He recalled being helped onto a buckboard in the driven rain. He recalled being brought in out of the rain and helped through the house to this room. He recalled strong yet gentle hands undressing him and later pressing a wet rag to his forehead. But the memories appeared and disappeared like pieces of lost dreams. He shook his head slowly, demanding more from his faculties, but not getting it.

"Ma'am, I don't know what to say. I want to pay you and your husband something for all your trouble. I have some money in my saddlebags."

Her voice turned a bit sharp. "We wouldn't accept payment for a simple act of kindness, Mr. Ellis."

"Of course not, ma'am," Ellis replied, realizing the error of his words. "Please forgive my lack of manners. I'm afraid I have spent too much of my life around those who do not think that way toward strangers."

"I understand," Callie nodded, as if in forgiveness.

"Ma'am," Ellis said, his eyes going to the empty holster on the chair, "was my Colt missing when you found me?"

"No, Mr. Ellis," said Callie, "we have your sidearm. My husband will return it to you as soon as you've regained your strength."

"I'm used to always having it at my side, ma'am," Ellis said. "I'd appreciate very much if you'd bring it to me."

As if not hearing his request, Callie said, "I'll prepare you a cup of tea, Mr. Ellis."

"I look forward to thanking your husband in person, ma'am," Ellis, not pressing the point about his Colt.

As the woman, the boy and the dog backed out of the open doorway, she said, with an air of civility, "It's Mrs. Mosely, if you please."

"Yes, Mrs. Mosely," Ellis replied.

"Mr. Mosely will look forward to meeting you as well, as soon as he returns this afternoon," Callie said. "Now, if you'll excuse us, please." She nodded toward an oak chest of drawers against the wall. "You'll find your clothes in there. Please join us when you've dressed." Without another word she guided the boy away from the doorway and shut the door.

CC Ellis sat staring blankly at the closed door for a moment before standing up slowly from the cot and walking back to the window. For a moment he stared out the window toward the barn, still curious about the woman's earlier activities. Then he set his curiosity aside, walked to the oaken dresser, took out his clean clothes and put them on. At the foot of the bed his high-topped boots stood clean and oiled. *Something the boy would have done*, he told himself, picking up one up and inspecting it with appreciation.

While CC Ellis stepped into his boots, the boy followed his mother around the kitchen restlessly as she prepared a cup of hot tea and set it at the head of the table. "Mother, aren't you going to tell Mr. Ellis?" he whispered secretively. "You said you might once he was up and around."

"I know what I said, Dillard," Callie Mosely replied firmly. As she spoke she thought better of setting the cup at the head of the table. Moving it to the side of the table, she nodded to herself, then continued. "But I've given it more thought. I don't think it would be wise to tell him anything. The less this man knows about our situation, the better." Instinctively she raised a hand to her hair and patted a strand into place.

"But, Mother, if you could have just seen how he handled those wolf hunters!" Dillard persisted.

"Indeed," said Callie, "and it's for that very reason we need to be guarded about what we let him know. For all we know, he could have been one of them."

"No, Mother, he isn't one of them!" Dillard protested shaking his head. "I'm most certain he's not one of the wolfers."

"The point is, we know nothing about him, Dillard," said Callie. "At least not enough to go pinning our hopes and our fate on him. It would be easy for a man like this to take advantage of our situation. Your father would tell you the same thing if he were—" She paused, then said, "Well, you know what I mean."

"Yes, I know," said Dillard, "but I believe Father would agree that we need somebody like CC Ellis on our side. I know he wouldn't take any guff off of Father Jessup and his men. He would send them running with their tails between their legs, the same as he did those wolf hunters!"

"That will be enough about it for now, Dillard," Callie said, her voice lowering to a whisper because she thought she'd heard the door to Ellis's room open. "We'll finish discussing this another time."

"Yes, ma'am," Dillard said reluctantly. After stepping away from his mother's side, he turned and stood as if at attention and watched CC Ellis walk into the room with a slight limp.

"Please be seated, Mr. Ellis," Callie said with only a slight show of formality. "I know you must be hungry. But the tea will be soothing on your stomach while I prepare you some solid food.

"Much obliged, Mrs. Mosely," Ellis replied, stopping a few feet from the table and looking around the clean, modest kitchen before stepping forward and seating himself where the cup of tea sat steaming before him.

As if he might have overheard what she and her son had been discussing, Callie thought, as she busied herself stirring a pot of thick beef stew in a kettle atop a small wood stove, "Dillard and I were just talking about the men you—" She paused, searching for a more delicate word. But finding none she said, "Well, that you shot, Mr. Ellis."

"Yes, ma'am." CC Ellis nodded, blowing on the hot tea, then sipping it. "I expect you must be wondering if others will come looking for them?" he asked.

Callie paused from stirring the stew and looked around at him. "Oh no, Mr. Ellis, I don't wonder if there will be others who'll come looking for them. I'm *certain* of it. These men are a part of a band of wolf hunters who work this entire mountainside. As soon as the men came up missing, the others must have begun searching the trails. I'm surprised they haven't been here already."

"Don't worry, ma'am," said Ellis. "I'll be going as soon as I can get my leg over my horse."

"Mr. Ellis, you mustn't try to leave until that wound in your side is properly healed. As for these men … they have a great amount of respect for my husband. Whatever we tell them is what they will have to accept."

"I don't want to bring harm to you and your family, ma'am," Ellis offered quietly.

"My husband will see to it that no harm comes to us, Mr. Ellis," she said a bit crisply. "You needn't concern yourself with our well-being."

"Of course, ma'am, begging your pardon," Ellis replied.

While the two spoke, Tic had turned his keen canine senses toward something outside. When he growled low, in the direction of the barn, Dillard hurried to the window, pulled the curtain back slightly and peeped out. "What is it, Tic?" he asked, as if the dog might answer him.

Callie turned from CC Ellis and hurried to the window beside her son. CC Ellis stood up stiffly and leaned on the table, using one hand for support and pressing the other to the wound in his side. "Is someone out there, ma'am?" he asked.

"Yes," said Callie, without turning to him, "it's Ace Tomblin, one of the men we were just talking about."

Dillard added in a hushed tone of voice, "It's Frank Falon's right-hand man, is who it is!"

CC Ellis hurried to the window with his hand pressed to his tender side. Looking out, he saw the rider leading his horse around the corner of the small barn toward the house, a rifle in his left hand. "Ma'am, I'd be obliged if you'd give me back my Colt now," Ellis said calmly.

"It's put away, Mr. Ellis," she said with firm confidence. "You won't be needing it."

"If this man is a part of the same bunch I ran into along the creek, I don't think he came looking for me just to talk things over."

"We don't know that he came looking for you, do we, Mr. Ellis?" Callie replied coolly. And when Ellis just looked at her, Callie said, "I mean, there is no reason why he should think you're here. I'll just go talk to him."

"Ma'am, I'd really like to have that gun in my hand," said Ellis. But his words went unanswered as Callie hurried over, opened the front door and stepped out onto the front porch. All Ellis could do was step back over to the window and peep out secretively. "Your ma has a stubborn streak in her, doesn't she, young man?" he whispered to the boy.

"Yes, sir," Dillard replied in the same tone of voice, "that's what my father always tells her."

"Well," said Ellis, eyeing the rifle in Ace Tomblin's hand, "I can't stand here like a tin target. Where do you suppose your ma might have hidden my Colt?"

Dillard stared at him blankly. "I don't know, sir."

"And you wouldn't tell me if you did?" Ellis asked.

"No, sir, I wouldn't," the boy replied.

"Stubbornness must run in the family," Ellis said under his breath, turning back to his guarded view through the window.

On the porch, Callie Mosely stood in front of the closed door and said curtly down to Ace Tomblin as he neared the house, "Is there something we can do for you, Mr. Tomblin?"

Ace Tomblin noted that there was no greeting. *No good day, go to hell, how are you? or anything else*, he mused to himself, taking a last quick glance around the yard as he swept his hat from his head. "Ma'am, we've had a couple of our hunters killed back along the creek right before the rain. Frank Falon sent me to check around, see if I can find their bodies and the body of the man who killed them … maybe even see if I can find out more about how it all happened. I need to speak with your husband, if you please."

"That's close enough, Mr. Tomblin," Callie said firmly, causing the man to stop short a few feet from the porch. "I'm afraid Mr. Mosely can't be disturbed right now. I'll tell him you were by. If he feels he can lend any help in the matter, I'm sure he'll go directly to Mr. Falon in person and discuss it with him."

Ace Tomblin's face reddened. He realized her words were intended to put him in his place. He wasn't important enough to get to speak to Mr. Sloane Mosely. "Ma'am, no offense intended, but if you would be kind enough to tell your husband I'm here …" He let his words trail.

"Mr. Tomblin," Callie said firmly, "I assure you, my husband realizes you are here. He does not wish to speak to you. I'm afraid you are forcing me to be blunt about this."

"Ma'am, in a matter such as this," said Tomblin, "it's up to all of us in these parts to stick together and help one another out. Frank Falon sent me to do a job, and I intend to do it." He took a bold step forward as if to walk up onto the porch.

Callie took a step forward to the edge of the porch as if to stop him. But not sooner had she stopped than she heard the door behind her open and close; and she heard CC Ellis's voice, say quietly, "You can discuss whatever it is you need to discuss with me, mister."

Callie Mosely stood silently, without looking around at Ellis, yet anxious to see how he intended to handle this.

Tomblin eyed him closely. "Mr. Mosely?"

Ellis suddenly realized that this man had never met Sloane

Mosely, at least not face-to-face. He shot a quick glance at Callie Mosely and saw that she too managed to keep the same flat, tense expression. Something in her eyes told him to go ahead and play out his hand. So he did, as he felt her eyes watching and knew she must be taking note of how effortlessly he'd lied. "What can I do for you?" Ellis asked, without answering Tomblin's question. "Like the missus said, I don't like being disturbed."

Stepping slightly to the side, Callie gave Ellis a glance. She saw him standing straight and looking much stronger than she knew him to be. His right hand lay atop his holster in such a way that it hid the fact the holster was empty. "I just returned home last evening after traveling three days along the creek until the water fell enough to let me cross it. If there were any bodies along there I failed to see them."

Tomblin looked him up and down, suspicious of something, but unsure of what it could be. "Begging your pardon, Mr. Mosely, but dead men don't just disappear without a trace," he said.

"You're right. Dead men do not disappear," Ellis replied. "With that in mind, I wish you luck. You'll just have to keep looking. I wish I could have been more help."

Glancing back and forth between the man and the woman, not knowing what to say next, Tomblin finally set his hat atop his head. "I apologize for any disturbance and I'll bid you both a good day and be off," he said.

"Good day, Mr. Tomblin," said Callie, politely but with a crispness to her voice, "and good luck in your search."

As Ace Tomblin turned and led his horse along the muddy path leading to the trail, Ellis stepped up beside Callie Mosely, his gunhand still shielding his empty holster. "Forgive me for intruding," he said softly.

"Forgive you indeed," Callie hissed without turning to face him. They watched Ace Tomblin mount his horse and ride up onto the trail. "Everything was going just fine, Mr. Ellis. I didn't need you butting in." Finally giving him a quick glance, she noted he had put on a clean shirt from her husband's drawer. "And who said you could wear my husband's shirt? Did Dillard fetch that for you?"

"Yes, ma'am, he did," said Ellis. "But don't be too harsh on him. I'm afraid I insisted he bring it to me. I couldn't be sure how things were going to go out here." He patted his empty holster. "After all, you've left us unarmed."

"Well, as you can see, things were well under control. I didn't need your help." As Ace Tomblin rode out of sight, Callie turned toward CC Ellis with his gun appearing in her hand as if it had sprung from out of nowhere. She pointed it toward his belly. "And as you can see, I'm far from being unarmed."

CC Ellis looked taken aback in surprise at having his own gun aimed at him. His hands rose chest high in a show of peace. "Yes, ma'am. I see what you mean."

Callie backed away a step and said coolly, "What you said earlier is a wise idea. As soon as you're able to ride, it's best you do so."

"Yes, ma'am," said Ellis, his expression turning serious. "You and your son have been more than hospitable. I don't want to leave here with ill feelings between us."

"Once you leave here," said Callie, "I assure you there will be no feelings between us one way or another."

Hearing their conversation, Dillard hurriedly stepped out onto the front porch. "But, Mother," he said in Ellis's defense, "he didn't mean any harm! He was only trying to help! Look at how quick Ace Tomblin cleared out of here, thinking this was my pa!"

"It's *Father*, not *Pa*," Callie said, correcting the boy.

"Either way, he sure didn't stay around long after that!" Dillard said.

"I understand, Dillard," said Callie, lowering the pistol slightly as Dillard stepped over closer to her. "I think Mr. Ellis realizes now that we don't need help. Not from him or anybody else. As soon as my husband returns, he'll go speak to the wolf hunters and see to it—"

"Begging your pardon, ma'am," CC Ellis said, "but I've seen enough to know that you're not expecting your husband to be coming home, at least not anytime soon. You're just putting up a pretense." As soon as he'd spoken, he saw her hand tighten around the gun butt. "Easy, ma'am. I'm not out to do you any harm. You and your son saved my life. That's not something I'm likely to forget."

"Mr. Ellis," Callie said, "if I thought you were out to do us harm, you'd be dead right now. I don't know what you think is going on here. But my son and I have reason to keep up our pretense."

"I'm sure you do, ma'am," Ellis replied. "That's why I mentioned it. Whatever problem you have with these wolf hunters, I'm offering my help."

"Thank you all the same, Mr. Ellis," said Callie, still keeping her hand tensed around the Colt. "But as I've already told you—"

"Mother, please!" said Dillard. "Let him help us if he can. That's what Father would tell you if he were here!"

"I won't pry, ma'am," Ellis said, seeing her consider her son's words. "But I will help you in any way I can if you'll allow me to."

"I hope I'm doing the right thing," Callie said at length, lowering the Colt. "Mr. Ellis, my trouble is not with the wolf hunters. My trouble is with the man they work for." As she spoke, she noted that Ellis had begun to lean slightly, favoring his wounded side. "Let's go inside and get you seated. I'll tell you everything." She sighed deeply. "To be honest, Dillard and I are both worn-out from dealing with this, day after day."

"Yes, ma'am, I can see that," said Ellis, reaching out and taking the Colt from her tired hand. He pressed his free hand to a sharp pain in his side as he gestured them toward the door. "But you can breathe a little easier now. You and Dillard aren't alone anymore."

Chapter 5

Once inside, Ellis and Dillard seated themselves as Callie walked to the stove, poured two cups of hot tea and brought them back to the table. When she'd set Ellis's cup in front of him and seated herself across the table from him, instead of telling him her problem, she sat in silence for a moment staring down at her folded hands because the words were not coming easily for her.

"Take your time, ma'am," Ellis coaxed gently.

After another moment's pause the words seemed to spill from her lips as if in confession. "I haven't seen or heard from my husband in almost a year, Mr. Ellis," she said. Then she turned her eyes back down at her folded hands as if embarrassed.

"I thought it was something like that," Ellis said gently, pushing her cup of tea closer to her folded hands. "You've been keeping up a ruse of him being here for your own protection, yours and Dillard's?"

"Yes, exactly," Callie replied, her hands unfolding and wrapping around the warm cup as she spoke. "Apparently my ruse wasn't good enough to fool you," she added. Dillard looked on, Tic's bony head on his lap, the boy's right hand idly stroking the dog's neck.

"I watch things much closer than most folks," Ellie said, shrugging off her comment. "I think I understand why you were doing it though, ma'am," he continued. "This is big country. A man's presence carries more respect than a woman on her own."

"Yes, but I'm afraid there's more to it than that, Mr. Ellis," Callie said. "You see, the town of Paradise is run by a religious sect. Their leader is a fanatic, the Reverend Father Malcom Jessup. He rules the lives of all his followers. When something happens to one of the men, Jessup takes the man's wife and family as his own." A frightened look came upon her. "If he knew that my husband has been gone all this time, there's no doubt he would force Dillard and me to go live in what he calls his *community family.*"

"I've heard of that sort of thing," said Ellis. "If that's religion, I'm glad I'm a sinner." He offered the slightest trace of a smile to lighten up the atmosphere, but it didn't work. Callie Mosely's expression didn't change.

"It's only his fear of my husband's reputation as a shootist that has kept him away so far. I'm afraid he'll see through me anyday and come riding in for me and Dillard."

"I'll fight him with our shotgun!" Dillard said. "He's not taking us anywhere."

"You're a brave young man," said Ellis. "You've already proved that to me, doing what you did for me along the creekbank." He paused for a moment, then said, "But maybe there's a better way."

"How do you mean, Mr. Ellis?" Callie asked.

Instead of answering, Ellis asked, "How many folks around here have ever met your husband, ma'am?"

Callie considered, then said, "No one that I know of has met him. He always kept his distance, and fortunately so for us. I've worn his old hat and riding duster and ridden the silver stallion along the ridges where I knew I'd be seen by Father Jessup's followers. They all recognize the stallion, but no one has seen Sloane except *from a distance.*"

"Including this Father Jessup?" Ellis asked.

"Yes, including Father Jessup," said Callie. "Jessup knew that my husband had very little use for him and his religious fanatics." She caught herself and stopped. But Ellis had already taken note of how she'd referred to her husband in the past tense. She let Ellis see her give Dillard a glance of consideration as she said, "That is, Jessup *knows* that my husband *has* very little use for—"

"I understood you, ma'am," Ellis said, cutting her off.

Dillard had also understood what his mother said, and he let them both know it by saying firmly, "My father is alive! And he's coming back soon. You'll see."

"Yes, Dillard," said Callie. "Of course he is alive. Of course he's coming back. I'm sorry I sounded as if I doubted it." She reached out and placed her hand over his.

Ellis watched in silence for a moment. Then, for the boy's sake, he said quietly, "Until Mr. Mosely returns home, I have an idea that I think will help." He gazed steadily at Callie and said, "I will pose as your husband."

"I was afraid you were going to say that," said Callie, shaking her head. "I won't hear of it, nor would my husband if he knew. If that's your idea of helping us—"

"Wait, listen to me," said Ellis. "You realize that I'm talking about posing as Sloane Mosely in name only. I didn't mean to suggest anything untoward."

Callie looked embarrassed and said, "Certainly I know you mean in name only. Still, it's out of the question."

"Do you mind if I ask why?" Ellis asked.

Dillard, who had listened intently, repeated Ellis's words. "Yes, Mother, why can't Mr. Ellis pose as Father? If it keeps us safe from having to go live with Father Jessup, why can't we do it?"

Callie seemed stuck for an answer.

"It makes sense to try it," Ellis interjected. "If it works, that's good. If it fails, I'll stay and see to it no harm befalls either of you. You have my word on that."

"No offense, Mr. Ellis," said Callie, "but I don't know you well enough to know if your *word* has any value."

A troubled look passed over his brow, as if he had something he could have said but decided to keep it to himself. He nodded and said in an even tone, "That's fair for you to say, not knowing me. But, ma'am, if this situation is as grim as you say it is, I don't see what other choice you have right now, unless you want to pull up from here and run." His expression remained the same, but his tone softened. "If that's your choice, I'll even escort the two of you out of here."

Callie took a deep breath and let it out slowly, considering his words. Finally she said, "Mr. Ellis, I don't think you realize what you are letting yourself in for."

"Let me worry about that, ma'am," Ellis said. He raised his cup of tea to his lips and took a sip. To Dillard he said, "Young man, why don't you and I go take a look at that silver stallion? It looks like I might be riding him for a while."

"There's something unnatural about a town that allows no drinking," Ace Tomblin grumbled to himself as he rode his horse the last few yards up the middle of the dirt street and reined it to the hitch rail, out front of the former Blue Diamond Saloon in the town of Paradise. Stepping down and wrapping the reins around the hitch rail, he looked up longingly at two dark spots on the clapboard building where at one time two large wooden beer mugs had stood tipped toward one another. Replacing the beer advertisement, a large painted wooden sign now read PUBLIC HALL.

Shaking his head, Ace stepped through the bat wing doors and walked to where Frank Falon sat at a table with a cup of coffee in front of him.

Upon seeing Tomblin enter, a rotund man with a shaved head hurried around from behind the empty bar, carrying a clean coffee mug and a pot of coffee.

While the man sat the cup down and filled it, Frank Falon

eyed Ace Tomblin. "Any luck?" he asked as the other man turned and left with the pot of coffee.

Ace Tomblin slumped down in a wooden chair and pushed the cup of coffee away from him with a sour expression. "No sign of any bodies on the other side of the creek," he said.

"You looked all around up near the Mosely place, I expect," Falon asked, trying to sound matter-of-fact.

"Not only did I take a good look all around there," said Ace Tomblin, in the same manner. "I also stopped by and spoke with Sloane Mosely. Asked him if he might have seen anything."

"Oh, you did … Mosely himself, eh?" Falon tried to hide his surprise and curiosity, but he did a poor job of it.

"Yep," said Tomblin, playing the situation down. "He said he didn't see anything. Said he'd just passed along the creek a couple of days before." Tomblin shook his head. "Said sorry he couldn't be of more help …" He let his words trail off.

Falon just stared at Ace for a moment. On second thought Tomblin pulled the coffee mug back to him, picked it up, blew on the hot coffee and took a sip.

"Sloane Mosely came on out and spoke to you?" Falon asked as if he might doubt Tomblin's word.

"That's right," said Tomblin. He set the cup down. "It's the first time I ever laid eyes on the man, up close anyways. He wasn't nearly as unsociable as I thought he'd be." Seeing the impressed look on Frank Falon's face Tomblin decided to stretch the story a bit. "Fact is, he and his missus invited me to stay and take a sit-down meal with him. I told him I was obliged, but that I had to get on with my search, then rode on into Paradise."

"Damn it!" said Falon, slapping his palm down on the table. "I knew I should have gone across the creek with you."

Keeping himself from smiling openly, Tomblin said with an air of self-satisfaction, "Yeah, I believe you would have enjoyed meeting ol' Sloane in person."

Falon's expression turned hard. "'Ol' Sloane?'" he said, mimicking Tomblin. "Ace, don't go cutting yourself too wide a spot. Meeting Sloane Mosely don't make you the cock of anybody's walk. I meant that I should have gone with you just so I could have heard in person that he didn't see any sign of our men's bodies, or the man who killed them."

Under Falon's harsh glare, Tomblin pulled back, saying, "I knew what you meant, boss. If you'd been there, Sloane Mosely would have paid you the same courtesy and respect he paid me—probably more."

"You're mighty damn right he would've," said Falon, "and don't you ever forget it." A tense silence set in for a moment. When it had passed, Falon asked in a more settled tone, "So what does he look like? How does he talk and handle himself?"

Tomblin shrugged as if having to think about it for a second. "Well, he just looks average-like, I reckon." Seeing that wasn't going to be enough for Falon, he added quickly, "But he does have a cold, hard look in his eyes, like at any minute he might just fly off into a rage—you know the kind of look I mean."

"Yeah, I know that look," said Falon, considering the image with a slight smile, realizing that some might say he had that same sort of look himself.

"As far as how he handled himself," said Tomblin, "even though he was hospitable enough, I noticed that all the time we talked, he never once took his hand off his gun."

"Yeah?" Falon liked that. His hand fell idly to his own gun butt. "I expect any serious gun handler is in the habit of doing that. I do it myself."

"Yes, you do, come to think of it," Tomblin said, placating Falon. He raised the cup of coffee to his lips, then frowned at it and set it down. Gesturing a nod toward the man behind the bar, he said, "Does Brother Lexar have anything out back that I might be interested in?"

"Yep," said Falon, "out in the barn. That's where Kirby and the rest of them are. I'm just sitting here for a while to keep up appearances."

"Do you mind if I go cut some dust from my throat?" Tomblin asked. "All this coffee is doing is aggravating me."

"No, go ahead," said Falon. But as Tomblin stood up from the table he added, pointing a finger at him, "Don't think that this is over though. We're finding them bodies. Every time we go to run the traps we're scouring the countryside till we find them."

"I understand," said Tomblin. He turned and stepped over to the open end of the bar, where Brother Lexar smiled, passed a small green bottle to him and nodded him toward the rear door leading out back and to a weathered livery barn. Slipping a small gold piece into Brother Lexar's hand, Tomblin said in a hushed tone, "Brother Lexar, you're the only *real* Christian in the bunch."

"I provide only what the Lord allows," Brother Lexar said with a sly grin, pocketing the gold piece.

Tomblin started for the back door, but stopped short when the sound of a brass bell rang out from the direction of the believers' meetinghouse. Looking around at Frank Falon, he said, "Does this mean I can't get on out back and catch a quick nip?"

"You know what that bell means," said Falon. "Don't bring trouble on us. Let's get out front and make a showing." He called out to Brother Lexar behind the bar, saying, "Hurry back there and tell all my men to hightail it out to the street, *pronto!*"

Out front, the bell rang again. "Yeah, yeah, we hear you," Falon said sarcastically. Looking back on his way to the front door, he saw Tomblin corking the small green bottle and sticking it inside his shirt. Tomblin grinned, running a hand across his lips. "Make damn sure that's hidden," Falon said. "You know what Jessup will do if he catches you drinking."

"Right," said Tomblin. "I just had to get a quick taste, is all." He adjusted the front of his shirt, making sure the bottle was not showing, then followed Falon through the bat-wing doors.

On the boardwalk Falon stopped abruptly at the sight of Jim Heady, his hands bound. Heady was being dragged along the middle of the street on the end of a short rope by two of Father Jessup's men. Heady resisted, cursing the two men loudly in a whiskey-slurred voice; but his captors yanked him forward, causing him to stumble along.

"Uh-oh," Falon said to Tomblin, "it looks like we've got a problem here. What's this young fool gotten himself into?"

"Beats me," said Tomblin, "but I can tell you what happens next."

"I know," said Falon. He looked back and forth nervously as more of Father Jessup's men appeared in doorways and gathered along the boardwalks and hitch rails. "There ain't a damn thing we can do about it though. We're outnumbered."

"We're always outnumbered," said Tomblin in a tone of disgust.

"What are you saying, Ace?" Falon asked coldly.

"Nothing," Tomblin replied in a clipped tone. Behind them, the rest of the men came through the bat-wing doors, having come from the barn at the sound of the bell, with Brother Lexar hurrying them. "But we can't stand by and allow this to happen to one of our own."

"It's the new man, Ace," said Falon. "He ain't exactly *one of us* yet, as far as I'm concerned." Falon stared away from Tomblin rather than face him.

From the street, Jim Heady called out in his whiskey-slurred voice, "Ace, Frank, Jaw, look at this! All of yas! Don't let them do this to me!"

One of the men leading him reached out with a long backhanded slap and sent him sideling to the ground. The other dragged him to his feet and shouted, "Now keep your mouth shut, *sinner*, if you know what's good for you. You're in enough trouble already!"

"Uh-oh," said Tomblin, "here comes Father Jessup." He called Falon's attention toward a large, powerful-looking man who stepped out of the doorway of the former sheriff's office across the street with a bullwhip coiled around his left shoulder.

"Aw, Jesus." Ace winced.

"What the hell did he do?" whispered Splint Mullins.

"Shut up and listen," Jaw Hughes replied.

"Whatever he done, he don't deserve no damn bullwhipping," said Quentin Fuller.

"Quiet, all of you!" Frank Falon hissed over his shoulder. Farther up the street, two more of Jessup's men came dragging another man along in the same manner.

"Look!" said Lewis Barr. "It's that young wolfer! The one from the boiling pits."

"I don't give a damn about him," said Lewis Barr, "but I ain't standing by and letting them whip Jim Heady. He ain't done nothing! Hell, he's been back in the barn with us all morning!"

"Everybody get ready to make our move," said Kirby Falon, standing directly behind his brother.

"You stand down," Frank Falon said in a harsh tone without turning to his younger brother. "I give the orders here. And I'm saying for everybody here to stand down and keep their mouths shut!" His right hand tightened around his gun butt. "Anybody saying otherwise?"

The men fell silent just as Father Jessup stepped into the middle of the dirt street to address the gathering crowd. "I want all of you to take a look at what we have here," Jessup's strong voice called out. "These men have both committed acts that not only bring shame to Paradise, but also bring offense to the Lord and His followers."

Jessup turned first to the young wolfer, who the two men

had stood up beside Jim Heady. "All of you remember Randall Turner, the man who ran up a burden of debt on himself and his family? Now that our community of believers has allowed him to work it off in a forthright manner, as any righteous man would want to do, instead of being grateful for the opportunity to redeem himself, he has chosen to go around talking against the very ones of us who have *helped* him!"

Randall Turner started to speak, but before he could say anything, one of the men holding him reached out and punched him soundly in his stomach.

Jessup smiled and turned his attention away from the young wolfer and toward Jim Heady. Pointing an accusing finger he said, "This man has been caught drunk, ignoring our town ordinance against alcohol." Jessup turned and faced the crowd of onlookers and said with finality, "Both men will be whipped publicly, ten lashes each."

"Like hell I will!" shouted Heady, hearing Jessup's words. He struggled violently against the men holding him. But it did him no good. The two men overpowered him and jerked him to the ground by the rope around his wrists.

Watching, Jessup called out, "Look at his *resistance* now! But where was this man's strength when it came to fighting Lucifer's temptation?" He pointed to the hitch rail. "Maybe this will open his eyes to the error of his ways. Take him to the hitch rail, Brothers," Jessup called out to the two men holding Heady by his arms.

Upon seeing the bullwhip come down from Jessup's shoulder and uncoil like a snake, Jim Heady managed to rise to his feet and call out in a sobered voice, "If you put that whip across my back, you better hope to God you kill me!"

Ace Tomblin murmured to himself, "Damn it, Heady, shut up."

The two men dragged Heady to hitch rail, where two other men helped to untie his hands and stretch his arms across the rail and retie them. Heady struggled with the men and turned toward Father Jessup, shouting, "If you don't kill me, I'm coming for you! You hear me, you rotten son of a—"

His words stopped abruptly as a pistol barrel whipped down across his bare head, not enough to knock him out, but enough to addle him while the men finished tying him. Jessup called out to one of the men, "Brother Paul, go to the blacksmith shop, fetch a pair of tongs. Jerk his tongue out and cut it off! He needs to be taught a lesson against blasphemy."

Brother Paul Chapin hurried away toward the blacksmith shop.

"Aw, Jesus, Frank," said Ace Tomblin, "we can't let Jessup get away with something like this!"

"You're right," said Falon, feeling that he wouldn't be able to control his men if he allowed such an act to go unchallenged. Stepping forward he said to Jessup, "Father Jessup, he didn't mean any blasphemy by it. Look at him." He nodded in Heady's direction, hoping to get Jessup to show some mercy on the young man. "This poor dumb ol' boy doesn't even know what blasphemy means."

"It doesn't matter if he knows it or not, he blasphemed me," said Jessup. "And whosoever blasphemes me, blasphemes the Lord almighty." Jessup's voice resounded powerfully as his eyes swept his gathered followers.

"He thinks pretty highly of himself, don't he?" Jaw Hughes grumbled among the men behind Falon. "I believe we ought to make a stand here. What say everybody?"

"Easy, men," Ace Tomblin warned them, speaking in a lowered voice. "This is likely going to get out of hand any second now as it is. Don't push it."

"Horsewhipping is enough, Father Jessup," Falon called out. "He's one *of us*. Anything else that gets done to him ought to be done by us."

"Defy *me* and you defy the Lord, Falon!" Jessup's voice boomed. As he spoke, he swung the whip out and cracked it in Falon's direction. "You are treading on dangerous ground."

But staring into Falon's eyes, Jessup saw more than defiance. He saw a warning. Falon's words were not meant to challenge him. Falon was telling him in his own way that he wouldn't be able to hold his men back if Jessup insisted on taking Heady's punishment any farther than a public whipping.

"Father Jessup," said Falon, "it's plain to see the man is drunk and talking out of his head. Whip him if you have to. But then give him to us. We'll see to it he never causes any trouble here again. You have my word on it. You have everybody's word on it." He gave a nod back toward the men gathered behind him, hoping Jessup would see that he was about to start a wildfire.

Jessup did see it. After considering his response, Jessup said, "I expect he'll loose his tongue soon enough once the whipping commences." Without looking at Falon he called out to Lexar, who stood off to one side watching, "Brother Lexar, you step out here and wield this whip for me. This man is a drunkard and will be punished." Looking at Chapin, who came running back to the middle of the street with a pair of iron tongs in his hand, Jessup said, "We'll not be using the tongs today. Instead Brother Lexar is going to whip this sinner until he cries out long and loud for God's mercy!"

Jim Heady shouted, "Don't bet on it, you big tub of—"

Again the pistol barrel silenced Heady.

In front of the former saloon, Jaw Hughes murmured to the other men gathered behind Falon and Tomblin, "This ain't right, Lexar bullwhipping Heady. Lexar's the man who sold him the whiskey."

"Shut up, Jaw," said Falon. "We're lucky we stopped him from cutting Heady's tongue out. Don't push the matter!"

As Lexar walked past them on his way to the middle of the street, Falon said secretively, "Go easy on him, Lexar. Me and the boys won't forget it."

Lexar gave no response. In the middle of the street he stopped and took the bullwhip from Jessup's outstretched hand. "Spare him not, Brother Lexar," Jessup said. "Let God hear this sinner cry out for mercy!"

"You ain't getting a word out of me!" Heady shouted defiantly, looking back over his shoulder as the two men tied his arms out along the hitch rail.

"Don't beg for nothing, Heady!" Jaw Hughes called out before Falon had a chance to stop him.

"Not a word, Jim, ol' pard!" said Arby Ryan. "Show them you can take it!"

"Shut up, both of you!" said Falon, although he felt like saying the same thing himself. Then he murmured under his breath, "This boy Heady is tough. He ain't going to give them the satisfaction." He stared confidently, watching one of the men rip the back of Jim Heady's shirt open, exposing his naked white back.

Preparing himself, Heady squeezed his eyes shut and called out to Lexar, who had taken the whip and spread it out for a long swing, "Do your worst! You'll get nothing out of me!"

Falon and his men winced as one when the first crack of the whip resounded and a bloody red welt appeared across Heady's back. Heady let out a long, shrill, agonizing scream, then began sobbing and crying aloud, "Oh, God, no! Please! No more! God have mercy! Oh mercy! Oh God! Mercy! Mercy! *Mercy!*"

Jaw Hughes swallowed a tight knot in his throat and said quietly to the others, "Well, I guess he held out as long as he could."

Chapter 6

Jim Heady screamed and begged until his words came in nothing more than a rasping whimper. By the fifth crack of the whip he lost consciousness and his head bowed beneath the hitch rail onto his wet naked chest. Lexar shot Falon and his men a look, but there was no letup in the way he swung the long whip, or the sound that it made slapping and tearing the pale fresh on Heady's bloody back.

"I'm not forgetting this," Falon whispered to the men gathered in close around him, their eyes fixed onto the grizzly scene.

"All this for having a few drinks to cut the dust from his gullet," Jaw Hughes whispered in reply. "And this son of a bitch the very one what sold it to him."

"I know," said Falon. "You ain't telling me nothing that I ain't already thought about."

When the final crack of the whip fell silent Jessup called out to Falon and his men, "You can have him now. Take him to the cells behind the believers' meetinghouse, where he'll spend today and tonight reflecting on his drunkenness and what it was brought him. Perhaps now he'll understand that this town is the Lord's town, and the Lord's vengeance will be come upon all who defy His ways."

"Yeah, let's hope so," Jaw Hughes murmured with an air of sarcasm. "Come on, Arby, let's cut him loose."

Without waiting for Falon's approval, the two ventured across the street to the hitch rail. Lexar handed the whip to Jessup and the two stood watching while Hughes took out his knife and cut the ropes that held Heady's arms tied to the rail.

Jessup called out, "Ordinarily I would demand that this man spend the next week behind the meetinghouse." He turned and nodded at the young wolfer who stood between his two guards. "But today we seem to have more than our share of transgressors to deal with in the name of the Lord. Brother Edmunds and Brother Searcy, take Randall Turner to the hitch rail and bind him good and tight." He swung the whip out on the ground before him. "I'll take care of this one myself."

"That's damn big of him," Jaw Hughes whispered to Ryan, the two of them lowering Heady between them as he moaned in pain. "Easy with him, Arby. He's cut all to hell."

"I'm easy with him," said Ryan. The two managed to drag Heady away, each holding him by an arm and a wrist, the toes of his boots leaving two snaking trails in the dirt behind him. Blood ran from his back down around to his belly and dripped steadily, leaving a string of dark spots on the dirt street. "Poor son of a bitch didn't deserve this," Ryan whispered.

"Am … am I through …?" Heady managed to ask in a rasping moan.

"Yeah, you're through, Heady," said Arby Ryan. "You might've held out just a tad bit longer, I'm thinking."

"Leave him be, Arby," said Jaw Hughes. "It's a hard thing, taking a whipping like that."

"I know it is," said Ryan. "I meant nothing by it, just that he might've held out a minute or two."

Hughes gave him a frown, then said to Jim Heady, "You're spending the day in a cell. Then you're done with all this. You can put it out of your mind."

"Give … give me a gun," Heady pleaded, his voice hoarse and spent from screaming.

"Sure thing, Heady," said Jaw Hughes. "That's the main thing you need right now is a gun. That would get you killed quicker than a cat can lick his whiskers."

"I mean to kill him," Heady moaned.

"Not right now you're not," said Arby. "Get yourself back in shape. Then go kill him. Nobody I know would ever blame you for it."

The two men dragged Heady the rest of the way to the meetinghouse, where three men standing guard dragged him inside. On the street the first crack of the bullwhip brought a tight, short yelp from Randall Turner, followed by a deep gasping sound as he fought to keep control of himself.

Not satisfied with how the young man managed to keep from screaming aloud for mercy, Jessup nodded slowly, slung the whip out on the ground and said, as he prepared for another swing, "So be it then. If you want to show us how tough and insolent you can be … I'll make this punishment a harsh example of the kind of malady that befalls the stubborn and wrongheaded." The next crack of the long bullwhip fell with more viciousness than the first.

"Good God almighty!" said Ace Tomblin to Frank Falon, keeping his voice down. "He's going to kill this one!"

"It sure as hell looks like it," Falon replied, squinting at the sight of the young wolfer writhing, clenching his teeth, tightening every muscle in his body against the slicing pain to keep from screaming his lungs out. "Poor bastard. He might be hoping Jessup *does* kill him before this is done."

Jessup stood silent for a moment, seeing if Randall was going to break. When he saw the young man seem to swallow the pain and slump, his weight pulling down hard on his tied arms, Jessup slung the whip out again, preparing to deliver an even harder blow, if he was capable of it. But before he could make the swing, a commotion from the direction of the meetinghouse drew his attention.

"Let me go!" a woman cried out. "Get away from me!"

Poised for the next lash Jessup turned and saw Delphia Turner come running toward the middle of the street, her thin gingham head cover flying free. Three women from the meetinghouse ran along behind her, grabbing frantically at her as she slung herself away from them and made her getaway. At the sound of his wife's voice, Randall Turner managed to turn his face enough to get a look at her and call out, "Run, Delph, run! Get away from here!"

But Delphia did not try to get away. Instead she ran straight to Jessup, stopping a few feet back from him, with her head lowered obediently, saying, "Father Jessup, please allow me a word with you regarding Randall Turner."

Jessup stood in stunned silence for a moment. This was the first time the young woman had ever showed him such behavior. So far all he had felt from her had been a cold undercurrent of defiance, even on those nights when she was forced to join him in his bed. As he stood staring at her, Edmunds and Searcy came running forward to grab her.

But Jessup called out, "No, leave her be, Brothers." To Delphia Turner he said, "What is it you have to say to me, *wife?*" He cut a glance toward Randall Turner, making sure the young man heard him.

Delphia brushed back a strand of long auburn hair, which had fallen loose when she lost her head cover. She glanced at Jessup, then looked down coyly at the ground and said, "It isn't something I want others to hear, *Father* Jessup. May I come forward? Can a wife ask a favor of her husband?"

It was the first time she'd ever called him *Father*, let alone *husband*. He smiled slightly, but managed to keep his joy showing too greatly. "Of course, dear wife. What is this favor you ask?" He draped the whip handle over his forearm as he spoke.

"I want to ask you to let this *boy* go," said Delphia, emphasizing the word *boy* in describing her young husband.

"Oh, and why would I want to do that," Jessup asked,

"after him saying so many terrible things about me and our community of believers?"

"He's young and foolish and he hasn't yet realized that I no longer belong to him … that I now belong to you, *Father* Jessup."

Jessup's smile widened. "I'm afraid that being young and foolish isn't enough reason to overlook what he's done. He has to pay for it."

"You'll see that whipping will do no good," said Delphia. "I know him well. He is stubborn and tough-skinned, and the only thing that will teach him anything is if he sees that I am going to make promises to you in order to spare him every time he does something rash and foolish like this."

"Delphia," Randall cried out, "please don't do this! Don't do this for me! Let him kill me! Please!"

Jessup's attention turned to Randall. With a bemused smile he said, "You might just be right, wife."

"I am right," Delphia said confidently. "I know him, and I know what would hurt him worse."

"Then speak up and tell me, wife," said Jessup.

Delphia blushed, and said in a lowered tone, "There are promises a wife makes to her husband that no one else should hear."

"Come over here, dear *wife*," said Jessup, feeling better about this by the second.

Edmunds and Searcy gave Jessup a cautioning look, but he brushed it aside, watching Delphia walk forward to him. When she stopped again no more than a couple of feet away, he looked closely at her hands, making sure they were empty as she cupped them and leaned toward his ear.

"I bet that *some* awfully pretty promise she's making," Falon whispered to Ace Tomblin. "Look how the good reverend's face is lighting up."

"This ain't none of our business, Frank," Ace offered in reply.

"I know it's not," said Falon. "I think we best get the men together and ride back up to the boiling shack."

"What about Heady?" asked Ace. "He can't leave until after Jessup says it's okay."

"Didn't you get a good look at him?" said Falon. "The shape he's in, he ain't going nowhere for a few days. Forget him for now. Once he gets his skin back on, he'll know where to find us, if he ain't too ashamed to come around licking his back." He walked out to his horse, his brother, Kirby, following him. He unhitched the reins and stepped up into his saddle. Looking back at the rest of his men, he saw them still standing on the boardwalk, with sullen expressions on their faces. Ace Tomblin stood in front with his thumbs hooked in his gun belt.

Falon called out in a forceful tone, "Damn it, boys! There ain't nothing we can do about it now! I said *let's ride!*"

Slowly the men looked at one another, then at Ace Tomblin. When Tomblin finally stepped toward his horse, the others followed. Falon backed his horse a few steps and leered menacingly at the men until they all rode away single file along the dirt street.

On the boardwalk a few yards away, stood four men in black business suits and long riding dusters. They'd ridden in after the whipping had started. The leader of the four—a tall, hard-faced man named Rudolph Banatell—held a carpetbag up under his left arm and said with a slightly dark chuckle, "Gentlemen, either tell me I'm stone blind or green-hog crazy, or else I just saw a man get the living hell whipped out of him for drinking whiskey."

"You're not blind, Rudy," said Ernie Harpe, the youngest of the four. "You saw it."

"You might be crazy, Rudy," said a large, stocky young man known only as Orsen, "but if you are, we all are. We saw it clear as day."

On the way into Paradise, Rudy Banatell and his men had

seen three crosses erected on a low hill on the outskirts of town. Beside the crosses a sign read WELCOME TO PARADISE, A COMMUNITY OF BELIEVERS. Thinking about the sign, Rudy said, "I reckon we'll walk the straight and narrow while we're here, men."

An older man named Shelby "the Gun" Keys, stepped forward and spit in the dirt in the direction of Falon and his men. Still talking about the whipping on the street, he said, "I can't abide his friends just riding off without firing a shot." His fingertips tapped idly on a big Smith & Wesson holstered across his belly. A big gold ring shaped out of a twenty-dollar gold piece glistened on his middle finger. "If that was any bunch I ever rode with, there'd already be buzzards already circling this shit hole. We'd've reaped vengeance, killed everything here that had air in it."

"Reaping vengeance is all we ever hear you talk about, Gun," said Ernie Harpe. "Why don't you get yourself another subject?"

"Hush, Ernie," said Rudy Banatell, grinning. "I like hearing that kind of tough talk. Gun was around when being a highwayman meant something. Right, Gun?"

"Yeah, I expect so," said Shelby Keys, ignoring Ernie Harpe. "Anyways, no man should take a whipping like that and not go back and cut that son of a bitch's arm off at the shoulder and beat him to death with it."

"See? There he goes again," said Ernie.

"I like it." Rudy grinned. Ernie and Orsen just shook their heads.

A young man with only a wispy thin line of a beard came hurrying along the street, and before he could pass the four, Rudy's hand reached out and snatched him to an abrupt halt. "Pardon me, lad," said Rudy, "but what we just saw here." He nodded toward the street where the onlookers were still dispersing. "Does this sort of amusement commonly take place on the streets here?"

Not understanding Rudy's dark humor, the young man gave him a serious look and replied, "Oh! No, sir. This wasn't public amusement. Those two men were being punished! They broke Father Jessup's town commandments. The one who got whipped the worst was drunk on strong drink!"

Seeing how serious the young man was about the incident, Rudy quickly adopted a serious expression himself, and said in a shocked tone, "No, you don't mean it! Drunk on strong drink?" He glanced at his three men and said, "Hear that, gentlemen? He was drunk on strong drink!"

"No wonder they whipped him then," Orsen commented, going along with Rudy, mocking the young man.

"Strong drink? I'm surprised they didn't hang him then," said Ernie, taking up the joke.

"Oh, no," said the young man, "Father Jessup would rather cure a man than take his life."

"That's big of him," said Rudy, wrapping an arm around the young man's shoulders. "What's your name, lad?"

"I'm Anderson Farnsley," said the young man. Proudly he added, "I'm one of the newest members of Father Jessup's fold."

"Indeed?" Rudy gave him an impressed look. "And how did that come about?"

"My father and mother both died last winter, and Father Jessup took me in when I turned over all of their earthly possessions to his community of believers."

"All their earthly possessions?" Rudy gave the other three men a knowing glance. "I'm sure you mean title to their land, money and such?"

"Yes, that's what it was. He took in me and my sister at the same time. I became a member of his fold and my sister, Martha, is to become one of his wives as soon as she turns twelve next month."

"One of his wives …" said Rudy, trying to contemplate the kind of situation that Jessup had going for himself. For a moment he stood silently, lost in that contemplation. Then, as if snapping out of a trance, he said, "Tell me something, Anderson. How would you like to show me and my associates around town? Sort of give us a welcoming tour, you might call it."

"Well, I'm on my way to Bible study."

"Well, we wouldn't want to keep you from that now, would we? Maybe you best run along then." But Rudy still kept his arm wrapped firmly around Anderson's shoulder. "We don't want to keep you from reading the Bible."

The young man made a slight tug, but then made no more attempt to free himself from Rudy's arm. "I don't read the Bible. None of us do. Father Jessup is touched by God and understands God's word perfectly. So he reads it to us—the parts that mean something, that is. Then he tells us what it means so we'll know how we're supposed to live by it."

"Oh, I see," said Rudy, giving the other three men another knowing look along with a bemused smile. "Well, again, I have to say, that *is mighty sporting decent* of him!"

"It inspires me," said Orsen, "and I'm not a man easily inspired."

"Me, too," said Ernie. "It nearly brings tears to my eyes."

Anderson looked around at the faces of the four men, feeling the arm around his shoulder begin to loosen its hold on him. "Perhaps it wouldn't hurt if I missed study, seeing it would be to show some newcomers around town." He offered a smile. "Who knows? You fellows might decide to stay and become members yourselves! Wouldn't that be something?"

"Yes, it *certainly* would," said Rudy, beginning to tire of the young man and his gullibility. "But these gentlemen and myself belong to too many other organizations as it is. I just don't see where we'd ever find the time."

Along the street Rudy saw another man approaching them as Anderson Farnsley started to say, "Oh, finding the time is—"

"There, there, enough said," said Rudy, cutting him off and patting his shoulder as he turned him completely loose. "You run along now. If we need you, we'll find you."

"But I want to be hospitable—" said Anderson.

Rudy gave him a little shove. "Then don't over-stay your welcome, lad."

"I hope young Anderson isn't making a nuisance of himself," said the man approaching them.

"This is Brother Beckman, our bank manager," Anderson said to Rudy Banatell, introducing the man.

"Yes, thank you, Anderson," said the man. "Now you get yourself on over to the study group"—he looked the young man up and down—"unless of course you already know it all."

"No, sir, Brother Beckman," said Anderson, backing away. "I'm on my way now!" He turned and broke into a run.

Forrest Beckman faced Rudy and his men. "You'll have to forgive Anderson. He's one of our newest brothers. I hope he hasn't been annoying."

"Not at all." Rudy grinned, touching his hat brim courteously. "We found the lad most informative. Didn't we, gentlemen?"

"A fountain of knowledge," said Orsen. Ernie Harpe and the Gun just stared.

"Well, in that case," said Brother Beckman, "as Anderson said, I am the bank manager." He spread his arms in a grand gesture. "Welcome to Paradise!"

"Thank you, sir," said Rudy. Then lying, he said, "I'm Mr. Able. These are my associates, Mr. Barnes, Mr. Carter and Mr. Dean." He swept a hand toward the others as he spoke quickly, using names he made up in alphabetical order. Then he stood grinning, waiting for Beckman to speak. Rudy Banatell was having fun seeing how far he could lead this banker. The man seemed awfully slow-witted to be in the money-handling business.

"So, then," Beckman said after a pause, "what brings you men to Paradise?"

"Your bank," said Rudy, flatly, just to see what look came to the banker's eyes.

"Our bank?"

Seeing only the slightest questionable expression come to Beckman's eyes, Rudy quickly said, "We have too much money on hand. We want to deposit it in your bank. Providing your bank is secure, of course."

"It isn't my bank. I only manage it for our community of believers. But let me assure you, gentlemen, this bank is safe! Safer than any bank I ever managed before I joined the fold."

"That's comforting to hear," said Rudy, with another grin. He dropped the carpetbag from under his arm, flipped it open and held it forward for Beckman to see. "Because as you can see, we're talking about some serious cash here. And we are prepared to pay a substantial fee to both you personally and your facility as well, for your help." He gave Beckman a quick wink.

Beckman's eyes widened slightly at the large amount of money piled in disarray; but they widened more as he saw the shiny Colt revolver lying nestled in the pile. He took a step back, saying, "Sir! Do you realize there is a gun in that bag?"

"No, kidding?" Rudy looked down, then picked up the Colt with two fingers and passed it over to Orsen, who took it and stuck it down in his belt. "I could have sworn I took that out before we left our camp." This fellow was unbelievably stupid, he told himself.

Beckman looked at the guns the men wore.

In response to Beckman's look, Rudy said, "As you can see, we are adequately armed anyway. I hope this doesn't frighten you?"

"Well, no," Beckman offered a bit reluctantly, "not now that you've explained your circumstances. I suppose if it were me carrying a large amount of money I'd be armed to the teeth. May I ask why you are carrying such a large amount across this hostile land?"

"Railroad money, sir," said Rudy, making a story up as he went along. He patted the carpetbag. "We're buying land for future rail speculation. Nothing helps like having the cash in hand when a deal is struck. It keeps folks from having doubts while they wait for drafts to be issued."

"Yes, of course," said Beckman. He reached for the door. "Let me show you gentlemen inside. I think you'll feel better once you see the new safe we've recently installed. It's large enough that a man could actually live in it!"

"My," said Rudy, stepping inside ahead of the others and looking all around at the polished oak woodwork and brass-trimmed counters. "I bet those thieving poltroons will think twice before taking you on, sir."

"Between having the new safe and the fact that the brothers are constantly on guard against any suspicious-looking strangers," said Beckman, "I can assure you this facility is a fortress."

"You know, sir," said Rudy, suddenly stopping as if something had just occurred to him, "now that I think of it, I wonder if the brothers might have been watching us moments ago, perhaps wondering if we were up to no good."

Beckman blushed. "A couple of them did mention that four strangers had arrived while Father Jessup was administering justice to those two lost souls. But after I took one look at you gentlemen, I assured everyone that you four were businessmen in need of banking services."

"Are we *that* obvious?" Rudy asked, giving Brother Beckman a helpless look.

"No, but when you've been in this business as long as I have, you learn to size a person up pretty quick."

"Indeed," said Rudy. To the others, he said over his shoulder, "Hear that, gentlemen? Mr. Beckman already had us pegged before we even said howdy." He grinned widely. "I find that to be a most comforting trait in a banker."

Chapter 7

Inside the bank in Paradise, Shelby immediately veered away from the others and started toward the far end of the long teller's counter to where he could keep an eye on everything. But before he could get there and into position, Rudy called out to him, saying, "This way, Mr. Dean! Let's all follow Mr. Beckman and not wander off on our own."

The Gun got Rudy's message, but he didn't like it. He stopped in his tracks, turned and gave Rudy a stern look, his hand resting tightly around his gun butt. He said with double meaning, "But I always like to look at a place from the long end, Mr. Able."

"Yes, I *know* that," said Rudy, the two of them understanding one another while the two tellers behind the counter seemed to see nothing out of the ordinary. "Only this time, will you *please* indulge me?"

"But I really want to do like I *always* do. I see no reason to change anything at the last minute."

Rudy gave the Gun a scorching look as Beckman unlocked a door in the counter and swung it open. Apparently nothing they had said made the banker suspect anything. "You'll have to overlook Mr. Dean," Rudy said to Beckman. Behind his back he made a motion with his hand for Orsen and Ernie to go deal with the Gun. "I'm afraid he's overcome with concern over all this money."

"Well, I can certainly remedy that," said Beckman, guiding Rudy through the door into an area behind the security wall and counter. "You'll soon see why I have such complete confidence in this facility."

Orsen and Ernie sidestepped a few feet across the floor, closer to the Gun, and Orsen growled as quietly as he could, "Gun, *gawdamn* it! You heard him! Get over here and do like he said!"

"Damn it! This ain't the way it was planned," the Gun grumbled to himself. He gave in and moved along toward the open counter door with Orsen and Ernie, but while doing so, he growled in reply, "I'm ready to do this thing! I'm tired of pussyfooting around about it!"

"Shut up!" Ernie whispered harshly, as the three of them tried to get through the counter door at the same time.

The Gun gave Ernie a slight shove from behind, snarling in reply, "Tell me to shut one more time, I'll crack this gun barrel across your jaw!"

The sound of their commotion and harsh whispers drew a glance from Beckman. Rudy stepped quickly in between the banker and the arguing gunmen and said in a raised voice to drown them out, "So this is the big fellow you were talking about, eh?"

"Big fellow?" Beckman looked confused.

Rudy gestured with a hand toward the partly open steel door of the safe that stood embedded into a solid stone wall. "*This* big fellow," he said with a smile. Behind him the commotion among the men quieted down. The Gun sidestepped and circled around to the front of the safe, his fingers tapping faster on his gun butt, the large golden ring on his middle finger flashing nervously back and forth. With his free hand he reached out, grabbed the big steel door and pulled hard, opening it the rest of the way. The sight of shelves stacked high with money and more bulging bags of coins sitting piled on the floor caused the Gun, Orsen and Ernie to gasp. Seeing the look on Orsen's and Ernie's faces, the Gun said, "Let's get on with it!" His fingers stopped tapping; his hand tightened around his gun butt and started to raise it from his holster. A startled look came upon Beckman's face.

"Mr. Dean!" Rudy said strongly. "Control yourself! I'll say when we *get on with it!*" He turned quickly to Orsen and Ernie. "Is that clear to everybody?"

Beckman stood stunned until Rudy turned to him and said in a consoling tone, "He's talking about getting on with making the deposit, Mr. Beckman. You'll have to forgive him … all of us for that matter. I'm afraid this money has us all four a little spooked."

"And rightly so," said Beckman, collecting himself and focusing again on getting that large amount of railroad money into the bank. "If you will, sir, I quite agree with Mr. Dean! Let's get that money to where it's safe and you gentlemen can rest easy and quit sniping at one another." He gestured toward the safe, and all around the well-secured area behind the counter. Along the inside of the counter the two tellers smiled. Near each teller's hand a shotgun rested on a shelf beneath the counter. Above each teller station a revolver hung on a peg, ready to be jerked down and put into use.

"I agree. Let's quit all this sniping," said Rudy, giving his men a quick, cold glance.

But when Beckman reached to take the carpetbag, Rudy tightened his grip on it and said, "Not so fast, sir. I have a concern or two about Paradise."

"Oh?" Beckman raised a brow. "And what might those concerns be?"

Rudy said, "When we rode in here we saw a man being whipped in the street for drinking whiskey. Public whipping strikes me as being a primitive way to maintain order."

"Father Jessup dispenses justice here with an iron hand," said Beckman. "But I think anyone you talk to will tell you that he is not only a fair, noble man, but indeed, a man touched by God."

"There's just something a little unsettling about a town run that way," said Rudy, pulling back slightly as Beckman reached for the bag again. "How do I know this town isn't on the verge of revolting against this kind of heavy-handedness? I put railroad money in here … first thing I know, the citizens have struck a torch to this place. *Poof!* It all goes up in a puff of smoke!"

"Mr. Able," said Beckman, shaking his head, "no offense, but that is absurd! This whole nation should be run as tightly and as benevolently as Paradise."

"All the same," said Rudy, with another quick look around that took in as much of the place as he could before leaving, "I believe I'll think about this for a short while before depositing this money. Perhaps it would be best if I first met the good Father Jessup in person—get an idea the kind of man he is."

"Oh," said Beckman, "I don't think Father Jessup would agree to that! He seldom meets with anyone who isn't a follower!"

"That's too bad then," said Rudy, patting a hand on the carpetbag. "I really feel it would help me make a decision."

"I'll ask." Beckman shrugged helplessly. "But I doubt if he'll even consider it."

"Yes, you ask, and let me know," said Rudy. "Meanwhile, I might want to look the town over, meet a few residents, hear what they have to say about Paradise."

Thinking of nothing more he could say to sway the man, Beckman shrugged and spread his arms. "Well, if you insist, sir. I know you will find no one here who can say anything but good things about our town."

"In that case, I'm obliged for your time and you will be seeing us, and our money again, as soon as Father Jessup decides to meet us in person," said Rudy, jiggling the carpetbag slightly. He turned toward the counter door.

But the Gun called out in disbelief from the open door of the safe, "What about all this money?"

Rudy turned and looked at the faces of all three of his men, each looking completely stunned by his behavior. "Yeah, the Gun's right! What about all this money?" Orsen asked, his face flush, his hand on his Colt.

Rudy gave Beckman a quick glance to see if had caught on to what they were talking about. But as soon as their eyes met, Beckman said, "Yes, what about all this money? Surely if it's safe enough for all these depositors, it should be safe enough for you!"

Rudy stared at him, bemused by his failure to see what they were referring to. "Well, that certainly is a valid point to consider." He turned to the men, and said, "Now, gentlemen, *let's go!*"

Reluctantly the three men filed past him and Beckman, through the safety door, then across the floor and out onto the boardwalk. "You will be hearing from us soon, sir," said Rudy, touching his hat brim, then turning and following his men.

On the edge of the boardwalk, out front, Rudy stuck his cigar between his lips and drew deeply on it, before letting go of a long, thin stream of smoke.

"What the almighty *hellfire* was that all about?" the Gun demanded, fighting to keep his voice down. "That's more money than I ever saw in one bank in my whole damned thieving life! All we had to do was take it! That stupid turd would've helped us pack it out of there!"

"The Gun's right, Rudy," said Ernie.

Smiling as he looked back and forth assessing the town, Rudy said without turning to face the men, "Tell these two why we decided not to rob the bank right then, Orsen."

The big, stocky gunman scratched his head for a moment. "To be honest, Rudy, I don't *know* why we didn't. Everything just sort of fell in place. We couldn't have asked for a better setup. You must've seen something you didn't like."

"That's right, I did," said Rudy, "but that's not the only

reason." He puffed on the cigar. "I always try to stick to a plan. The plan was that we would meet CC Ellis here in Paradise. We won't make a move until he shows up. I was just checking that bank out, making sure it was going to be ripe for the pickings. But it didn't feel right making a move until we first hear something from CC. The other thing is, that whole deal was going just too damn perfect to suit me. It's a trap, a setup of some sort."

"Trap my aching ass," said the Gun, his finger with the golden ring back at work tapping on his gun butt. "There are few things in life that just fall right into a man's lap. This was one of them. We might have just hexed ourselves, not taking advantage of it. I don't get it!" He shook his head.

"It's called patience, Gun," said Rudy. "We're going to put off the bank for a day or two and hope CC shows up. Meanwhile, I want to just look around a bit. It's my first trip to Paradise. I want to take my time and enjoy this lovely hamlet." The three looked at one another not knowing what to make of Rudy Banatell's attitude.

Rudy puffed on his cigar and looked back and forth along the street again in contemplation. "What do you suppose is taking CC Ellis so long to get here? He was supposed to get here days ahead of us and look this place over."

"I think this job had CC spooked from the beginning," said Orsen. "He must've seen something he didn't like here and hightailed it on us."

"Watch your mouth, Orsen," said Ernie. "CC is steady as a rock."

Orsen said to Ernie, "Boy, you're getting awfully quick to reprimand a person."

"Easy, both of yas," said Rudy. "I hate to make our move here without CC. I don't like being a man short on a job this size."

"This bank ain't nothing," said the Gun, looking around with an appraising eye, his fingers still tapping his gun butt furiously. He shrugged. "We don't need CC. We hit hard, take what we can grab, kill a bystander or two to make sure folks see we're serious, then ride out."

"That's what I like about you, Gun," said Rudy. "You keep things simple. I bet you sleep well of a night, don't you?"

"Like a baby," said the Gun.

"All the same," said Rudy, "we'll give CC a couple more days before we make any move." He puffed his cigar and smiled to himself. "This little waiting spell might just be good for the soul. I want a better look at this Father Jessup—see what he's all about."

"He's all about hot air and bullwhips—it looks like to me," said the Gun.

"You're missing the picture, Gun," said Rudy. "A whole string of wives, a fat bank—Father Jessup lives awfully high, from the looks of it all. Maybe I ought to be a preacher myself."

"He might have it made now," said Orsen, "but that sort of thing doesn't happen overnight. I bet it's taken him a while to put together something this big. He had to find people foolish enough to live under his thumb. Like that dumb ol' boy Anderson."

"Yeah," said Rudy, grinning, "or those three young ladies … the one who ran out to Jessup and the two who tried to stop her. I can't say which of the three was the prettiest. Ol' Jessup has them warming his bed of a night, *all three* of them, maybe even more!"

"That wasn't something easy to find either," said Orsen. "Women are scarce in these parts, especially the pretty ones."

"So much the better," said Rudy, reaching inside his duster and taking out a match. "He's already rounded them up and sorted them out." He struck the match and held the flames to his cigar, turning it as he puffed. Blowing out a stream of smoke he continued, saying, "It looks like all I'd have to do is squeeze this Jessup fellow off his roost, take this flock over and make it my own."

"What about this bank?" the Gun asked in a guarded tone. "I came here to make myself a raise ... not turn preacher all of a sudden." He spit and kept his fingers tapping his gun butt.

"Relax, Gun." Rudy chuckled, stepping down off the boardwalk and into the street, the carpetbag still up under his arm. "We're just speculating ... looking at every possibility so to speak. We'll take the bank before we're finished here." He walked toward a tall white clapboard hotel across the street, his eyes going along the edge of its blue-trimmed facade and showing no visible notice of having seen two riflemen duck down behind it. He gave the Gun a glance and a short gesture that asked if he had also seen the riflemen.

"Yep, I see them! It *was* a damn setup," the Gun said in a hushed tone. "You *were* right!"

"Of course I was right, Gun," Rudy beamed confidently. "The longer you ride with me, the more you're going to realize I'm seldom wrong on matters of robbing and the like. Watch me close and you might even learn something. Right, Orsen? Right, Ernie?"

Ernie and Orsen snickered and each gave a grunt of agreement. The Gun grumbled under his breath and said, "All right then ... when will we make our play here?"

"Soon, but don't stand in a strain waiting," said Rudy. He gave another glance back and forth along the street, his eyes going across the street to the meetinghouse doors, where he'd last seen Delphia Turner and the other two women. "I'm going to take my time, decide what it is I really want out of Paradise."

In a locked, cell-like room behind the meetinghouse, Jim Heady lay on his stomach on a hard wooden bench, shivering uncontrollably. Kneeling beside the bench, Randall Turner dipped a bloody rag into a bucket of cool water, wrung it, shook it out and laid it gently on Heady's tortured back. Heady clenched his teeth, gripped the sides of the bench and held his breath for a moment, then settled and began shivering again. "I'll kill that son of a bitch if I have to walk through fire to do it," he said in his hoarse voice.

"Shh," said Randall. "Let it go. This isn't the time or place to be talking about it."

"Let it *go?*" said Heady. "You must be crazy!" He gave a sidelong glance at Randall, seeing that the other man's shirt had been torn away also. A streak of dried blood led down the young wolfer's shoulder onto his chest. "You got the same thing I got, *wolfer,*" said Heady. "Don't tell me you ain't ready to gut hook that rotten bastard yourself!"

Calmly, Randall said as he carefully touched down on the wet rag, helping it soak up the blood from Heady's back, "I'm not telling you one way or the other. Talking won't do anything, as far as I'm concerned."

"Oh?" Heady gave him another sidelong glance, fighting another round of uncontrollable shivering. "Are you saying I'm all talk, wolfer?"

"No," Randall said flatly. "I'm just saying talking is no help. I'll do what I do. But I won't talk about it first. I'll just do it." He winced a bit, feeling the pain in his own whip-cut back.

"Why ain't you shaking like I am?" Heady asked. "I don't see how you can keep from it."

"I didn't get it as bad as you did," he added. Then his voice took on a bitter twist. "My *wife* stopped him before he got that far."

"Oh, yeah," said Heady. Realizing what the young man meant, he spoke in a kinder tone, saying, "Sorry I brought it up."

"No reason to be," said Randall. "She's still my wife, even though he's forcing himself on her."

A shiver ran the length of Heady's body; then he looked around again at Randall and asked, "You forgive her?"

84

"Forgive her for what?" Randall replied. "It's not her fault. She's done no wrong."

Heady shivered. "No, I reckon not. But still, you'd take her back? I mean, knowing that her and him … you know."

"Yes, I know," said Randall. He gently peeled the wet rag up from Heady's back and dipped it into the bucket. "And yes, of course I'd take her back. I *will* take her back. She's my wife, I told you. No matter what else happens she'll still be my wife when it's all finished."

Heady grimaced and shook his head. "You wolfers are strange folks. I know that much. Falon says you're all a cut apart from ordinary folk. I suspect he's right."

"I'm not a wolfer," said Randall. "I'm a farmer. At least I will be once I get my wife back and get on into Oregon. And my name is Randall Turner. Skinning and boiling wolves is just something I'm forced into doing right now. It'll pass. What a man does at a particular time doesn't make him what he is. It's what a man is for his whole life that makes him something." He wrung out the wet rag, shook it out and laid it across Heady's upper shoulders, where the blood had begun welling again.

"Whatever you say, Randall," said Heady, fighting off a shiver. "I'm in no shape to disagree about anything right now. All I ever saw was you fellows boiling wolves for their bones. I never talked with any of you enough to know who you are or what else you might be." He shivered and lowered his head. "Damn, I'm hurting deep down. I know that much."

"Try not to think about it," said Randall. "It'll pass." He pressed down on the wet rag with his fingertips.

"I know one thing," said Heady. "If this son of a bitch is what religion is all about, I don't want nothing to do with it. Nothing to do with God, the devil or nothing else. It can all go straight to hell, for my part."

"You can't blame God for what Jessup's doing," Randall said. "Just because a man does something in God's name, it

85

doesn't mean God is behind it."

"Well," said Heady, giving in a little as his shivering lessened, "it's supposed to mean it. Preachers are supposed to be part of God's world and the way God wants things ... or so I always heard."

"I don't know how things are supposed to be," said Randall. "All I know is, if a man blames God for what some foul piece of work like Jessup does, he didn't believe much in God to begin with. I expect God is as angry at Jessup as we are, maybe more so for all the wrong he's doing in God's name."

Heady forced himself to turn over onto his side, facing Randall. "Then maybe God won't mind when I go blow his head off, huh?"

"I told you I've got no answers," said Randall. But Heady saw something dark glisten in the young wolfer's eyes. "I've just got to do whatever I've got to do to go on. I don't know if God or the devil dealt me this hand. All I know is I've got to play it out, best I can."

Studying Randall's eyes, Heady said in a whisper, "I wasn't just talking when I said what I'll do. Maybe I should've just kept quiet and gone on and done it. But it wasn't just hot air blowing. I'm going to do it."

"I know," said Randall. "I believe you will if you get the chance."

"We ought to swear an oath between us," said Heady. "Both of us vow to do whatever we have to do to kill him. What do you say?"

"That oath has already been made," Randall said in a guarded tone. "I didn't need you to make it."

"Yeah, but the two of us together have a better chance of doing something than we do on our own."

"What about Frank and Kirby Falon and all the trappers you ride with?" Randall asked. "Won't they be siding with you?"

"They didn't lift a finger to stop Jessup," Heady said bitterly. "Far as I'm concerned, they can all go to hell. I'm on my own from here on." He reached out with his shaking bloodstained hand and said, "What do you say? Want to make a pact with me?"

Randall thought about the offer for a second, almost reaching out and taking Heady's hand, but stopping himself just short of doing it. Shaking his head he said, "I expect I'd make a pact with the devil himself, if that's what it took to get Delphia away from that evil man. But I think you and I are after two different things. I better go it alone."

Heady shivered, gave Randall a look and shrugged off the rejection. "Go it alone then, if that's the way you feel about it. We both still want to kill the same son of a bitch. Pact or no pact, I'm still offering my hand in friendship." He reached out again.

"None of you trappers ever offered any of us wolfers a hand in friendship before," said Randall. "I reckon it takes some getting used to." The two shook hands. Heady lay back down flat on his belly. Randall carefully peeled the wet rag from his back again, and dipped it into the bucket of water.

PART II

Chapter 8

In the night Callie Mosely had dreamed of her husband's embrace; and in the morning she had awakened still imagining the feel of him on her skin. The sensation of him making love to her in the night had been strong and vivid, more so than anything she had felt throughout the length of his absence. "Damn you, Sloane Mosely," she had murmured to herself, hearing how close she was to tears. Then she had pushed herself up from the bed and gone about her daily chores, more aware than ever of CC Ellis being there with her and Dillard.

By midmorning a dark cloud had moved in from the west, and its presence, along with her dreams of her husband and the presence of CC Ellis in her home, so close to her, had cast a pensive, wait-and-see aura to the day. She had been a bit too sharp telling Dillard *no* when he asked to take Tic and go down along the creekbank. When he had walked away across the yard, both boy and dog looking crestfallen, CC Ellis had stepped nearer to her from where he sat cleaning his Colt and asked if anything was wrong.

"Nothing is wrong, Mr. Ellis," she snapped at him. With a look of disdain toward the disassembled Colt lying atop a nail keg, she said to him, "When you're *through* cleaning your gun, perhaps you'll ride the stallion up along the ridgeline."

Ellis had turned away without a word, but he gave her a

look that let her know he saw more of her than she had wanted to show. "And damn you, too, Mr. Ellis," Callie said under her breath as he walked away, as if continuing the conversation she'd begun earlier on the edge of her bed. She stood and watched the man walk away to the barn, noting that his wound had greatly improved. He would ride away any day, she told herself. Sighing to herself, she looked up and out across the graying sky, then walked back into the house and stood at the window watching Ellis ride away, upward toward the ridgeline that wreathed the trail into Paradise. After he was long out of sight she continued to stare at the hills and the dark sky above them until rain blew across the yard and ran steadily down the window-panes.

It was afternoon when she heard the sound of the barn door creak open; she walked to the window and looked out at Ellis stepping down from the saddle and leading the stallion into the barn. Stepping in beside her, peeping out through the rain, Dillard asked, "Shall I go help him, Mother?"

"No, Dillard," she said absently, staring out at the open barn door. "You and Tic stay here out of the rain. I need to speak to Mr. Ellis privately."

"What about, Mother?" Dillard asked.

She looked down at him for a moment, lost for an answer. "Never you mind," she said at length. "Stay here like I told you."

She avoided her son's eyes as he watched her take a shawl down from a peg beside the door and drape it around herself, covering both her head and shoulders and giving the end of it a toss around her neck. "Will it ever stop raining?" she murmured, opening and closing the door behind herself. She stood against the door for a moment as if having second thoughts. Then she hurried from the porch, across the muddy yard, and through the open door of the barn.

Just inside the barn door, she stopped short at the sight of CC Ellis lifting the saddle from the big stallion's back.

She unwrapped the shawl from her head and let it rest on her shoulders. She shook out her hair. Ellis wore her husband's long riding duster and broad-brimmed, which usually hung in the barn; and seeing him from behind in the afternoon gloom she had to remind herself that it was not Sloane Mosely standing there with his back to her. *Damn you, Sloane Mosely....*

A moment of silence passed as she stood watching him heft the saddle onto a stall rail and turn and stroke the big stallion's muzzle with his gloved hand. Then the silence was broken when she heard him speak gently without turning toward her. "Are you coming inside ... or staying out in the rain?"

She didn't know if it was the sound of his voice, or simply the surprise of him knowing she was there, but something caused her to gasp.

"Sorry," he said, still without turning to face her. "I didn't mean to startle you."

"You didn't startle me," she said, a bit defensively. "I don't startle easily." As she spoke, she studied the wet hat brim and the duster darkened wet across the shoulders. She waited for a reply, and when none came she realized that once again that he saw through the tough exterior she had been hiding behind these past few days. "Well, a little perhaps," she said, her voice softening, something inside herself no longer able to sustain the pretense. Another silence passed and she said, "It's seldom we get this much rain this time of the year." She paused, then said a bit awkwardly, "But we need it ... the land, that is."

He turned facing her, finding her change of tone and further conversation encouraging. "Yes," he said, "the land needs it." Holding the stallion's bridle in one hand, and a rope lead he'd slipped over the big animal's head in the other, he stroked the stallion's chin and studied Callie Mosely's face in the grainy light.

Ellis noted a change in her: her demeanor, her eyes, the sound of her voice. She was not the same as she had been only hours ago. She had abandoned something—*a barrier*, he told himself. That wall of formality she had kept raised guardedly between them was suddenly gone, and Ellis knew why she had come to the barn, and why she had acted the way she had acted earlier. A decision had been made while he was off riding the ridgeline. He saw it in her eyes. This was the first time she had held his gaze this long without looking away as if something about him annoyed her. "It's been a year," she heard herself say, her voice sounding like someone else talking through her. She took one step forward and stopped, her hand still clutching the shawl at her throat.

"I know," he said. Ellis dropped the stallion's lead rope and gave the stallion a gentle shove, his eyes never leaving Callie's. He peeled the gloves from his hands as he moved past her, closed the barn door and returned to her. He stood near her, nearer than he had ever stood, nearer to her than he ever thought he'd be allowed to stand. He put his hands on her shoulders, a questioning look coming to his eyes. "No, don't," she said. "We mustn't."

"I know," he whispered, and at first he felt the slightest resistance as his lips met hers. But before he could move away, rejected, she opened her lips to him and drew him into her mouth, kissed him with deep urgency.

At the end of the kiss he pulled the shawl back from her shoulders and pitched it aside onto a pile of fresh straw, all the while keeping his mouth to her throat, pressing her against him. "My husband ..." she moaned, not trying to push him away, but rather wrapping her arms around his neck as he lifted her up off her feet.

"I know," he whispered. Her legs went around him and he carried her into a bin of fresh dried hay, her dress seeming to come undone on its own.

"He'll kill you...." She fell beneath him into the softness

of the hay, the fresh scent of it stronger than the smell of rain and earth.

"I know …" he whispered again.

She gave herself to him completely, the sound of rain on the tin roof only partially muffling the sounds of their passion. When they were finished, they lay only for a few moments in the fresh hay before hearing the door creak open slowly. "Mother?" Dillard said from the crack of dim daylight, his restlessness having gotten the best of him.

"Yes, Dillard," Callie said calmly, rising onto her knees, slipping into her dress and brushing hay from her hair as she spoke.

"Can I come in?" Dillard asked.

"We're still talking, Dillard," she said, rising to her feet, watching Ellis step quickly into his trousers and pull his boots onto his bare feet. "Close the door and go back to the house. I'll be there shortly."

"Yes, Mother," said Dillard. "Come on, Tic."

Callie and Ellis stood in tense silence until the door creaked shut. "I meant what I said," Callie said barely above a whisper. "My husband must never know about this."

"Yes, I understand," Ellis said. He stepped forward and brushed a strand of hair from her eyes. As gently as he could, he said, "But, Callie, listen to me. Sloane Mosely isn't coming back."

She had lowered her eyes from his, but now she raised them and said in a stronger tone, "You say that like you know it for a fact." She searched his eyes, seeing something there that she found puzzling, almost a guarded yet knowing look. "Do you know my husband, CC?" she asked pointedly. "Is there something you know that you're keeping from me?"

Ellis grimaced a bit. "I'm just going by what I see, Callie. Like you said, it's been a year. If he was coming back he'd be here. You have to face it."

Silently, she began weeping, but the only sign of her grief

was a single tear that ran slowly down her cheek.

"I don't want to see you go through this, Callie," he said, coming even closer, taking her in his arms. "I don't know what might have happened to him out there, but you have to accept it, for your sake and the boy's. Sloane Mosely is *not* coming back to you."

She spoke against his chest. "But how can you be so—"

"Shh, please," he said, cutting her off. "Don't do this to yourself. Let him go, Callie. He's gone ... but I'm here. I'll be here, and I want to stay here. I won't leave you. You have my word."

"What about Father Jessup?" she asked. "He'll soon know my situation. What then?"

"We'll go on the way we've been going," said Ellis. "Nothing has to change. Nobody here seems to have ever seen your husband. As far as they're concerned, I'm *still* Sloane Mosely. When we get ready, we'll leave here, take the boy and go somewhere far away. We'll make a new start, both of us."

"Do you mean that, CC Ellis?" she asked. "If you don't mean it, please don't say it. What happened here doesn't make you obligated to me in any way."

"I want to be obligated to you, Callie," he said, sincerely. "I mean what I said more than I've meant anything in a long, *long* time." Holding her against him, he stared off into the grayness, reminding himself that starting over might not be an easy thing to do. There had been a reason why he'd come here to Paradise. That reason could not be ignored—not if he expected him and the woman and the child ever to live in peace.

* * *

In a private office above the bank, Beckman and Lexar awaited Father Jessup's arrival. Beckman stood looking out the window, watching Randall help Jim Heady walk stiffly along the dirt street from the meetinghouse. "Those poor men," he whispered aloud to himself, seeing the pair pass the front of the hotel, where they both stopped and turned toward Rudy Banatell and his men when Rudy called out to them.

"Who's that you're talking about?" Lexar asked, taking a step toward the window and looking down himself. "Oh, those two," he said before Beckman could answer. "Yes, I quite agree. Those are a couple of sad cases. I'm afraid neither one learned anything from that whipping."

Beckman only stared at Lexar for a moment before the two turned and seated themselves in two wooden chairs facing the door. On their way to the chairs, Lexar picked up two full water glasses from atop a linen-covered table and handed one to Beckman before seating himself. They sipped the cool water, Lexar looking wistfully at the clear liquid and wishing it was something stronger. Swirling the water around in the glass he said quietly, "I'm not complaining mind you, but I think it looked bad, me using the whip on that wolf trapper after being the very one who sold him the whiskey."

"It might have looked bad to the trappers and to you and me," said Beckman. "But Father knew what he was doing. It was his way of letting Falon and his men know that in Paradise they live only by Jessup's law. He's the one who says what's fair and what's not. They have no right to question it."

"I understand," said Lexar. "Like I said, I'm not complaining. I'm sorry I brought it up."

"You needn't worry, Lexar. I'm not going to say anything about it," said Beckman. Lowering his voice because someone might hear, he said, "There is something I might say to you, providing you swear a solemn oath never to repeat it."

Seeming to consider the request for a moment, Lexar raised his right hand and said, "All right. Here is my hand to God that whatever you say to me will never be repeated to Father Jessup." He stared intently at Beckman and asked, "Do you swear the same?"

Beckman hurriedly raised his thin hand. "Yes, of course, I swear the same thing." Fidgeting in his chair he said, "All right, here goes. The truth is, I'm having trouble understanding all this public whipping, *period*. There's been too much of it of late. I think it's hurting our community instead of helping it. I wish Father would stop it completely. I think I'm going to have to tell him my thoughts on it."

Lexar gave him a cautious look, saying, "Are you serious? You're going to mention it to Father?"

"I'm afraid I must," said Beckman, "for the good of all of us here in the community. If we're going to grow and prosper, we've got to show ourselves as more hospitable to outsiders."

"Father Jessup doesn't want any more outsiders passing through here than is absolutely necessary," said Lexar. "That's why we have no telegraph lines, or no rail spur. The more outside influence we allow into the community, the more corrupt our values become,' he always says, 'until we fall short of God's glory.' I don't think you're going to change his thinking on that."

"I feel I've got to try," said Beckman, nervously straightening his stiff white collar. "Now that I've told you, I'm hoping that perhaps you will side with me on it."

"No," Lexar said flatly. "I don't want to end up tied to the hitch rail! And that's where you'll be if you try to change his mind. First of all, it's not his words, but God's, don't forget. Try to change God's words and Father will show no mercy. You ought to know that by now."

"I do know that," said Beckman. A tense silence passed; then he said reluctantly, "Although, just between the two of us, I have to say, there are times when I wonder if maybe Father Jessup lets his own beliefs seep into God's word. I know I shouldn't say it and I pray you'll never tell him I said it, but if God wants this community to grow and thrive the way Father Jessup said he does, I think the people are going to have to see more freedom and less bull-whippings." He glanced around nervously as if making sure his words went no farther than to Lexar.

"Careful," said Lexar. "Don't tell me so much that I begin thinking it's a test of faith and loyalty set up by Father— because I will tell him if I think this is a trick you and he have concocted on me."

"This is no trick, Lexar," said Beckman. "Didn't we both swear an oath? So help me, God, this is just you and me speaking our minds in the strictest of confidence." He leaned in even closer to Lexar and said, "We're losing believers, Lexar. And there have been grumblings from those who live away from town. Even the wolf trappers patrolling the hills and plains can't keep them from slipping away in the middle of the night."

"It's a hard four-day ride across Wolf Valley," said Lexar. "They know that Falon and his men will catch them before they get out of the valley and into hiding." He shook his head. "No, I haven't heard anything about this. I think you're mistaken."

"I'm not mistaken, Lexar," said Beckman. "You haven't heard about it because it's not something that you *would* hear about. But running the bank makes it important for me to know everything going on that might affect our community's financial standing. Believe me, we have lost some people … and we can lose more if we're not careful. These whippings don't help attitudes any."

"I think you're right," said Lexar, "I heard about the railroad men not depositing their money in our bank. I'm certain that upsets a banker like yourself."

"Indeed it does," said Beckman. "There's no excuse for that happening. Those men saw us as a barbaric religious sect. They said they might make the deposit after meeting Father Jessup in person. But personally, I'm afraid they will never deal with us after witnessing such behavior. And this at a time when we need money badly!"

"Need money badly?" Lexar gave him a curious look.

But Beckman didn't seem to hear him. He sipped the cool water and touched a handkerchief to his moist lips. "Now that you and I have shared these thoughts, I wonder how many others of our community might feel the same if we discussed it with them."

"Probably more of them than we think," said Lexar. "But about needing money—"

"Yes, I'm sure of it," said Beckman, cutting him off, turning talkative all of a sudden now that he realized he had someone to talk to. "I believe that's the reason Father Jessup's law is so strict against gossip. He doesn't want us talking too much to one another. He wants us to be afraid to speak our minds. There is a large cloud of distrust hovering over all of us. We fear *the whip*, and it appears that our fear of the whip is costing us our freedom." He reached over and grasped Lexar's sleeve, saying desperately, "Do you see it?"

"Yeah, yeah, I see it," Lexar said, tugging his arm free. "But calm down. Tell me what you meant about us needing money so badly. I saw piles of money in the safe only this morning."

"Of course you did." Beckman gave him a grave stare for a moment, then started to say more on the matter. But before he could speak, footsteps coming up the stairs and down the hall caused him to stop, straighten upright in his chair and fidget with his stiff collar. "We'll talk more about it later," he whispered as the doorknob turned.

Brothers Edmunds and Searcy stepped inside the room first, giving a quick look around before taking a position on either side of the door. Father Jessup stepped inside and stopped for a moment, allowing Beckman and Lexar to stand up respectfully. Then, motioning the two to be seated, he stood with his arms crossed and stared from one to the other with a strange half smile on his large face. Finally he stepped closer to the banker and fixed his gaze down on him.

"Brother Beckman," Jessup said, towering over the frightened banker, "is there any *reasonable* excuse in this world for those four men not depositing their money in our bank. If there is please tell us. I'm sure we'd all like to hear it."

Beckman cowered in his chair, looking up at Jessup. "They were concerned, Father," he said meekly. "Seeing those men whipped in the street has caused them to rethink trusting the railroad's money to us."

"Hmph!" said Jessup. "What a coincidence that they should express such a belief at about the same time you've been going around behind my back harping about doing away with public whippings."

"Oh, no, Father," said Beckman, his voice turning broken and unsteady, "I haven't gone around harping about anything behind your back!" His eyes widened in terror. "It's true. Their leader, Mr. Able, is greatly put off about the whipping incident! He insists on meeting you personally before entrusting the money to our bank. But, Father, please don't think I have said anything against you or our community. I would never do such a thing!"

"Is that so?" Jessup turned his attention to Lexar, asking, "What say you, Brother Lexar? Has our dear Brother Beckman said anything against me or the way this community is being ministered?"

With a wide smile of satisfaction Lexar gave Beckman a glance, then said very calmly to Jessup, "He hasn't shut up complaining about how this community is being run since he walked in here."

"What?" Beckman looked stunned. "I—I discussed some concerns I have had about the whippings of late! But, my goodness! I never meant it to sound as if I had any—"

"Now he's lying," Lexar said, chuckling slightly, wearing the same grin. "He made me swear an oath not to reveal anything he said about you, or how the town is being run, or about our finances being short right now."

"Did he indeed?" said Jessup, giving Beckman a dark stare.

"My God, Lexar! How can you do this to me?" Beckman sobbed, knowing he'd made a terrible mistake confiding in the man. "We both *swore* an oath!"

"That's true," Lexar said smugly, "but I just *unswore* mine. I only swore it to flush out someone who is undermining the well-being and the brotherhood of our community. I don't believe I've committed any wrongdoing. Have I, Brother Jessup?" He gave the religious leader an expression of innocence. "I bow to your wisdom in such matters, of course."

"You've done just fine, Brother Lexar," said Jessup. "This community is grateful to you for doing your Christian best to weed out one of the fallen."

"Fallen?" said Beckman, his face contorted by fear, a sheen of sweat across his brow. "I remain ever true to our beliefs and the doctrine of our Lord! I only stated what was on my mind. I only did it out of care and concern for our community!"

"That's difficult to understand, Brother Beckman," said Lexar, motioning for Edmunds and Searcy to step forward for the trembling banker. "At any rate it isn't for me to judge you. That is the Lord's job. I will only do as He leads me to do in this matter."

Beckman looked back and forth between Edmunds and Searcy with a terrified expression. Then he pleaded, "Father, please don't do this to me. Please don't kill me!"

"I wouldn't dream of *killing* you, Brother Beckman," said Jessup in all sincerity. "But you will have to be punished. After which you will return to the bank. However, your job will no longer be bank manager. Instead, you will teach Brother Lexar everything he needs to know about running the bank for us." Turning his gaze to Lexar, he said, "Congratulations, Brother Lexar. I know we can count on you to do a splendid and *loyal* job."

"I will do as the spirit leads me," Lexar said humbly.

Brothers Edmunds and Searcy reached down and pulled Beckman up from his chair. "Come with us, Beckman," Edmunds commanded.

Beckman couldn't keep from coming to his feet. "Please, Father Jessup! What is to become of me? Are they going to torture me?"

"What men of weak spirit call torture, men of greater spirit call redemption," said Jessup. "Let us see which of the two you are." He gave Beckman a cruel smile and gave the two men a nod toward the door. "Take him outside, Brothers. I'll be right along."

"No!" Beckman pleaded loudly. "Please, no!" His voice became shrill, hysterical. "Father, I have sinned! All right? I admit it! I was wrong saying anything! I should have kept my mouth shut! But I've learned my lesson! God help me, I have learned!"

"Not quite yet, you haven't," said Jessup. "But I'm confident that Brothers Edmunds and Searcy are going to put you on the right path."

Lexar gave a dark muffled chuckle as the two men led Beckman from the room, the banker sobbing aloud and struggling with them. Father Jessup stepped over and closed the door behind them. Turning to Lexar he said quietly, "I think I will meet with those railroad men, Brother Lexar. After all, they have money and we need money. Perhaps the Lord is giving us a sign." As he spoke he walked to the window and looked down on the hotel across the street. Out front of the hotel, Shelby Keys stood smoking a cigar and pacing back and forth restlessly. "After all, Lexar," Jessup added, "the Lord does truly work in mysterious ways."

"His glory to fulfill," Lexar said, finishing the verse for him. He took a long sip of water, then asked, "Would you like for me to arrange for them to meet you in the bank, maybe tomorrow sometime?"

"Yes," said Jessup, "tomorrow early, before the heat of the day is upon us. I think these railroad men might be the answer to our prayers."

Chapter 9

In a corner of the lobby inside the hotel, Rudy took a bottle of whiskey from inside his black suit coat, pulled the cork and offered it to Randall, who looked around nervously and at first seemed reluctant to take it. "Oh, I almost forgot," said Rudy with a taunting smile. "This is the same stuff that caused you to get the hell beat out of you. Maybe you better leave this alone." He swished the contents of the bottle as he started to withdraw it.

"Wait a minute," said Jim Heady with defiance in his voice. He snatched the whiskey from Rudy's hand. "To hell with Jessup! He's a dead man anyway, as soon as I get a shot at him." He swigged long and deep from the bottle, then wiped his mouth with his hand as he passed the bottle on to Randall Turner. "Is *this* what you brought us in here to talk about?" he asked Rudy.

"Obliged," Randall said, taking the bottle from Heady, but passing it back to Rudy without taking a drink.

Instead of answering Heady, Rudy commented on Randall turning down the drink of whiskey. "What's this?" he said. "A man spends the night licking his wounds in a cell and doesn't even want a stiff drink or two to make him feel better?"

"I wasn't whipped as bad as him," Randall said, nodding at Heady. His voice turned more solemn. "Besides, I don't drink."

Rudy, Ernie and Orsen studied Randall closely for a moment before Rudy said with an incredulous expression, "You mean after Jessup taking your wife, whipping you and all, you're still one of his followers?"

"I never was one of his followers," said Randall. "I just don't drink. I never did."

"But you still believe in all that religious stuff? All that Bible malarkey anyway?" Rudy asked, searching for insight into Randall's character, as if sizing him up for a job.

"The Bible's not malarkey," Randall said firmly, "and yes I believe in religion. But I believe in my *own* religion, not Jessup's. As *blasphemous* as it might be considered here in Paradise, a person can believe in God and still not follow the teachings of Malcom Jessup."

"Oh …?" Rudy narrowed his gaze. "Then what brought you and your young wife here in the first place?"

"Jessup lured my wife's folks into his community of believers. When they died, we spent everything we had to come here and claim their land and belongings. We thought we'd try homesteading the place. But we found that Jessup had taken over everything, because her folks owed him money … or so he claimed."

"I see," said Rudy with contemplation. "So you *do* have some dirt that needs settling with him, the same as this young man." He pointed at Jim Heady.

"I want my wife back," said Randall. "That's all I care about."

"No vengeance, no pound of flesh?" Rudy asked. "Not even the land and the belongings that brought you here to begin with?"

"Not anymore," said Randall. "Just my wife. That's all I want."

"All right, I understand," said Rudy, as if dismissing him. Turning to Heady and handing him the bottle again, he said, "What about you, young man? You say you're going to kill

Father Jessup ... but how serious are you?" He looked Heady up and down as if for the first time, noting his bare shoulders, the ends of the whip marks showing around on his chest.

Heady took a drink, his eyes staying on Rudy's. Lowering the bottle from his lips he said, "Hand me a gun, point me toward him and I'll show you how serious." He reached a hand out toward Rudy's belly gun.

"Whoa now!" Placing a protective hand over his gun butt, Rudy laughed with approval and nodded at Orsen and Ernie. "See, I told you both, this young man was going to come out with one hell of a grudge against Jessup! Damn, I was right! He wants to kill him before he even gets a shirt on!"

"You don't know *how* right," said Heady, his bare shoulders stiffening in anger at the very thought of what Jessup had done to him.

"That's good to hear," said Rudy, "because we're going to bring Jessup to you." Raising a finger as if to have Heady hold his thought for a moment, Rudy turned to Randall and said, "I believe you ought to run along now. I've got things to talk to this man about—things that you don't want to be a part of."

Without a reply, Randall turned and walked toward the door, his shirt torn open down the back and the two long red whip cuts showing. "Hold on, Randall," Heady called out, causing the other man to stop at the hotel door. To Rudy, Heady said, "This man is my friend. You can't tell him to leave." He stepped over to Randall. "You're welcome to stay, Randall. You don't have to listen to him."

Looking past Heady, Randall saw the look on Rudy Banatell's face. He also saw the same grim looks on Orsen's and Ernie's faces. "I best go, Jim," Randall said quietly. "These are dangerous men. You watch out for yourself."

"I can see what they are, Randall," Heady whispered, "but you heard what he said. He's going to bring Jessup to me! They're after the same thing we're after!"

"You and these men have the same intentions in mind,"

said Randall. "But I can't be a part of it."

"We both want Jessup dead," said Heady, whispering. "Stick with me. These men will help us. We'll get your wife back. I promise you."

"No," said Randall. "You go on with them if that's what you need to do. I got to go it on my own." He reached for the door knob.

"You're still my friend, Randall," Heady said. "I'm not forgetting what you done for me."

"You're still mine, too, Jim," Randall replied without turning to face him.

When the door closed and Heady turned back around, he saw Rudy let out a long stream of smoke from his cigar and smile at him. "All right. Now that you and your friend have parted company, let's talk some serious business about that whip-swinging preacher. You really *will* kill him, won't you, if I go to all the trouble of setting him up?" Rudy asked.

"I swear on my mother's grave!" said Heady. "Just help me get him in my sights."

"Good enough." Rudy nodded in satisfaction. "The way I figure it, Jessup never goes around without his two big bodyguards. It'll be me and the boys' jobs to get them covered. So when you make your move, they won't be able to do anything to stop you."

"How will you manage that?" Heady asked.

Rudy grinned and narrowed his gaze. "You let me worry about that. Just make sure when you come in … you come in shooting." He nudged Heady with his elbow and nodded toward the door. "Now come on. I'll tell you more about it upstairs, while we get you into a clean shirt.…"

Out front of the hotel the Gun continued to pace back and forth restlessly while Rudy, Orsen and Ernie accompanied Jim Heady to their room upstairs, found him a clean shirt, and helped him slip it on carefully over his pain-racked back. As Heady stiffly buttoned the shirt, Rudy continued to tell him how he planned to meet with Jessup in the bank office, and how he would arrange to have Heady waiting outside the rear door.

But before Rudy could finish telling Heady his entire plan, from the street below, the Gun let out a short warning whistle that drew Rudy and the others to the open window.

"What the hell is this?" Orsen murmured, the three of them peering out the window, gazing off in the direction the Gun pointed them to. On the street at the far end of town, CC Ellis rode the big silver stallion slowly alongside a buckboard driven by Callie Mosely.

Rudy's eyes narrowed; a grin came to his face. "I'll be double-dog damned," he said, his eyes fixing on Callie and staying there. "Look who's riding beside him! Sloane Mosely's wife!"

"Jesus!" said Orsen. "That woman is a *looker!*"

"A *looker* hell!" Rudy said almost breathlessly. "Boys, that is pure honey still warm in the cone!"

"You wouldn't say that if Sloane was around," Ernie chuckled.

"I wouldn't say it if I thought he was within a hundred miles," Rudy chuckled in reply. "But he *ain't*. And it ain't likely he ever will be." His gaze went back to CC Ellis, who rode along watching the boardwalk and storefronts. Chuckling again, Rudy said, "I swear, Paradise gets more and more interesting every minute we're here."

"What do you suppose CC's up to?" Ernie Harpe asked, hovering near Rudy's shoulder.

"Damned if I know," said Rudy. "But knowing CC, I bet it's going to be worth listening to." He turned away from the window, crossed the floor quickly and headed out the door toward the stairs.

"Hey! Where's everybody going?" Jim Heady asked, one hand stuffing his shirttails inside his trousers. "What about the plan?"

"I'll tell you later," said Rudy over his shoulder. "Hurry up and join us once you've found yourself."

On the street, Callie and Dillard sat in the buckboard seat, Tic the hound sitting in the plank bed behind them. Passing the meetinghouse Callie cut her eyes sidelong toward the open door, then said quietly to CC Ellis, who was riding the stallion close beside her, "Well, I suppose there's no turning back now."

"You're going to do just fine," Ellis assured her. "Just remember everything we talked about. Stick to our story. I'll do most of the talking when the time comes." He smiled and touched his hat brim courteously toward two women who looked their way. But then his smile melted away as he caught sight of Rudy Banatell and the others standing alongside the street twenty yards ahead of him.

"Well, well," Rudy said to the others, seeing the expression change on Ellis's face, "looks like we've caught our ol' pard unawares." He jerked his head sidelong gesturing for Ellis to meet him in an alley beside the mercantile.

"What's going on?" Callie asked, catching sight of the four men and noting the effect they seemed to have on Ellis.

"Nothing, Callie, just some men I know. Stay calm. This doesn't change anything." He turned the stallion to the hitch rail out front of the mercantile. Callie turned the buckboard, following him.

"Are you sure about that, CC?" Callie asked, watching him step down and hitch the big stallion.

Ellis grimaced slightly. "It's Sloane, remember?" he said in a hushed tone, reaching up to give her a hand as she stopped the buckboard, set the brake and wrapped the reins around the brake handle.

"Yes, I remember," she replied, shooting a nervous glance back and forth as if worried that someone might have heard her. "It won't happen again, I promise." She stepped down, allowing CC to assist her.

"I trust you," Ellis said, giving her arm a reassuring squeeze. "You and Dillard go on inside and get the supplies." he added. "I'll go speak to these men and come right back."

From the buckboard seat Dillard asked with a concerne look, "Mother, is everything all right?" He bounded dow from the seat and stood looking up at her.

"Yes, Dillard, everything is fine," Callie replied, turning to him as Ellis walked away toward the alley. "Just rememb r what we decided to tell folks in Paradise." Her voice bec secretive.

"Don't worry, Mother," Dillard responded in the same tone. "I won't forget that Mr. Ellis is supposed to be Father."

Callie smiled at her son and brushed a hand across his forehead. "I know I can count on you. Now make certain that's the last time you call him *Mr. Ellis* while we're here."

At the corner of the alley, CC Ellis gave a quick glance over his shoulder. Seeing Callie and Dillard walk into the mercantile store, he stepped down from the boardwalk and followed Rudy and the others a few feet farther back into the alley. They turned and faced him, Rudy giving him a strange look.

"Damn it, CC!" Rudy said. "Where the hell have you been? We'd about given you up for dead!"

Ellis nodded to each of the men, then said to Rudy, "You would've been close to right. I got jumped by some riders out in Wolf Valley. I took a bullet in the side."

Rudy looked him up and down. "You look fit enough." He nodded in the direction of the big silver stallion hitched out front of the store. "Do you realize who that stud you're riding belongs to?" He raised a brow before CC could answer and asked, "Do you realize who *that woman* you're escorting belongs to?"

"Believe me, I do." Ellis let out a breath. "It was Callie Mosely and her son who found me and took me in. Hadn't been for them, I'd be feeding the wolves along a creek."

111

"Yeah …?" Rudy gave the story some thought, noting how CC called Sloane Mosely's wife by her first name. "Did you tell her what happened to Sloane?"

CC took on a troubled look. "No, I didn't. I never found the right time to tell her." He stopped, then said, "To tell you the truth, I couldn't bring myself to tell her. She didn't seem to know her husband turned outlaw. I couldn't tell her he got himself hanged."

Rudy said, "He was still alive when I went through Fort Griffin two months back. But he was due to hang most anytime. That's why they allowed me a visit with him." Rudy shook his head, recalling the visit. "I hated looking at him through them bars. He managed to hire Snake-eye Warly as his attorney. I told him it was a waste of time."

"Then he *is* dead by now?" CC Ellis asked.

"Yep, I'm sure of it," said Rudy. "Even *Snake-eye* Warly couldn't keep him from pulling hemp. He had eyewitnesses swearing he killed that guard right out front of the bank, clear as day!"

Orsen cut in, saying to CC, "You better hope he's pulled hemp, the way you're escorting his wife around."

"It's not what you think, Orsen," CC replied.

"Hell, it never is." Rudy grinned. "Maybe I ought to tell you, it was Sloane himself who told me about this place. While he was sweating it out waiting to hang, all he talked about was for all of us to be sure and come to Paradise. He wanted this bank here robbed some awful!" Rudy grinned and added, "I wasn't too keen on doing it a man short, but now that we see you're back in the saddle, I expect everything is back as planned."

"No, Rudy, you're going to have to count me out of this one," CC said firmly. "I've made other plans."

"I don't suppose those other plans have anything to do with that warm-looking Mosely woman, do they?" Rudy asked, insinuating.

"No," Ellis said. "But the truth is I'm impersonating Sloane Mosely for a while, just to keep the woman and her land from being taken over by Malcom Jessup, a preacher who runs Paradise."

"Damn!" said Rudy. "You sure took on a big set of boots!"

"I know, but that's how it is," Ellis said firmly. "I owe her for saving my life."

"What about what you owe us?" the Gun cut in, his thumbs hooked in his gun belt. "We've been waiting here for you. You should have found us sooner and let us know something."

"I figured as long as it's been," Ellis said, addressing Rudy instead of the Gun, "that you'd already been here, got tired of waiting and left."

"We wouldn't do that without first checking around," said Rudy, "to see what happened to our ol' *pard*, would we, boys?"

Orsen and Ernie murmured in agreement; the Gun grumbled under his breath, then fell silent.

"I'm obliged," said CC, "but I'm still not in on this one." He gave Rudy an unyielding gaze. "I've always held up my end, Rudy. This time I'm out."

"You're out only if we say you're *out*," the Gun cut in, using a strong tone and taking a step closer to CC Ellis.

Ellis took a step forward himself. Rudy stepped in between the two, saying, "Easy now, both of yas." He looked back and forth, then said to Ellis, "The fact is, since I thought we might be a man short, I've changed our plans some."

"You never told me that," said the Gun.

"Not in so many words, Gun, but I told you," said Rudy. "You just haven't been paying close enough attention." He said to CC Ellis, "If you want out of this one, you're out." He raised a finger for emphasis. "But if you're out, stay out. I've got something I want to do here. I don't want anybody butting in once I've started picking this place clean."

"Don't worry, Rudy," said Ellis, with relief. "Whatever you've got in mind, it's all yours."

Rudy grinned. "It's a damned good one though! Don't you want to know what it is?"

"No," said Ellis. "It's none of my business."

"You're not even a little bit curious?" Rudy asked. "All the riches there are for the taking here in Paradise, and you're not even tempted to know?"

Ellis smiled in reply. "No, I'm not tempted. I've got money. I've found all I want in Paradise. The rest is all yours."

"No long rider ever finds *all* he wants," said Rudy. "There's always one more thing he wants to snatch up on his way out of town. It's an outlaw's nature."

"Not mine, not anymore," said Ellis. "Sometimes a man has to look at all he's got and be satisfied with it. That's where I am right now."

"That sweet little Mosely woman has you turned around and walking backward, CC," Rudy said. "But I won't argue with you. Just don't jump in the middle of my game. I'm glad to learn that you're still alive. While we're both here in Paradise, let's stay off each other's toes."

CC Ellis nodded in agreement and backed away, returning Shelby the Gun's cold stare and bidding a respectful farewell to Orsen, Ernie and Rudy. As soon as he was out of hearing distance, the Gun said, "I don't like a man walking around who knows my business ... especially one who's fallen for a petticoat. A man falls for a woman shows himself weak as far as I'm concerned. You never know when a man like that might decide to trade you in to the nearest lawdog."

"Not CC," Rudy said, gazing off in the direction CC Ellis had just taken back onto the boardwalk and toward the mercantile. He gave the others a glance, then said, "Damned if I might not feel the same way if I had Callie Mosely warming my back of a night."

"How do you know she's warming his back?" Ernie asked.

All three gave him a bemused look. "Ernie," Rudy said with an exaggerated show of patience, "did you ever notice that the longer you keep your mouth shut the less stupid you sound?"

While the others chuckled at Ernie, Rudy Banatell gazed out again toward the street. "We best get back and find Jim Heady, help him get his shirttail stuffed and get ready to meet the preacher this morning." He grinned. "I find myself in a religious mood all of a sudden."

Chapter 10

From the window of the private room above the bank, Malcom Jessup watched Ellis, young Dillard, and a clerk stack a large amount of supplies into the bed of the buckboard wagon. While they loaded the wagon Dillard toyed with a stick of candy in his mouth. "It appears that the Moselys are living well these days," Jessup commented to Lexar. "Do they owe the bank anything?"

"I haven't gone through all the ledgers yet," said Lexar, "but it doesn't appear that Sloane Mosely owes us anything."

"That's too bad," Jessup said almost to himself, staring closely at Callie, who had stepped out of the mercantile and up into the buckboard seat, Ellis giving her a hand. "I like to see folks support local businesses." He watched Ellis step up atop the silver stallion. "But I suppose in time he'll come to us for financial assistance, like all the other settlers … and of course we'll give it to him." He watched the buckboard wind its way out of town, the silver stallion and its rider right beside it.

On the street, Callie glanced back over her shoulder, then said to CC Ellis as they continued on, "Do you think it all went well?"

"I think it all went fine, Callie," Ellis replied. Beside her, Dillard sat sucking a stick of candy; in the wagon bed Tic sat in a clear space among the tarpaulin-covered supplies. For everyone's sake Ellis hoped he was right. "Now we'll just have to wait and see what comes of our visit."

"What about those men you talked to," asked Callie. "Will they tell Jessup who you are?"

"They said they wouldn't," Ellis replied. Yet even as he said the words, doubts crossed his mind. It was not his custom to stay around a place where anyone knew too much about him. But here he was, his safety and the safety of the woman and the boy in the hands of a man like Rudy Banatell.

"And you trust them?" she asked.

"I trust them as long as things are going their way. But I think it would be wise if we got things in order and got out of here. We need to be leaving here as soon as we can."

"Once everything appears normal, we'll leave," Callie said. "We want to leave here looking as though we're going on a trip and will be returning soon. If Jessup should have any reason to want to stop us, we could never outrun his men across Wolf Valley."

"Judging from the looks I got from townsfolk," Ellis said, "your husband commanded a great amount of fear and respect. Jessup is going to think twice before he tangles with a man who has that kind of reputation."

"Yes," said Callie. "It's that reputation that has saved me from him so far. But no matter what fear and respect my husband has, when it comes to the Community of Believers, Jessup has more. Jessup is all powerful in Paradise. If he decided to send his men against you, they would all follow his orders blindly … to their death if he demanded it of them. Their faith in him is that strong."

Ellis shook his head. "Religion," he murmured under his breath, "who needs it."

"We *all* need it," Callie replied, gesturing a glance toward Dillard as if saying it for his benefit. "We just don't need Malcom Jessup's version of it."

"Yeah," said Ellis, also for Dillard's benefit, "that's what I meant."

Looking at her, he debated whether or not to sit her down in private and tell her about Sloane Mosely. She needed to know, and he knew he couldn't put it off forever. But he also knew it was going to hurt her. Maybe it was something he should wait and tell her after they had left the valley, he thought, nudging the stallion forward with a touch of his bootheels. Now that the wheels of their plan were in motion, he didn't need to complicate their leaving Paradise by telling her that those men, himself and her husband were all at one time members of the same gang.

A feeling of doubt tugged at his stomach. He resisted the urge to look back over his shoulder at the town behind them, knowing that in all likelihood they were being watched. Instinctively he laid his hand on the gun across his stomach and nudged the stallion forward, rounding a wide turn out of town.

Above the bank, seeing the wagon and horseman ride out of sight, Malcom Jessup turned to Lexar and said, "Let's get downstairs and meet the railroad men." Together they walked out the door and were joined by Brothers Searcy and Edmunds who flanked Jessup and remained close to him as they descended the stairs and walked to the manager's office. "The Brothers and I will wait here until you've shown them in," Jessup said to Lexar. "Once they've given over their firearms, we'll come in and you'll announce me while I enter appropriately."

"Will I have trouble getting their guns?" Lexar asked.

Jessup grinned. "Not if their hearts and minds are right."

Returning his grin, Lexar said, "Then I won't be but a moment." He stepped away from Jessup and the two bodyguards, through the office door and over to the security door separating the office from the bank lobby. Jessup and the two bodyguards listened to the sound of voices and footsteps as Lexar brought Rudy, Orsen and Ernie into the office. Straightening his tie and smoothing down the front of his black coat, Jessup folded his hands in front of himself and waited.

On the other side of the door Lexar said to Rudy, "I will have to have your firearms, gentlemen." Seeing the look of hesitancy on Rudy's face, he added quickly, "Only for a few moments. It's our rules here, for security sake."

Rudy looked at Orsen and Ernie and said in a relenting tone, "Fellows, if it's security we're looking for, I suppose we ought to be glad to see a place operate with such efficiency." Realizing that the Gun was close at hand outside the bank building should they need him, Rudy lifted his weapon from his holster and handed it over to Lexar. Ernie and Orsen followed suit stiffly, not liking the idea, but going along with their leader.

With all three gunmen's firearms in his hands, Lexar stepped away toward the front door, saying, "Please excuse me for one moment please, gentlemen, and we'll be under way."

"Of course." Rudy grinned.

As soon as Lexar left the room, Orsen and Ernie gave Rudy concerned looks. But Rudy whispered, "Relax. We've got the upper hand here."

Before either man could respond, Lexar walked back into the room, crossed the room and stood for a second beside the other door. "And now, gentlemen, I give you the most reverend Malcom Jessup."

When Lexar opened the office door, both bodyguards flanked the doorway as Jessup entered. "Gentlemen," Jessup said with enthusiasm, his folded hands coming undone and his arms spreading as if embracing the three of them, at the same time avoiding any offer of handshakes. "Welcome to Paradise! Please tell me who you are and what I might do for you!"

"I'm Mr. Able, Reverend," said Rudy, stepping forward as he unsnapped the carpetbag. "As I'm sure Brother Lexar has told you, we have a rather large amount of cash. I'm hoping you can make me feel safe about leaving our railroad's money in the bank of Paradise."

While Rudy introduced the other two and opened the carpetbag for Jessup to take a look inside, outside the back door of the bank, the Gun had already jimmied the lock on the door and held it open an inch with the toe of his boot. But instead of allowing Jim Heady to enter right away, he held him back while he kept track of the passing minutes on a large pocket watch. Beside the Gun, Jim Heady fidgeted impatiently, saying, "Has it been long enough yet? Let's get on with it!"

"Take it easy, *assassin*," the Gun said with sarcasm. "Rudy said the preacher would keep them waiting for a while. We're going to do this just as we said we would." He looked at the pocket watch in his gloved hand.

Heady grew even more restless, the pain across his back throbbing with no letup. "I can't stand this waiting!" he said. "I want to get this over with. I want to kill this son of a bitch so bad I can taste it!"

Finally, the Gun lowered the watch into his vest pocket and said, "All right, it's time. Slip on in there real quiet-like and do your killing." He drew an extra Colt from beneath his black suit coat and shoved it into Heady's hand.

"It's about damn time," Heady growled. He checked the gun quickly, then eased into the dark back storage room behind the bank. The Gun waited outside the door, keeping an eye on the alley.

Inside the bank office, Malcom Jessup and Rudy had just finished getting acquainted and were about to get down to business when all heads turned toward an urgent sounding knock on the office door. Brothers Searcy and Edmunds both stood in the doorway as Searcy opened it and caught young Anderson Farnsley before he could barge in. "Please!" said

Anderson, out of breath. "I have to see Father! Something terrible has happened!"

Searcy turned toward Jessup.

"Yes, let the lad in, Brother Searcy," Jessup said with a slight smile. To Rudy and the others he said, "Excuse me for one second, gentlemen." He leaned near to Anderson, who bent over and whispered in his ear. "Oh! I see," said Jessup, sounding perplexed by the news.

Rudy Banatell, Orsen and Ernie gave one another a glance, realizing that at any second Jim Heady would come charging in from the back room to kill Jessup.

But before that could happen, Jessup stood up quickly and said, "I'm afraid we'll have to meet another time, gentlemen. The lad just informed me that one of my wives has been abducted! I have to leave now and go find the wretch who did this." He looked intently at Rudy and offered a slight smile. "But if you would like to see what makes our bank and our town so safe, Mr. Able, come ride with us. I think you will feel more secure after you see how impossible it is to escape Wolf Valley."

Rudy, Orsen and Ernie looked at one another, not sure what to say for a moment. Finally Rudy jiggled the carpetbag. "I'm afraid it would be irresponsible of me to take this money on a jaunt of this nature."

"Nonsense, sir," Jessup insisted. "Leave the money here for the time being with my *personal* guarantee. If your money isn't safe until we return, it will be reimbursed out of *my* pocket."

Feeling all eyes upon him, Rudy knew he had to make a move. "Yes then, of course we'll come along! I can't argue with an offer like that! What better way to see how you handle things here in Paradise." As he spoke, he handed the carpetbag to Lexar.

"I'll take very good care of your money, Mr. Able. You have nothing to worry about."

"Now then," said Jessup, watching Lexar step back with the carpetbag in his hand, "while Lexar prepares your receipt, the Brothers and I will go gather our horses. Please join us at the livery barn." He raised a finger for emphasis. "Be prepared for a rather short adventure, gentlemen … but one whose outcome has already been determined. I predict that we'll catch this miscreant and return to Paradise before nightfall."

Before Rudy could say another word, Jessup and his bodyguards turned and left. So did Lexar, with the carpetbag under his arm. No sooner was he out of sight than the rear office door swung open and Jim Heady stepped in quickly, the Colt cocked and ready in his hand. He looked stunned when he saw no sign of Malcom Jessup.

"Get out of here, Heady, you fool!" Rudy hissed. "The plan has been changed. You'll have to wait!"

Heady started to speak, but Orsen stepped in and gave him a shove backward and closed the door in his face.

The three stood in silence for a moment, then turned to Lexar when he returned with a receipt in his hand and handed it to Rudy. "Now then, gentlemen," Lexar said, "we'll go to the livery barn and you'll be off. Fortunately for Father Jessup that someone witnessed this incident."

"Yes, he's a lucky man all right," Rudy said, glancing toward the rear office door, where Jim Heady had stood a moment earlier.

"We can call it *luck*," said Lexar, "but the fact is, it never hurts to have the Lord on your side, does it?" He grinned, sweeping a hand toward the door to the lobby and on out to the street.

"Amen to that, Brother Lexar," said Rudy. "But what about our guns?" Rudy asked bluntly.

"I had them sent on to the livery barn," said Lexar, directing the other men ever closer to the door with his gesturing hand, "Shall we …?"

Both horses had tired quickly in a high-paced sprint across the stretch of flatlands between Paradise and the narrow pass leading into Wolf Valley. Randall Turner slowed the spindly chestnut bay he was riding and sidled the horse up closer to Delphia, who sat atop a shorter roan gelding. Glancing back over his shoulder, Randall said hurriedly "Are you all right, Delph?"

Delphia tried to hide the fear in her eyes and the pain in her stomach. She swallowed once, hard, and replied, "I *will* be all right, as soon as we get clear of the valley."

Studying her face closer, Randall said, "Delph, you look pale."

"It's the heat, Randall," she said, turning her eyes away from him. "Let's not stop again until we know we've gotten away from him!" She started to gig her horse forward, but Randall grabbed its reins and held her back for a moment. Lifting a canteen from his saddle horn, he shook it to see if it had water in it, then uncapped it and handed it to her.

"Take a drink, Delph," he said firmly, "and cool this horse out a little. We won't make anywhere if we blow these horses down. Getting clear of Wolf Valley is the thing that keeps everybody from getting away from Jessup. We have to pace ourselves. There's no place in the valley to hide from him. The stretch of land is too long. Lose our horse, and him and the Brothers will ride us into the ground."

Delphia knew Randall was right. She forced herself to calm down, take the canteen and sip the tepid water. After handing the canteen back to Randall, she wiped her dress sleeve across her lips.

Randall capped the canteen and looked back at his wife, seeing her turn her head to the side and clutch her stomach. Sickness spewed from her lips to the ground. "Oh, no, Delph!" said Randall. "You've got the fever!"

"No, I don't!" Delph insisted. "It's this heat, the hard riding! Please! I'll be all right. Get me away from him!"

123

Randall sat for only a moment longer looking at her, knowing they had no choice but to run. "Hang on!" he said. After backing up his horse a step, he slapped her horse's rump, sending it forward. He stayed behind, where he could watch about her.

For the next hour they pushed the horses until both animals were covered with white foam and slinging sweat from their wet manes. Feeling desperate, they both slowed to a halt at a turn in the trail and looked all around at the distant high rock walls surrounding Wolf Valley. "We've got to find a way to get out of sight! If not, we're done for." As he spoke he reached out and held her hand, feeling a clamminess.

"If that is the case, husband," she said, "I'd rather die beside you than go back and live with him."

"The only folks living around here are believers," Randall said, shaking his head. "They'd never hide us from him." He searched the distant walls more intently. "I've heard Falon's trappers talk about the high trails up there. There's a creek, a man named Sloane Mosely lives there. He has little to do with Jessup's people."

"That doesn't mean he'll do anything to help us," Delphia remarked.

"I know," said Randall, "but he's our only chance." They rode on, veering north toward the distant rocks. Before they had gone a thousand yards, Randall nodded at the hard ground beneath them where their horses' hoofprints joined a dozen other sets of fresh prints filling the trail. "At least this is going to hide us some," he said, grateful for this sudden stroke of luck. "If we can cut away from the trail high up in the rocks, maybe they won't find our tracks."

"Yes, you're right!" said Delphia, sounding hopeful. "Hurry! We have to get up there!" She hammered her small heels to the tired horse's sides. Randall did the same, his horse almost staggering a bit as it hurried along behind her.

Looking back over his shoulder at a long rise of dust

on the distant sky toward Paradise, he whispered under his breath, "I don't care about myself, God. Just let me get Delph away from this devil."

But by late afternoon, when the prints of the trappers' horses continued up the high trail into the rocks surrounding the valley, their own horses had grown too weak to support them any longer. At a spot where the hillside leveled onto a wide stretch of flatlands, they turned the horses loose atop a rocky ledge and watched them stagger off along the winding trail. From the ledge Randall and Delph looked down and halfway across the valley floor at the rising dust that had grown ever closer to them throughout the afternoon.

"Look at them, Delph," Randall said. "They haven't even had to speed their horses up any. They figure it's just a matter of time before they've got us."

Delphia heard the almost beaten tone in his voice. Taking his hand she said quickly, "But they *figured* wrong, didn't they, husband?"

Randall found the strength to nod his head. He looked at her sweat-streaked face, her tired sunken eyes. "Yes, they did," he rasped. Holding hands tightly, the two struggled away from the trail through a sparse growth of scrub juniper clinging to the rough ground. Above them the sky had begun to darken into night. "I've heard there's a creek somewhere north of here. We'll find it, get ourselves some water and see if we can find Mosely's place."

Chapter 11

Outside the small room where Dillard slept, Callie Mosely listened closely for a moment until she was satisfied her son had settled into his bed for the night. In her white cotton nightgown, with a candle in her hand, she walked softly across the rough wooden floor to the master bedroom, where CC Ellis lay beneath a blanket waiting for her. Upon seeing her enter the room and close the door behind herself, Ellis at first felt a bit awkward being in another man's bedroom, ready to sleep with his wife. Yet, watching Callie move to the side of the bed, set the candle down, slip the cotton gown over her head and lay it on a chair, Ellis let the thought slip from his mind.

"Jesus …" he whispered, turning back the edge of the blanket for her and feeling her warmth move over him. In the candle glow she smiled and moved closer, their faces only inches apart on the soft pillows.

"I think we've done it," she said, her voice sounding relieved, as if a terrible burden had been lifted from her shoulders.

"Yes," said Ellis, "I think our showing up in Paradise will keep Jessup at bay long enough for us to leave here."

They looked into each other's eyes until at length Callie asked, "Where will we go once we leave here?" She reached out with a hand and brushed a strand of hair from Ellis's forehead.

"I haven't thought things out that far ahead," he replied. "But I know lots of places we can go to. There's good farmland in Oregon. We could take on a place, set out crops."

"Farming?" She smiled and fondled his hand. "These don't feel like the hands of a farmer."

"But they could," Ellis said, "given the right team of animals, a good plow and some land worth tending. I come from farming country."

"Oh? And where is that?" she asked in a whisper, her hands moving to his chest, his neck, toying with the back of his hair.

Ellis had to think about it for a moment, to make certain that he hadn't already mentioned a place to her. Finally, satisfied that he hadn't, he said with a slight shrug, "Missouri … but that doesn't matter. Neither does farming as far as I'm concerned. I can make a life for us, Callie. Anywhere you want to live, we'll live there. I always have a way to make us a living."

A silence passed while her hand stopped and lay still on his shoulder. "What is it you do for a living, CC?" she asked quietly, but firmly.

"I'm a businessman, Callie," he replied. "I do whatever suits me and turns a profit on my investment in it."

"I see," she said, seeming to think about his answer for a moment. "I trust you, CC Ellis … and I don't give my trust easily. Don't let me down."

"I won't," he said, drawing closer to her. When the kiss ended, she turned from him long enough to snuff out the candle. Then she turned back to him with nothing more to say on the matter.

They made love until the two of them drifted to sleep in each other's arms. In the middle of the night, while Callie slept on his shoulder, Ellis was awakened by the sound of the dog growling toward the front door. After lifting Callie's head gently, he slipped from the bed naked and stepped into his trousers, whispering to her as he took his gun from the holster hanging from the bedpost, "Callie! Wake up! The dog's growling. There's somebody outside."

Callie stirred, then sat upright and hurried quietly from the bed and into her gown. "Are you going out there?" she asked.

"Yes, I am," said Ellis. "Get your shotgun in case you need it. Wait until I'm out the front door before you light the candle. As soon as you light it, hold it over in the window where it can be seen."

"Be careful," said Callie, watching him slip out the bedroom door. When he closed the door behind himself, she hurried to a wooden wardrobe, took out the ten gauge, checked it and held it poised, waiting before lighting the candle, the way Ellis had asked her to do.

At the front door, Ellis held the big hound back with the side of his leg as he eased quietly out the front door and down off the porch into the dark yard. He hurried across the yard and out into the darker shelter of an overhanging spruce, where he could see the window clearly. He waited, his eyes studying the darkness until the light of the candle glowed in the window and cast two black hovering silhouettes on dim-lit ground. With his Colt out and cocked, he moved forward silently. Ellis managed to get within six feet of the two dark shadows before he stopped, pointed the gun and said, "Raise your hands real easy-like. I've got you covered."

Randall and his wife turned with their hands chest high, their faces sweaty, covered and streaked with trail dust. Randall spoke on both of their behalf, saying, "Please, Mr. Mosely, don't shoot! We mean you no harm! We need your help awfully bad!"

Hearing the man call him by Sloane Mosely's name, Ellis eased his finger on the trigger, but only slightly. "What kind of help are you talking about?" he asked. "Are you on the run from somebody?"

Before Randall could answer, Delphia stepped forward and said in a shaky voice, "Mr. Mosely, we're running from Father Jessup and his Brothers. This man is my husband, Randall Turner. He and I are just trying to get out of this valley alive! I've heard that you are a freethinking man who follows his own mind in spite of Jessup's believers. Is that true? If it is, you *have* to help us."

Ellis looked them both over closely again while Callie saw what was going on, opened the window and stood with the candle in one hand the shotgun in her other. "Who are they? What do they want?" she asked.

"They say they're running from Jessup," said Ellis. He made a gesture for Randall to turn around with his gun barrel. Randall did so reluctantly, revealing that he had a length of a white oak limb shoved down in his waist. "Said they mean us no harm." Ellis grinned slightly. "But when I see a man carrying a club down his trousers, I have to wonder about him."

"Mr. Mosely, let me explain, please!" said Randall, his back still turned. Ellis reached out, pulled the oak limb from his trousers and pitched it away.

"I think I already understand," said Ellis. "You figured you'd come here, ask for help, and if you didn't get it freely, you'd get it at the end of that club. Isn't that about it?"

Randall sighed deeply. "Yes, you're right. I meant to get what I wanted one way or the other. There's no denying it. But that's the kind of straits we're in, my wife and I. Jessup has forced my wife to become his property, like he has so many other women in this valley. I mean to take her away from here, no matter who I have to knock in the head. There, does that satisfy you?"

Ellis and Callie looked at their tired, frightened faces and realized that what the man said was probably true. The two bloody strips from Jessup's whip showing through the back of his torn shirt confirmed his story to them. "Yeah," said Ellis, "that satisfies me. Both of you lower your hands."

129

"Mr. Mosely," said Delphia, letting her hands fall to her sides, "thank God for you. Thank God for both of you!" Tears fell down her dust-caked cheeks. Callie stepped over to her and directed her toward the house.

"Do you have a horse?" Ellis asked Randall Turner.

"No, sir. We rode them down, just like Jessup knows everybody will do if they try escaping this blasted valley!"

"You were going to take ours then?" Ellis asked.

Randall nodded, looking ashamed of himself. "You have to understand, Mr. Mosely. This man is *living* with my wife! Making her his own! No man should do that to another man, should he?"

Glad that Callie had stepped out of hearing range, Ellis said quietly, "No, no man should. Now come on. Let's get you inside and get yours and the woman's footprints hidden. If Jessup and his men are on your trail, they can't be far behind."

After helping the worn-out man limp into the house and collapse into a chair, Ellis hurried outside with a broom in one hand and his Colt in his other. He had already begun sweeping away the couple's footprints when Callie joined him, carrying a lantern now instead of the candle. "We're so close to getting out of here," she said. "I hope this isn't going to ruin our plans."

"What could I do, Callie?" Ellis asked. "You heard him say what Jessup did to them. It's the same situation you was afraid he'd put you in if we hadn't done something about it."

"I know," said Callie. "We've got to help them. I'm just so afraid."

"Don't be," said Ellis. "We'll be all right." He swept the broom back and forth, fanning the ground to get rid of the prints without making the ground look too recently swept. "If our trip to Paradise was worth anything at all to us, I can handle Jessup one more round before we clear out of here."

Looking off across the night sky in the direction Jessup and his men would be coming, Callie said, "God, I hope so."

Inside the house, Delphia huddled at her husband's side,

sharing a dipper of cool water with him. "We're safe now, Randall," she said with tears in her eyes.

"Not yet," Randall said, placing a hand on hers, "but we're better off now than we were, thanks to Sloane Mosely and his wife. If he can turn Jessup and the Brothers away, we can slip along the creek until daylight, hide in the cottonwoods by day and travel by night until we're shed of this valley." He squeezed her hand, reassuring her.

Delphia took a deep breath and said, "Randall, I have to tell you something and this might be the only chance I get."

As if in fear of what she might say, Randall said, "No, you rest and save your strength. There's nothing you have to tell me right now. We're going to be together the rest of our lives. Whatever you need to tell me can wait until we're away from here."

But Delphia pulled her hand from his. "No, I must tell you now. Don't stop me." Then before Randall could say anything, she blurted out, "I'm carrying Father Jessup's baby, Randall." Her voice turned shaky and tearful as she spoke. "I'm afraid you won't want me after hearing this."

"Oh no. God, no. Please don't think that, Delphia," Randall said in a whisper, pulling her face to his chest as he shook his head. "Don't ever think that I wouldn't want you, no matter what."

"I prayed every night that God would keep me from being with child, but God just didn't listen to me, Randall." She sobbed quietly.

"Delph, it will be all right. I swear to you it will," said Randall, feeling tears well in his eyes. "There's nothing that devil has done to us that we can't undo. Maybe God didn't hear your prayer. Maybe He did. We can't say what God is up to … only how we can bear up under it and not let this destroy us. I'm your husband, Delph. So the baby in your stomach is my child, even if it is begotten by Father Jessup. It's *not* his, it's *yours and mine*."

"I suppose I knew you'd say that, my good and decent husband." She stroked his cheek and sobbed against his chest. "I want you to know that every time I lay with him, as far as I'm concerned, I was violated. I know it's something that maybe you can't understand."

With tears in his own eyes, Randall said, "Of course I understand. Delph, you are a part of me. Every time he violated you, he violated me as well. I nearly lost my mind, knowing what he was doing to you, knowing that you didn't want him doing it ... couldn't *stand* him doing it. More than once, God forgive me, I came near taking my own life rather than live with the thought of it."

"Thank heavens you didn't do it." She raised her face and looked into his eyes.

"This minute right here is the only reason I didn't," said Randall. "The only thing that kept me going was knowing that this minute would come, and that someday I'd look into your eyes again before I died. I believed that, Delph. I *had* to believe that." They held each other's hands tightly. "I don't know what God means by all this ... by putting this on us." He shook his head.

"There must be a reason, Randall," she said. "We mustn't question what God puts upon us."

"I do," said Randall, his voice turning bitter in defiance. "I question God doing this to us. I don't understand why it all began or how it's going to end. All I know is that we're right here in the middle of it, having to do our best to live through whatever God has allowed to happen to us. I don't curse God, nor do I blame Him. But if He allows a devil like Jessup to act in His name without striking him down, then I have to question Him for it. I most surely do."

Out front, Callie and Ellis finished sweeping away the footprints and checked their work over thoroughly before turning off the lantern and coming inside. In the doorway to his room, Dillard stood with his hand on Tic's back, the big hound's hackles still slightly raised from all the commotion. "Mother, is everything all right?" Dillard asked.

"Yes, Dillard," said Callie, stepping over and stooping down to him, seeing the questioning look in his eyes. "These people are having the same trouble we had with Father Jessup. We're going to help them hide from him when he and his men arrive. So we're all counting on one another to do our part."

"Don't worry about me, Mother," Dillard said. "I won't tell Jessup anything, ever!"

"I know, Dillard," said Callie, turning him and directing him and the dog back into the bedroom. Over her shoulder she said to Ellis, "Show them the trapdoor that I showed you the other day."

As soon as Callie closed the door behind Dillard, the dog and herself, Ellis stepped over to the hoop rug and peeled it back from the floor, revealing a trapdoor leading down beneath the house. He said to Randall and Delphia, "At the first sign of Jessup and his men, the two of you get down here. It leads out through the rear of the house and up into the rocks … from back when the Blackfoot roamed these parts."

Randall gave him a questioning look. "She said she showed you where it was *last week?*"

Ellis caught the slip and said, "I've been gone for quite some time. I must have forgotten. Are we clear on what to do?"

Randall still stared at him, finally saying just between them, "You're not Sloane Mosely, are you?"

"Of course I am," said Ellis.

"Huh-uh, you're not," said Randall. "I don't know what you're trying to pull, but you're not him."

"You're not the only one trying to get away from Father Jessup," Ellis said tightly. "Now are you going to trust me or not?"

Hearing only that part of the conversation, Delphia spoke

up, saying, "Yes, we trust you. We'll go down there as soon as you tell us to, Mr. Mosely. Thank you and your wife for all your help."

Randall seemed to consider Ellis's words for a moment before snapping out of his thoughts, saying, "Yes, Mr. Mosely, thank you both … and God bless you."

On the trail a few yards behind Father Jessup and his Brothers, Rudy Banatell turned slightly in his saddle and said to Orsen and Ernie Harpe, "This doesn't look like a be-back-by-evening chase to me. It's starting to look to me like this fellow and his wife have outfoxed the good reverend."

"Me, too," said Orsen. "I'm all for turning around and heading back to Paradise. Tell the reverend we've had enough of his manhunt." He looked all around, then added in a lowered voice, "We need to clean out that bank and ride somewhere a man can get some whiskey without getting condemned to hell with a back full of whiplashes."

"Let's give Jessup a few more miles," said Rudy, "just to show good faith. If nothing happens before then, we'll turn back. I've got a feeling they will, too." He gave a nod toward Jessup and his men.

Ahead of the three, Father Jessup slowed his horse at the creekbank, still looking around in the dark for any hoofprints. Beside him, Lexar held a torch down toward the ground. "If you want me to, I'll ride with some of the Brothers along the main trail while you take some riders across to Mosely's place," said Lexar.

"No," Jessup said firmly, "we'll all stay together!"

"But, Father," said Lexar, "always before we split up if it looked like someone might get away from us."

"Nobody's getting away, Lexar!" Jessup growled. "Do you hear me? Nobody is going to get away, and we're not going to split up this time. I won't take a chance on the woman being harmed!"

Behind them Rudy and his men rode up on the tail end of the conversation, hearing Lexar say to Jessup, "I wouldn't want her harmed either, Father. But what so special about this woman, if I might ask?"

Jessup spun an angry stare his way. "This woman is carrying my child! That's what makes her so special!"

Rudy and his men stopped and listened quietly.

"Oh, I had no idea, Father," Lexar said, not knowing what else to say. The other Brothers stared in stunned silence.

"Yes," said Jessup, "there you have it. All these wives, all have the power to bear as many children as I want. Yet this is my only one … my *only son*, if I dare reveal what the Lord has promised me."

The Brothers all looked at one another, then back at Jessup in reverence at what they had heard. "God be praised," one of them whispered.

"Yes, praised indeed," said Jessup, seeing the good response he'd received from the Brothers. "Now keep this in mind when we run those two down. The woman must not be harmed. She must be given special care! She carries my only son!" He spurred his horse out across the creek, saying back over his shoulder, "Now on to Sloane Mosely's place. We'll see if he's knows anything of these two!"

Rudy whispered sidelong to Orsen, "How the hell does he know he's got a son coming?"

Oren grinned. "You heard him. He said the Lord told him … even *promised* him to boot." He leaned closer to Rudy in his saddle. "I'm telling you, Rudy, it's getting time we rob the bank and put this place behind us. These religious fellows are apt to go hog-wild nuts on us at any time."

Rudy grinned in reply. "The crazier they get, the better I like it." He slapped his reins to his horse and rode forward into the shallow creek, following Jessup and the Brothers. "If he's headed for *Sloane Mosely's*, I wouldn't miss it for the world."

Chapter 12

At the first sight of the torchlight moving up from the creekbank, Ellis and Callie hurried the couple down through the trapdoor beneath the house. Before climbing down the ladder, Delphia reached out, grasped Ellis by his forearm and said, "Mr. Mosely, we're putting our lives in your hands."

"I know," said Ellis, speaking to her and looking down the ladder past her to Randall. "Don't worry. I won't let you down. Just remember if everything sounds all right up here, stay put. But the minute it sounds like something might be going wrong, get out of there, take to the hills and find cover for yourselves."

"We will, Mr. Mosely, and much obliged," Randall called up to him as he helped Delphia down into the darkness with him.

Closing the trapdoor and smoothing the hoop rug across it, Ellis turned to Callie when she said to him from the window, "Here they come! Dillard, go into your room and stay there."

"But, Mother," said the boy, "Tic and I can help!"

"Please, Dillard," Callie said calmly, in spite of tenseness she felt at the thought of Jessup and his men riding into her yard. "Staying out of sight *is* helping."

Before Dillard could protest, Ellis said, also in a calm voice, "Dillard, I'm counting on you and Tic to stay out of sight. Will you do that for me?"

"All right," Dillard said with reluctance, pulling the hound by its leather collar toward the bedroom door. "Come on, Tic, let's go."

After the boy led the dog into the room and shut the door, CC Ellis took off his shoulder holster, hung it loosely over his shoulder, then drew the big Colt, checked it quickly and shoved it back into the holster. Seeing the curious look on Callie's face, he explained, "It's the middle of the night. It might look strange, me stepping out already wearing my shoulder harness."

She only nodded without answering.

Stepping over to the window, Ellis looked out at the torchlight and the riders moving into the yard single file and half circling the front of the house. "Here we go," he said quietly to Callie. "Let's just play it like we played it in town. We'll do all right."

"I hope so," Callie replied.

Before Ellis could say anything to further reassure her, a voice called out from the front yard, "Sloane Mosely! The Reverend Father Malcom Jessup is out here. He would like a word with you!"

Sitting back from Jessup and the other riders, Rudy Banatell chuckled and said to Orsen sitting atop his horse beside him, "Right about now I bet ol' CC is wondering what all he's took on, looking after Sloane's wife for him." He stepped his horse closer to the front of the riders, for a better view, as the front door opened slowly in the glow of torchlight.

Standing inside the door, Callie held the shotgun close to her and watched CC turn to face Jessup and his men. Lifting the loose harness from his shoulder, Ellis looked around at the gathered riders as he slipped his arm through it and buckled it. Looking like a man disturbed in his sleep he said, "You pick a peculiar time of night to come calling, Mr. Jessup."

Beside Jessup, Brother Searcy called out sharply,

correcting him, "It's *Reverend* Jessup, not Mr. Jessup."

Ellis shrugged slightly. "Suits me. Now that we're meeting face-to-face, what can I do for you, *Reverend* Jessup?"

Searcy started to speak but Jessup silenced him with a gesture of his large hand. "My apologies for having awakened you at this hour, Mr. Mosely," said Jessup, "but one of my wives is missing, taken from our family by a scoundrel and a debtor. We found two spent horses along the trail. Since there are few ways across this valley we're checking with everyone." Looking all around, he settled his eyes on the barn door. One of his men had ridden and circled the barn, holding a torch down close to the ground. "Yours would appear to be the most likely place to have come looking for fresh horses."

The rider by the barn door, rose up in his saddle and shook his head *no*, indicating that he had seen no sign of any fresh footprints. Jessup noted his gesture; so did Ellis, who said calmly, "In that case, feel free to check inside my barn. I'll join you, although if anybody but me tried to take my stallion from the barn, I would have heard quite a ruckus."

"And you have heard nothing?" Jessup asked, his eyes boring into Ellis's.

"Not a sound all night, Reverend," Ellis said, poker-faced. He took a step forward on the porch, as if to step down. "Let's take a look. If I have horses missing, this man you're after will have more than you and your men on his trail. I hate a horse thief."

Listening, Rudy smiled to himself and sat watching Ellis, knowing him well enough to see that he was hiding something. But whatever it was, he was doing a good job of covering it from Jessup and his men. "That's our boy," he whispered faintly to himself, the torchlight glistening in his wary eyes.

"That won't be necessary," said Jessup, relaxing a bit in his saddle. "Again, I apologize for awakening you and your family." His eyes searched the closed door as if trying to pierce it.

"If I see these two in the next few days," said Ellis, "I'll get word to you."

"Rest assured, Mr. Mosely, this poltroon will not manage to run free that long. I'll have his hide … and of course the hide of anyone he tells me tried to aid and assist him. And believe me, he *will* tell me."

"I've heard all about your whippings in the streets of Paradise, Reverend," said Ellis, "so I'm sure he will." He took a step back on the porch. "Now, if there's nothing else I can do for you … you'll excuse me, please."

Jessup almost turned and gave his men a signal to back away. But along the trail behind them, a voice called out, "Father Jessup! Wait! I've found something!"

The rider had fallen back and searched the rocky ground off to the side of the trail while the others rode into the yard. Now he came pushing his horse forward at a quick pace, almost sliding it to a halt beside Jessup. "What do you have there, Brother Arnold?" Jessup asked, reaching out and taking a strip of soiled gingham fabric from his hand.

"Found it stuck to some brush back there," the rider said, sounding excited by his find. "It could be hers!"

"Indeed, it could," said Jessup, examining the two-inch scrap of fabric closely in the flickering glow of torchlight. "Any footprints?"

"No, Father Jessup," Arnold Yuley said. "Just that! But it's white, just like the dress she was wearing!"

"But no footprints, eh?" Jessup said idly, almost to himself, raising his eyes back to Ellis on the porch.

"That's been out there for days," Ellis said, unshaken, trying to keep up his confident demeanor. "It belonged to my wife."

"Oh …?" said Jessup. He studied Ellis's eyes in the torchlight. "You must live well, Mr. Mosely, if your wife can afford to leave a good piece of patch-work lying in the wilds."

Reminding himself to make no excuses, Ellis said,

139

bluntly, "Yes, we do live well. My wife doesn't have to patch her dresses—not that it's any of your concern."

Jessup stiffened a bit in his saddle; his men did the same. Rudy stifled a dark chuckle and whispered to himself, "Easy, CC, don't overplay your hand here."

"Perhaps there is something more you can do for us, Mr. Mosely," Jessup said, his tone turning colder as he clenched the two-inch strip of cloth. To the men around him he said, "Search this house thoroughly! If my wife has been here, I want to know it!"

"Uh-oh," Rudy said, backing his horse a step, seeing the look on Ellis's face.

Ellis's hand came up quickly, the big Colt cocked and leveled in Jessup's direction. The men froze. "The first man that *tries* to come into my house will be the first man to die *trying* to come into my house," said Ellis. "Call them down, preacher, or I'll open you up."

"Wait, men!" said Jessup, seeing that the Colt was pointed straight at him, too close for him to escape. A man like Sloane Mosely couldn't miss at this range.

The men eased back down into their saddles and sat tensely, careful not to lower a hand close to their holstered weapons.

"I demand permission to search your house, Mosely!" said Jessup, still pushing, but not nearly as hard. "What do you have to hide?"

"I'm hiding nothing," said Ellis. "But I'm not a man who submits to another man searching my house. Privacy is something I hold *dearly*."

"I serve the Lord, Sir!" said Jessup. "The Lord rules this country and he has seen fit to give me dominion over it, and all who dwell herein!"

"You forget yourself, *preacher*. I'm not one of your flock like the rest of these *sheep*." Ellis looked from one to another, making it clearly known that the word *sheep* was by no means meant to be a compliment. "I told you that cloth belonged to my wife. Unless you're calling me a liar, you better take my word for it. That's all you're getting here."

"I demand proof!" Jessup bellowed, pointing a finger at Ellis. "These men must be allowed to—"

His words cut short at the sound of the front door creaking open. He stared as if dumbstruck as Callie Mosely stepped out onto the porch, her hair still down, brushed and glistening upon her shoulders.

"Oh, now that's a good touch," Rudy murmured to himself. Orsen and Ernie were too transfixed at the sight of the woman to hear him.

Ellis looked at the folded dress in Callie's hands, then said in a strict, husbandly voice, "What are you doing out here?"

"Trying to prevent trouble with our good neighbors, *the Believers*," she said boldly, stepping past him barefoot, her robe slightly low on her right shoulder, her pale bare skin aglow in the torch light. She stepped down from the porch and out to Jessup's horse. Holding the dress up to him, showing him the torn hem where a piece of cloth was missing, she said, "Father Jessup, forgive my husband. He wakes up cross in the middle of the night." She offered an alluring smile. "Sometimes it takes hours before I can get him back to sleep."

Jessup's men almost gasped at her words, at the images her words suggested. Jessup gave his men a stern look, then let his eyes sweep over Callie, as if he could not control them. He lifted the dress from her hands and held it close to his face, breathing in the scent of her from it. "Yes, it does appear that this could be the dress that the strip of cloth came from."

"I told you. It *is* the dress," said Ellis, keeping the right amount of pressure on the situation. "Now take your hands off it."

"Please, husband," Callie said softly. "Father Jessup is a *holy* man. He means no harm."

Glancing at Ellis, then looking back down at Callie, at

her bare shoulder, her soft eyes in the torchlight, Jessup said, "Don't judge your husband harshly, ma'am. If you were my wife, I would not allow another man to hold your dress either." Dropping the dress into Callie's hands, Jessup stepped his horse up closer to the porch, saying to Ellis, "I am indeed a holy man. Otherwise, against your and your wife's bidding, I would order my followers to ransack this house and see what secrets you might be keeping from me."

Ellis only stared, seeing that things were about to wind down, and that he and Callie had won.

Callie offered a smile that bordered on suggestive. "In the future we'll look forward to seeing you again, at a more favorable time of evening, Reverend," she said.

Jessup smiled, barely able to control himself in the presence of a woman wearing only her night-clothes. He said down in a quiet tone just between himself and Ellis, "It's unfortunate that we meet face-to-face under these circumstances, sir. Perhaps in the future we'll better acquaint ourselves with each other and what we do or do not hold *dearly*."

"Perhaps," Ellis replied, tight-lipped.

Jessup turned his horse and gestured for his men to follow him. "Let us not intrude here any longer," he said, smiling down at Callie in her robe as he spoke. "A beautiful young lady must get her rest."

Callie and Ellis stood watching the men step their horses close to the porch as they circled behind Jessup and moved away into the night. When Rudy Banatell led Orsen and Ernie past the porch, he gave Ellis a dubious look and chuckled under his breath. "Mighty good show." Looking at Callie, he tipped his hat slightly and said, "Ma'am, good evening then."

Watching Banatell and his men trail off behind the reverend and his believers, Callie said cautiously, "I don't trust those three men any more than I do the Father and his Brothers."

Watching the torchlights disappear into the night, Ellis

said, "You know what, Callie? Lately, neither do I."

They walked back inside, Callie going to the window to make sure Jessup and the riders were really gone. Ellis threw open the trapdoor and said down into the darkness, "It's all right. They're gone. You can come up."

But when no answer came right away, Ellis didn't bother repeating himself. Instead he stood up and said to Callie, "They're gone. Come on, let's check the barn!"

"Mother? Can Tic and I come out now?" Dillard asked from the doorway to his room.

"Yes, but stay here in the house," Callie said, taking time to warn him. "Jessup's men might still be out there." She hurried away through the open front door, Ellis having already run out to the barn.

Callie caught up to him just inside the open barn door. "That fool!" Ellis said, realizing even as he spoke that Randall was no fool. "He must've heard me and Jessup having words and figured he couldn't risk us bluffing Jessup away from here."

"I suppose we can't blame him," Callie said, quietly, watching Ellis take a lantern down from a wall peg and light it.

Ellis held the lantern up, the two of them seeing the empty stall where the two wagon horses and his own horse had been stabled. Only one of the team horses stood there, staring at them blankly. In the next stall the big stallion stared at them in the lantern light. "Now we're stopped cold," Ellis said. "They took my saddle horse, so we've got no speed leaving here. They left only one of the team horses. So now we can't depend on the wagon."

"I know they didn't mean to strand us," Callie said. "I'm sure they couldn't even see what they were doing in the dark. They just took whatever was closest to them."

"It doesn't matter whether they did it intentionally or not," Ellis said. "Either way, we're in trouble if Jessup catches up to them and they tell him we helped them."

"Maybe they'll get away from him," said Callie, hoping desperately for the couple.

"Not with one of them riding a wagon horse, Callie. It'll never keep up with my big bay. They'll be down to one horse within an hour."

"God help them," Callie whispered. "I don't think they'll tell Jessup anything," she added. "Not after us hiding them the way we did."

"Jessup will torture it out of them, some way or other," said Ellis. He stood in silence for a moment, then said, "Randall knows I'm not Sloane Mosely."

"He what?" Callie looked frightened. "How could he know? You didn't tell him, did you?"

Ellis said, "Of course not. He figured it out by the things we said, the way we said them. I don't know how he figured it out. He just did. I told him he was wrong, but I know he didn't buy it. He knows. And under enough torture, he'll tell Jessup."

"What do we do?" Callie asked, her voice sounding weak all of a sudden.

"I've got to go after them," said Ellis. "I've got to tell them that right *here* is the safest place for them—for now anyway."

"Maybe we should just sit tight, hope they manage to get away," Callie said.

"We can't risk it," said Ellis. "With both Rudy Banatell and Randall Turner knowing I'm not your husband, I'm afraid it's only a matter of time before Jessup finds out. Jessup wants you, Callie. I can see it in his eyes. He'll come calling again." Ellis's face grew dark in contemplation. "This time he'll be harder to handle ... knowing it's not a big gunman like Sloane Mosely he's facing."

Callie watched him walk toward the stall where her husband's big stallion stood waiting as if it understood everything going on.

While Ellis hastily saddled the stallion, he thought about what Rudy Banatell had told him about Sloane Mosely insisting that Rudy and his gang rob the bank in Paradise. *Why would he do that?* Ellis asked himself.

Ellis's answer struck him with such a profound realization that for a moment he had to stop what he was going to consider it closer. Mosely knew that this valley was almost inescapable. Standing in his cell, knowing his time had run out, had he directed Rudy Banatell toward Paradise, knowing that somehow Rudy and his gang coming here would mark the end of Malcom Jessup's iron rule? Was this Mosely's last desperate try at looking out for his wife, Callie, and their son? Did Sloane sic Rudy on Paradise, knowing that once he'd hang, his family had no way out of this valley?

"What's wrong?" Callie asked, stepping in closer to Ellis after seeing the look on his face.

"Nothing," Ellis said, shaking free of his thoughts, then going back to his task. He tightened the cinch, dropped the stirrup and tested the saddle with both hands. If what he thought was true, he had news for Sloane Mosely, Ellis told himself. He would have come here as a favor, if Mosely had asked him to. He wouldn't have had to be lured here by the promise of a big fat bank waiting to be robbed. *Stop it!* he demanded of himself. This was all nothing more than speculation, and he had no time for idle speculation.

Leading the stallion toward the barn door, he said, "I'll be back as soon as I can. Meanwhile you and Dillard lay low." He stopped at the door, kissed her and climbed atop the stallion. Without another word, he turned the stallion and headed out toward the hills rising up behind the house. As he swung out of sight into a stand of pines, he tucked his hat down more firmly on his forehead and whispered to himself, "Damn you, Sloane Mosely.…"

Chapter 13

"The wagon horse can't keep up, Delph!" Randall said, sounding harried, looking back and forth along the dark trail, where only moments before, he thought he'd heard the scraping sound of horses' hooves on the rocky ground.

"We'll never get out of this valley riding double," Delphia said, anticipating what Randall was about to say. Yet even as she spoke, she slipped down from the shorter, stockier wagon horse and let the tired horse's reins fall to the ground.

"We have no choice!" Randall said, circling back on Ellis's big bay and reaching a hand down to her. Without protest, she grabbed his hand and forearm and swung up behind him on the bay.

"All right then, let's go!" she said, throwing her arms tightly around his waist, adjusting her seating and bracing herself as the big bay lunged forward into a run. Behind them the worn-out wagon horse began making his way back down the steep path toward the main trail across the floor of Wolf Valley.

Over an hour later, crossing the valley floor, Brother Searcy spotted the tired horse in the light of the half-moon. Pointing up along a rocky ledge, Searcy said, "Father Jessup! Up there! I saw something!"

Seeing the outline of the animal, Jessup replied, "Yes, an abandoned horse I believe." Drawing the riders to a halt, he said to Searcy and Edmunds, who rode flanking him, "Quickly, you two go get it and bring it down here to me."

As the two bodyguards rode toward a path leading up toward the wagon horse, Rudy Banatell said to Orsen and Ernie in a sly tone, "See what I'm seeing?" He stared forward at Jessup sitting alone and unprotected at the head of the column of believers.

Orsen and Ernie looked at one another dumbly and shrugged. "No," said Orsen, "what *are* you seeing?"

"I'm seeing opportunity stare us in the eyes. Right now would be the best time in the world to slip up beside the good reverend, put a gun to his *holy* head and tell him we're taking over Paradise. I bet he'd melt like soft wax on a stove."

Orsen grinned and said eagerly, "Want to do it right now? Just for the hell of it?"

"Real soon, Orsen, real soon," said Rudy. "Once a man starts letting down his guard, it ain't long before you can splatter his nose all over his face."

"Why do we want to do that?" Ernie asked, not understanding the example Rudy gave them.

"Damn, Ernie," Orsen growled under his breath. "Please tell us that you ain't *really* that stupid."

"How stupid?" Ernie looked more confused.

Shaking his head, Rudy gigged his horse forward, saying over his shoulder to Orsen, "Talk to this boy some. See if you can teach him something. I'm going up there and test the water some."

Orsen said wryly to Ernie, "You *do* know what he means by 'testing the water some,' don't you?"

Ernie gave him a scowl without answering.

At the head of the riders, Jessup appeared a bit startled when Rudy sidled his horse up close to him, on his right side where Searcy usually rode. Seeing the look on Jessup's face, Rudy jerked his horse away quickly and said quickly, "Begging your pardon, Reverend! I didn't mean to scare you, riding up the way!" Rudy's eyes had been busy, checking to see if Jessup made any sudden moves toward a gun. Then, satisfied that the reverend was unarmed, Rudy grinned and relaxed in his saddle.

"You didn't scare me, Mr. Able," said Jessup. He turned his face away from Rudy and toward the two bodyguards riding away in the darkness.

"Of course not, Reverend," said Rudy. "*Scare* wasn't the right word. I meant to say *surprise*." Rudy grinned.

"Yes, *surprise* has a better sound to it." Jessup nodded and sat staring off in the direction Searcy and Edmunds had taken.

"Yes, *surprise*." Rudy gazed off with him for a moment, then said, "Well, anyway, I was just telling my two associates that, since this hunt is taking much longer than you had expected it to, perhaps the three of us should turn back and await your arrival in Paradise."

"Never fear, Mr. Able," said Jessup. "It's the Lord's will! I'll capture this man and take him back before this night is over."

"Nothing like confidence, I reckon," Rudy said, again smiling broadly. As he spoke, he raised his Colt from its holster, cocked it and started to take aim at a large jackrabbit that had loped into sight thirty yards away.

"Fire that weapon at your own peril, sir!" Jessup warned him. "We are on a manhunt here!"

Rudy lowered the gun, unlocking it. "Excuse me, Reverend," he said. Then in a defensive tone he said, "I left Paradise thinking I'd be back before dinner. My belly must've gotten the better of me." Holstering the Colt, he turned his horse away from Jessup's harsh gaze and rode back to join Orsen and Ernie.

Moments later, Brothers Edmunds and Searcy came riding back down from the ledge, leading the tired wagon horse by its reins. Even in the pale moonlight Jessup recognized the Mosely wagon horse at once. Sidling up to it, he ran a hand along the sweaty horse's mane, saying, "It appears that either Sloane Mosely has deceived us, or that he himself has been a victim of Randall Turner's rash undertaking." He looked all around and continued, saying, "Whatever the case, he will owe us an explanation when we return."

Having ridden up closer to hear what was being said when Edmunds and Searcy brought the horse down to Jessup, Rudy, Orsen and Ernie listened and watched, Rudy noting eagerly that even with his bodyguards back beside him, Jessup was not staying as safely tucked between them as usual. "Prepare yourselves, boys," he said to Orsen and Ernie out the corner of his mouth. "It won't be much longer."

"You mean the bank?" Ernie whispered.

"Bank, hell," said Rudy, grinning. "I'm going to get everything this arrogant fool has."

* * *

Having pushed Ellis's big bay hard throughout the night, in the grainy hour before dawn, Randall and Delphia finally rode the big bay across the last stretch of flatlands to the narrow pass leading out of Wolf Valley. Before entering the pass, Randall stopped the horse, let out a breath of relief, raised his face toward the sky and cried out loudly, "Thank God!" Then, listening to his voice echo before them, he tilted his head back to Delphia and said, "Wife, this big bay has done well. He's brought us to freedom."

Delphia reached a hand up and ran it across her husband's clammy forehead. Tearfully she said, "Take us on, husband. Let's not waste a minute."

Randall nudged the big bay forward into the narrow pass, but before they had gone a hundred yards, they stopped abruptly at the sound of horses' hooves descending from the rocks surrounding them. Randall circled the big bay, seeing the dark outlines of riders closing in around them. He nudged the horse forward, preparing to charge through the riders. "I wouldn't try to make a run for it if I was you," said a voice.

Randall stopped at the sound of a rifle cocking. Behind him Delphia said in a shaky voice, "Oh no! Please God, no! Randall, go on!" Wildly she tried to bat her heels against the horse's sides; but Randall held the big bay in place, seeing the rifle pointed at them.

"Stop it, Delph," he said over his shoulder. "They've got us cold."

Delphia slumped against her husband's back.

"Better listen to him, little lady," said Frank Falon. "You don't want to both die out here, do you?"

"Yes!" Delphia said defiantly, recognizing Falon and his men as they drew in closer. "I'd rather die than go back to that *pig,* Jessup!"

"I'll be damned. It's that wolfer," said Falon, looking them over as he held his rifle on them. "I heard you *thanking God*, wolfer." He grinned, saying, "You should've thanked Him a little quieter, eh?"

Randall only stared.

To Delphia, Falon said, "A *pig?* Now that's a shameful thing to call your husband—your *real* husband that is."

"Jessup is not my *real* husband," said Delphia, "and you know it. This is my real husband!"

"That ain't what I heard Jessup say that day in the street," Falon said, wearing a tight smile.

"Randall and I were man and wife before we ever laid eyes on Wolf Valley or Jessup and his whole wicked community," said Delphia.

"You best settle down, little lady," Falon cautioned her. Then to Randall he said, "Last I saw of you, Jessup was ready to give you a good skinning with his bullwhip." He grinned, looking from Randall back to Delphia. "She was all that kept him from killing you. Made quite a trade to Jessup for you would be my guess." His eyes went up and down Delphia's bare leg. "I expect I can't blame ol' Father Jessup for that, can you, Ace?"

Ace Tomblin, Colt in hand, sidled up to Falon. The rest of the wolf hunters drew in tighter around the couple. "Naw, I can't blame Jessup either," said Tomblin, "women being at such a premium hereabouts."

"Indeed they are," said Falon. "Of course her being the reverend's wife and all, I suppose we ought to be on our best behavior," Falon said.

Seeing the men's eyes explore his wife hungrily, Randall said firmly, "Frank, let us go. I'm begging you! You've seen how Jessup does people. He takes their land, their possessions, their wives!"

"You're breaking my heart, wolfer," said Falon.

"Listen how you always call my kind *wolfer*," said Randall, trying to appeal to whatever humanity the man might have inside himself. "You say it like you're so much better than me! But can't you see we're no different? You trap and kill them. I skin and boil their bones. Jessup is the only one who reaps the rewards from it! We are both slaves to the same cruel *Lord!*"

"No, there is a difference, wolfer," said Falon. "I'm a whole lot farther up the ladder than you are. Jessup ain't my Lord. He just pays me to do his killing for him. Or in this case, getting a flea out of his whiskers." He grinned. "I know he's a no-good son of a bitch. So what? Ain't we all?"

"No, we're not! We don't *have* to be! You can be a better man than he is, Falon," Randall said, trying to reason with him. "Just let us pass through here. He'll never know you did it."

"Listen to you carry on, wolfer," Falon said, chuckling slightly. "I suppose you're right. I *could* be a better man than him—" He paused and grinned at Ace Tomblin, then shrugged and said, "But hell, maybe I don't want to!" He nodded to his men, saying, "Neither do they." Looking back at Delphia, he said, "Of course, a pretty woman could always change our minds. Right, Ace?"

Ace Tomblin only grunted a reply.

"I'm carrying a child!" said Delphia, hoping to discourage Falon and his men from forcing themselves on her.

"No kidding?" said Falon to Randall with a dark grin. "Then congratulations are in order." Looking back at Delphia he said, "I never knew of that stopping anybody from doing what folks do. Some folks even say they like it better when a woman is—"

Delphia cut him off, saying, "Father Jessup will kill all of you if you force yourselves on me!"

Falon laughed. "Whoa! Let me get this straight. A while ago, Jessup was a *pig*. Now that you think his name can protect you, he's Father Jessup!"

"Yeah," said Ace Tomblin. "Next thing you know, she'll be saying Jessup *really is* her husband." He threw up a hand. "I give up! Woman, how many husbands *do* you have?"

Falon shook his head while the others laughed at Ace's little joke. "Funny, ain't it," said Falon, "how a woman gets to pick and choose all she wants. A man has to take what he can get, whenever he can get it." His mood seemed to darken. "Climb down off that horse, both of yas."

Delphia refused to move. "I'm warning all of you. I will tell Jessup. He will kill you!" She clenched her arms tightly around Randall's waist.

But Randall, who had been observing Falon and Tomblin as they spoke, said to Delphia in a calm voice, "Let's step down, Delph. They're not going to bother you, are you, Falon?"

"Hell no," said Falon. "I'm doing what we always do for Jessup when we catch somebody escaping the valley. Except this time, he is going to reward me beyond belief!"

"You're going to take us back to him, aren't you?" Randall asked in defeat, letting Ace Tomblin take the bay's reins from his hand as Delphia slipped down from the horse's back.

"That's right," said Falon, "her anyway. I've got a feeling the reverend doesn't want you around any longer. He's going to think I'm the cock of the walk, bringing this sweet little wife back to him." He made a slight gesture with his eyes toward Delphia, then said to Randall, "Believe me, there are worse things that could happen to her than us taking her back to Father Jessup—if you know what I mean."

Delphia heard the suggestion in Falon's voice and said quickly, her voice rising in panic, "What are you saying? What are you going to do to him?"

"Tell her what I'm going to do to you, wolfer," Falon said.

Randall slid down from the saddle and faced Falon, seeing no way out for himself. "Promise me you won't harm her, Falon."

"No! Don't kill him!" Delphia screamed, realizing what Randall already knew Falon had in mind for him. She tried to lunge forward to Randall, but Ace Tomblin grabbed her and held her back.

"Get over there, wolfer," Falon demanded, using his rifle barrel to gesture Randall to the rocks alongside the steep walls of the pass. "The quicker we get this over with, the quicker everybody can get on back to their own business."

Before taking step, Randall said, "You're taking her right back? You're not going to let any of your men bother her, are you?"

"Damn, you're getting on my nerves, wolfer!" said Falon, giving him a shove with the tip of his rifle barrel. "You heard the woman. Jessup would kill us all deader than hell if we did what we feel like doing to her. She's going back. You're going to hell. We're going to get a lick on our cheeks for solving Father Jessup's problem. What more can a man get out of life?" He stopped walking along behind Randall. Allowing Randall to get a few feet farther away from him as he raised his rifle and aimed it at the back of Randall's head.

Hearing the hammer cock, Randall continued to walk, but began to recite a prayer from the Bible. Hearing Randall pray, Falon gave a dark chuckle and said, "You're a dumb one, wolfer. God hasn't done a damn thing for you yet, and He's about run out of time."

Randall's voice continued, low and calmly, "Though I walk through the valley of the shadow of death, I shall fear no evil, for thou art with me."

The sound of Randall praying seemed to anger Falon. He clenched the rifle tighter, taking closer aim, his hand trembling in rage. "Damn it! I told you, it was hearing you talking to God that brought us down on you! Don't you ever learn, you damned fool!" The rifle hammer dropped with a loud explosion, silencing Randall's prayer abruptly as he flipped forward, the bullet striking the back of his head.

Delphia screamed long and loud, twisting her face free of Ace Tomblin's grip, but unable to free herself from the other two men and run to her fallen husband.

More angry now than before, Falon turned quickly from his gruesome handiwork and stomped past Ace and the others as they struggled with the woman. "Shut her up, Gawdamn it!" he shouted. "Everybody mount up. Let's get moving!"

Ace Tomblin stepped around in front of Delphia while the other two held her. Walking to his horse to slide his rifle into his saddle boot, Falon heard the sound of the punch landing on the woman's jaw. Spinning quickly toward Ace he said, "Have you lost your mind? What the hell was we just talking about? Jessup will kill us if something happens to her!"

"So?" said Tomblin, looking at Delphia, who had slumped back into Kirby Falon's arms. "Tell him the wolfer did this to her. If she denies it, tell him she's accusing us just to cause us trouble." Ace laughed a little and said with a hand up to his ear, "Anyway, listen how quiet it is without her wailing and carrying on."

"Damn," Falon grumbled under his breath. "You better

hope she doesn't have a bruised jaw out of this. That's all I can say." He jammed the rifle down into the saddle boot, stepped up into the saddle and rode his horse over beside the big bay. "Lay her up here. We're headed for Paradise."

Chapter 14

CC Ellis had ridden the big silver stallion hard throughout the night, staying on Randall and Delphia's trail ahead of Jessup and his men. When he'd heard the single rifle shot echo up around the rim of the rock walls encircling the wide valley, he pushed the stallion hard in that direction until he slowed to a stop where the ground beneath him lay covered with fresh hoofprints. He started to turn the stallion and follow the prints, but the boot prints leading off the side of the trail caught his attention and he followed them instead, his Colt drawn and ready.

"Oh, Jesus," he murmured, seeing Randall Turner, facedown in the rocky dirt. In the grainy morning light, he saw the large dark puddle of blood surrounding Randall's hidden face. Holstering his Colt, Ellis stepped down from his saddle and walked over to body. "You didn't deserve any of this," he said quietly.

Ellis stooped down, turned Randall onto his back and dragged him out of the puddle of blood, back toward the stallion. In the silence of morning he asked himself if there was any way in the world to save the woman from Father Jessup now that her young husband was dead. But in asking, he also had to remind himself that none of this affair was his business. He owed this man nothing. He owed this man's young widow nothing. He reminded himself that the way this thing was playing out, he would be lucky if he could get Callie,

Dillard and himself out of Wolf Valley without a fight. Yet, having witnessed the grim outcome that had befallen Randall and Delphia Turner, he found it hard not to take Jessup's trail and kill him upon sight.

For the sake of Callie and the boy Ellis forced himself to stop thinking about killing Jessup. He reached his hands under Randall's blood-soaked shoulders and prepared to move him up. "At least I can see to it you get in the ground proper like, you poor son of—" He stopped abruptly at the gurgling sound that rose up from Randall's chest.

"Help— Help me," Randall said in a voice so faint it could have been easily missed had Ellis not been stooped down close to him.

"Jesus!" Ellis exclaimed. "You're alive!" He lowered Randall quickly, keeping a hand behind the mass of blood on the back of his head.

"Help me," Randall whispered.

"Hold on, Randall! Just hold on! I'll be right, back," Ellis said, hearing the surprise and urgency in his own voice. Turning Randall's head sideways as he laid it back in the dirt, Ellis hurried to the stallion and took down a canteen of tepid water as he untied his bandanna and pulled it from around his neck.

Back at Randall's side, he washed the heavy blood from around Randall's weak and trembling lips. "Don't try to talk," Ellis told him. "I see what happened here."

"My—my wife," Randall managed to say, the words seeming to deplete his strength.

"I know," said Ellis. "Some of Jessup's men caught up to you. They must've circled around the main body and ridden on ahead."

"No," Randall whispered. "Falon …"

"Falon?" Ellis asked, surprised by the information. "Falon and his wolf trappers have your wife?"

"Yes," Randall answered, his hand managing to find

Ellis's forearm and squeeze it slightly. "A horse …"

"A horse?" Ellis shook his head as he wet the bandanna. He carefully turned Randall's head sideways again for a closer look at the wound beneath the mass of dark-jellied blood. "I've got no more horses for you," he said. "Besides, you're not going to be riding for a while." Judging from the severity of the wound, Ellis was doubtful that the young man would live throughout the coming day.

"I've got to. God help me…." His pleading whisper trailed off into the grainy morning light.

Ellis felt him go limp and almost stopped cleaning the wound, thinking him dead. But he felt Randall take a shallow breath, and remarked to himself, "If I was God, I sure would, as much as you've been through."

But you're not God, a warning voice sounded in his mind. Ellis clenched his teeth and concentrated on examining the bloody head wound.

As the mass of blood gave way to the probe of the wet bandanna, he saw that a flap of loosed scalp lay to the side and exposed a long strip of white skull bone before blood began to well and cover it. Before blood obscured it, Ellis saw what he thought to be thin vein-like cracks in the bone matter. He winced at the sight of it and carefully laid the layer of scalp in place. Rather than remove any more of the blood mass and perhaps start the heavy blood flow all over again, Ellis laid the wet bandanna atop the wound and pressed it gently into place. "We're going to make us a camp here," he said to the unconscious man in his arms, still doubting if Randall would make it through the day. "As soon as you're able to ride, we'll take you somewhere and get you some proper medical care."

Ellis looked all around in the grainy morning light, realizing with an almost eerie feeling in his gut that every step he took with the young couple drew him in deeper toward a reckoning with Jessup and his followers.

At the rear of Frank Falon's riders, his brother, Kirby, and

Willie Singer rode close together, arguing back and forth secretively between themselves. Warily, Kirby Falon stared forward, watching Frank and Ace Tomblin ride along, with Ace leading Ellis's big bay behind him. Delphia Turner sat slumped in her saddle, half-conscious, still groggy from the earlier punch to her jaw.

"I don't know, Willie," Kirby said. "Seeing that big bay makes me think we better come clean and tell Frank everything the way it really happened that day on the creekbank."

"I'm telling you, Kirby, that might not even be the same bay the man was riding that day. You act like there's only one bay horse in the whole damned world!"

Kirby said firmly, "Willie, you know as well as I do, that's the same bay horse that man was riding the day we all got the hell shot out of us. The man said he was CC Ellis, and I believed him."

"Well, whoever he was, he's deader than hell," said Willie Singer. "And I don't see how telling your brother, Frank, is going to do anything but get me killed, and you skinned from top to bottom! Now keep your mouth shut and let's ride this thing out."

"That wolfer was riding CC Ellis's bay, Willie," Kirby insisted. "I don't know how that happened, but I don't like it a damn bit."

"The wolfer could have gotten that bay anywhere, including finding it walking along the trail after the shooting," said Willie. "Damn it, Kirby! Learn to hold your water! You're acting as fidgety as a schoolgirl!"

"Watch your mouth, Willie," Kirby said, his voice rising, drawing attention from the rest of the men riding along the trail.

"Easy, Kirby," Willie whispered, trying to settle him down. "All I'm saying is let's keep this thing to ourselves. Odds are CC Ellis is dead. Don't let this horse undo everything we told Frank!"

At the head of the riders, Frank Falon turned in his saddle at the sound of the two men's voices. "What's going on back there, Kirby? Are you and Willie Singer at it again?"

"Now you've done it," Willie whispered sidelong to Kirby. "Go on then. Ride up there and tell him every damned thing. See what it gets us." He gave Kirby a cold stare. If Kirby made a move toward riding up to his brother, Willie had already made up his mind. He would put a bullet in the young gunman's back, turn his horse and make a run for it.

"It's nothing, Frank," Kirby called out. "You know how Willie and I are always fussing about something."

"Yeah, well keep it to yourselves," Frank called back to his younger brother. "You're both starting to get on my nerves."

"Sure thing, Frank," Kirby said, turning his gaze to Willie, seeing how relieved he looked.

Willie settled back into his saddle, saying, "Sometimes I wonder about you, Kirby. You don't always seem to have good sense."

Kirby grinned to himself and stared ahead.

The riders pushed on until they came to the trade shack in the clearing where the old wolfers gathered at the doors of their smaller plank huts and stared at the big bay with Randall Turner's wife sitting slumped in the saddle, her jaw bruised and puffy from the blow Ace Tomblin had dealt her. "Better come take a look, Soupbone," said one of the grease-smeared attendants wearing dirty rags tied around his hands in place of work gloves. "It looks like Randall and his wife didn't get very far."

"Out'n my way, all of yas!" said a gruff voice. From amid the station attendants, Soupbone Pitler shouldered his way to the front of the open doorway and said aloud to himself upon looking out onto the mud street and seeing the woman, "Poor Randall. God help him if this bunch caught him for Jessup. Falon would kill his own kin if he thought it would gain him favor with Father Jessup."

Beside Soupbone the attendant with rags around his hands said, "I'll give Randall this much. He said he was going to make a break for it, and by God, he did it!" He looked all around at the other dirty, half-starved attendants and said in a sour tone, "That's more than the rest of us sorry bastards can say for ourselves."

"Speak for yourself, Dooley," said Arch Tidwell, another of the attendants. "Jessup has done right by me. I would have starved to death long ago had he not taken me in."

"Yeah, you sorry old scab," said Lloyd Dooley, turning his attention back to the riders coming along the middle of the muddy street. "That's why you run to tell Jessup everything that anybody says about him."

"Careful Dooley," said Soupbone, "or he'll be telling him what you've got to say about him." He gave Tidwell a dark stare. "Every time I think he mighta been the one to tell on Randall Turner, it's all I can do to keep from sinking a hatchet into that ugly skull of his."

Hearing Soupbone, Tidwell turned and slinked away toward the back door of the shack.

"I couldn't care less what he tells Jessup about me," Dooley hissed without taking his eyes off the riders. "I'm getting like Randall. I just don't give a *damn* anymore. What's the worst he can do to me, kill me?" He spit and ran a hand over his mouth. "Dying ain't the worst thing can happen to a man."

"Hear that, Tidwell?" said Soupbone, calling as Arch Tidwell stepped out of the shack and disappeared from sight. "It's getting to where folks ain't worried about Jessup anymore!" But upon realizing that Tidwell hadn't heard him, he said to the others, "Randall Turner has shown us all something, the way he stood up to Jessup and tried to take back what was his."

"He might've *tried*," said Dooley, nodding out toward Delphia Turner, "but he didn't get very far with it. The trail out of Wolf Valley is too long and hard for a man to get away! It's impossible!"

"The whole point is he *at least tried!*" Soupbone snapped. "Everything is impossible until a man puts his shoulder to it and shoves. Even if it defeats *him*, others see his effort and it causes another man to step up and try his hand at it." He gave the others a solemn stare. "Look around, those of you who want to leave this hellhole! This whole valley is turning into a keg of black powder. All it's going to take is the right spark to set it off."

"You might be right about that, Soupbone," said Dooley, scratching his dirty beard in contemplation.

"I am right about it," Soupbone replied. "I just hope I'm standing near that betrayer Arch Tidwell when it happens, so that I can gouge both my thumbs into his sorry eyes."

"There goes Tidwell now," said Dooley, staring out across the muddy street.

Crowding in beside him, Soupbone and the others stared out at Tidwell as he ran through the mud past the boiling caldron toward another party of riders coming into sight from the opposite direction of Falon and his men. "What the tarnation is that skunk up to now?" said Soupbone to no one in particular.

Squinting for a better look, Dooley said, "Speak of the devil. Here comes Father Jessup and his believers right now."

"To gather up Delphia Turner and force her back with him, I reckon," said Soupbone with a bitter note in his voice. They watched Tidwell hurry along, casting a backward glance in their direction as he slipped, stumbled and raced on through the mud.

At the head of the riders, Father Jessup also saw Tidwell running to meet him and his men. But his eyes only looked toward the running man for an instant, then went to the woman sitting atop the big bay across from the attendants' shack. "Brother Searcy, get rid of this fool!" Jessup shouted, kicking his horse forward toward Delphia Turner, swerving a bit to avoid Tidwell.

"Father! Father! I have to talk to you!" Tidwell shouted, waving his arms, seeing Jessup hurrying away from him. He started to run along behind Jessup, but Brother Searcy sidled his horse over in front of him, blocking his way.

"What do you want, Tidwell?" Searcy asked in an impatient voice.

"I've got to talk to Father! It's important!" Tidwell cried out, his face turning white because the other wolfers had seen Father Jessup ignore him. "These wolfers are talking awfully harsh! I expect trouble from them!" He glanced back quickly and saw all eyes on him from the door of the shack. "Father's got to listen to me! He's got to talk to me! Please! He's got to!"

"Oh does he?" said Searcy, giving a tap to his horse's sides, the horse bumping Tidwell backward a step. "You're forgetting yourself, *wolfer!*" Searcy gave him a cruel grin. "Father listens to whoever he feels like listening to. No amount of begging or shouting is going to change that!"

"But they'll kill me!" Tidwell pleaded. "I've always done what Father asked me to do! He can't just let a follower die!"

"Sure he can," Searcy grinned, seeming to enjoy Tidwell's pleading. "It happens all the time!" He gave the man another bump backward with his horse. Tidwell went down on his back in the mud, and struggled up to his knees, knowing the others were seeing all of this. "Beside, who said that you're one of the believers, you grubby, sour-smelling wolfer? Nobody ever let you into the believer's group."

"But I've done everything I was asked," said Tidwell. "I just figured after all that I was the same as the rest of yas! That's how God would want it!"

"You figured wrong!" said Searcy, turning his horse back toward the other riders, who had already followed Jessup toward Falon's men across from the attendants' shack. "Don't tell me how God would want it!" He pointed a gloved finger toward Jessup as he rode away. "As far as I'm concerned, he is God—leastwise in Wolf Valley. Anything you've got to say to God, you better take to him!"

"That's all I'm trying to do here," Tidwell pleaded, slinging mud from his hands. "But I can't get to him with you standing between us!"

Searcy looked back, chuckled and winked, saying, "Now you're starting to understand how this thing works, *wolfer*." He gigged his horse away toward Jessup and the rest of the riders, leaving Tidwell standing alone in the mud trail. Tidwell looked around at the grim dirty faces watching him from the doorway of the shack.

"Get back over here with us where you belong, Arch Tidwell," Soupbone called out.

"Yeah," Dooley called out. "From now on, stick with your own kind."

Tidwell looked in fear and longing toward Father Jessup and his followers, then turned slowly and trudged through the mud toward the shack.

Chapter 15

Father Jessup reined up close to Falon's men at the very moment Ace Tomblin reached up, took Delphia in his arms and lowered her to the ground. No sooner had her feet touched the ground than Jessup lunged his horse between the two of them, butting the big animal into Tomblin, almost knocking him off his feet. "Never put your hand on a wife of mine!" Jessup bellowed at him.

Tomblin looked stunned. "But I was just helping her down from her—"

"I said *never!*" Jessup shouted. "Do you hear me, man!"

Falon interceded on Tomblin's behalf. "He hears you, Father. It won't happen again."

"Where is the man who stole her?" Jessup demanded, turning his attention from Tomblin to Falon.

"Randall won't be coming around bothering anybody else," Falon said, offering a proud expression Jessup seemed not to notice.

"Don't speak that blackard's name in Paradise again," said Jessup, without so much as even a thank-you for a job well done. Instead, he reached down from his saddle, scooped Delphia up with an arm and raised her onto his lap. He looked her up and down closely, then demanded, "What happened to her face?" He touched his fingertips gently to her bruised puffy cheek.

"She must've fell before we got to her, Father," Falon said, lying to protect Tomblin.

"Or perhaps *he* struck her," Jessup said, brushing Delphia's hair from her forehead, fawning over her.

Falon shrugged. "I suppose that could be. If so, *he'll* never do it again," he added, still reaching for some recognition from Jessup.

Instead Jessup said to Delphia, "Which one of these men struck you?"

"Wait a minute, Father," Falon began to protest. "You can't take the word of a woman whose been through—"

"Silence!" Jessup shouted, cutting him off.

Delphia did not answer, but Jessup saw the way her eyes moved to Ace Tomblin before quickly looking away from him.

"He did this to you?" Jessup asked her.

Delphia didn't answer.

"Tomblin, did you strike my wife?" Jessup asked, trying to keep his angry voice under control.

"We couldn't handle her, Father," said Falon, still speaking on Tomblin's behalf. "She was a wild woman. I was afraid she'd hurt *herself!*"

"I see," said Jessup, turning a hard stare to Tomblin. "So you hit her to keep her settled down."

"Well, yes," said Tomblin, "something like that. The main thing is, we brought her back for you … no harm done."

"Shoot him," Jessup said matter-of-factly to his two bodyguards.

"No, wait!" shouted Falon. But his words were drowned out by the roar of both the bodyguards' big Colts firing as one.

From a few yards away Rudy Banatell and his two men saw Ace Tomblin fly backward with a scream, two bloody mists exploding front and rear from his upper body. "Gawd-damn!" Rudy said to Ernie and Orsen. "For a couple of church boys, these fellows are awfully fast."

"I've seen faster." Orsen shrugged and spit. "I suppose the preacher makes them keep in practice, since it's his ass they're protecting. That's something you might want to keep in mind when we go taking these fellows on."

"Ha, no problem there," said Rudy, "not the way we're going to take them on." He turned his attention back toward Jessup and Frank Falon, seeing Falon's men ready to jerk up their guns and shoot it out with Jessup's believers.

But Falon held up a hand to keep his men in place. He said to Jessup in an enraged voice, "For God's sake, Father! Ace Tomblin was the best man I've got! You had no cause to kill him!"

"Stand down, all of you!" Jessup warned Falon's men, bypassing Falon altogether. Surrounding Jessup, the rest of the mounted believers sat braced in their saddles, their rifles cocking almost as one and pointing toward Falon and his riders. Jessup turned back to Falon, saying in a fatherly, almost soothing tone, "Frank, you allowed this man to harm my wife. You're very lucky I didn't have you shot as well. Lately you've been slipping away from me. You haven't been as attentive to my orders … to running this trapping crew for me. I don't know what's wrong, but I hope that what just happened here will jar you back to your old self—the Frank Falon I can count on, the Frank Falon we all have admired and respected."

"Father, he did her no harm," said Falon weakly, already relenting in submission to Jessup. "Ace was a good man." His eyes went to the crumpled body lying on the ground.

"Of course he was," said Jessup, "at one time. But I'm afraid he let himself get too unruly." His eyes moved across all the riders facing him, then went back to Falon. "That is so often a good man's first downfall. He gets too big and too proud to follow the rules of both God and man. He begins to think that whatever he wants to do is just fine! He soon forgets that we are *all* here to serve in some capacity or another."

As he spoke, he continued brushing his hand gently across Delphia's head, as if stroking a favorite house pet.

"But enough of Ace Tomblin and his downfall," Jessup said, his tone of voice changing, sounding more agreeable. He stopped stroking Delphia's hair and said to Falon, "Frank, you and these men have done a wonderful thing, bringing my wife back to me! I know that God had His hand on this thing from start to finish. But it's the people God chooses to do His good work that show us who among us are blessed in His eyes." He raised a finger for emphasis "We are all on a religious quest in this life. We do not always know what it is we are seeking, but the fruits of our quests are always revealed to us in the end."

"Amen," said a voice from among the believers.

Jessup nodded in acknowledgment and said, "Never forget that as you do *my* bidding, so do you do God's bidding." He gave Falon a beaming smile, then swept a hand toward Ace Tomblin's body. "Aside from this *ugly* incident, Frank Falon, you have much to be thankful for this day. Don't think that the fruits of your labor will go unrewarded."

Out of hearing range, Rudy said to Ernie and Orsen, "Jesus, this preacher can beat them down and butter them back up, all in the same breath." He backed his horse a step and turned it toward the doorway where the attendants stood watching.

"Where are you going?" Orsen asked.

"On a little religious *quest* of my own." Rudy raised his thumb to this lips as if secretly taking a drink of whiskey.

"Are you kidding?" said Orsen. "You're not going to find anything like *that* in a place like this. This preacher would have them skinned and scalped if he caught them."

"Look around this shit hole," said Rudy. "If you had to live here, wouldn't you find yourself something to drink even if it cost you your life?"

Orsen looked all around at the muddy shabby buildings and the piles of decaying wolf carcasses lying near the boiling caldron. Without answering he nudged his horse forward behind Rudy toward the attendants' shack. "Let the quest begin," he said over his shoulder to Ernie who nudged his horse along close behind him.

At the shack, Rudy stepped own into the mud and trudged over the open doorway, neither seeing nor caring that Jessup's bodyguards watched every move he made. While Orsen and Ernie stopped their horses behind him and stepped down, Rudy stood at the open doorway, stamping mud from his boots and saying to the gaunt dirty faces staring at him, "All right, who do I see about getting a jug of whiskey in this place?"

"Mister, we don't want no trouble," said Soupbone.

"Good," said Rudy, offering a firm but friendly smile. "'Cause I'm after whiskey, not trouble."

"We don't have no whiskey, mister," said Soupbone. "It's against Father's rules."

"Oh, the *rules*." Rudy shouldered his way into the shack, causing the attendants to take a step away and form a circle around him. Orsen and Ernie stepped into that circle with him, their hands on their gun butts. "I've seen and heard a lot about Jessup's rules. But let me tell you *my rule*. I just made it a rule that I ain't leaving this place without some whiskey." He turned a slow harsh stare from one pair of eyes to the next.

"Mister, that's bold talk, and we all take it seriously," said Soupbone, "but the fact is Jessup's whippings scare us more than your guns. For all we know, you're here checking up on us for him."

Rudy tossed a head gesture toward Jessup and his men across the street, saying, "If you think I'm working for that snake oil-selling son of a bitch, you're crazier than yas look."

A gasp went up from the attendants. Nobody would dare call Jessup such a name, even if that person was here to check up on them. After a tense silence, Soupbone said in a hushed tone of voice, "Mister, if I was to find a jug of whiskey for you, how would you hide it?"

Rudy grinned at Orsen and Ernie, then said to Soupbone as he pulled out his battered whiskey flask and shook it, saying, "Forget the jug. I'll just have you fill this little fellow up for me."

Soupbone took the flask and passed it along to someone behind him. "Go fill this up for him, Dooley." Turning back to Rudy, he said, "Dooley is from Kentucky. He makes some of the best whiskey you ever poured down yourself." He looked back and forth warily. "Whatever you do, don't let Jessup know."

"You can count on that, mister," said Rudy. "While we're on the subject of Jessup. How would you boys like it if somebody new came along to run this valley? Would there be any objections?"

A silence set in for a moment. Finally Soupbone said, "Objections? My God, man, that would be an answer to all our prayers!"

"No kidding," said Rudy, grinning and giving Orsen and Ernie a look.

"Who would you be talking about, mister?" Soupbone asked. "Yourself, maybe?"

"Maybe," said Rudy, "but I've already said more than I should." He leaned slightly and looked past Soupbone and the others toward the rear door Dooley had hurried through only a moment ago. "How's that whiskey coming along anyway?"

Just as he asked, Dooley opened and closed the rear door behind himself. He stepped quickly over and handed Rudy the whiskey flask. "Here I am. I've got you all fixed up."

Rudy took the flask and shook it slightly, saying to Orsen and Ernie, "See there, men. My *quest* has worked out pretty damn good."

On the ride back to Paradise, Rudy pushed his horse in between two of Falon's men and sidled up close to Falon himself. Seeing Kirby and the others give Rudy a warning look, Falon said to them, "It's all right, men."

"Damn shame they didn't act that way when Jessup was about to gun down your pard, eh?" said Rudy. He grinned, watching the others drift away, leaving him and Frank Falon to talk.

"What's on your mind?" Falon asked him gruffly, not liking Rudy's implication.

"I just thought I ought to come back here and properly introduce myself," Rudy said. "Able's the name. I work scouting land for the railroad."

"Like hell," said Falon, staring straight ahead.

"Well, I can see it ain't going to be easy winning you over, is it, Falon?" said Rudy.

"I don't give a blue damn what your real name is or what the hell you're doing in Paradise," said Falon. "I lost a good man back there. I ain't in much of a sociable mood right about now."

"I can't blame you," said Rudy. "I'd feel the same way about losing either one of those boys back there." He nodded toward Orsen and Ernie riding a few yards ahead. "I expect if it was me, I would be thinking of all kinds of ways to get even right now." He looked at Falon expectantly.

But Falon only shrugged and looked away, saying, "Whatever I'm thinking about, it's none of your business."

"Ordinarily I'd say that's true," said Rudy. "But what I'm considering doing is going to be just as important to you as it is to me. I thought I better try to see where you stand on things. It might be the difference between you living and dying."

Falon jerked his horse to a halt and stared at Rudy, his hand poised on his pistol butt. "Is there a threat in there somewhere?"

"Depends on what you call a threat," said Rudy. "What one type of man sees as a threat, another kind of man sees as an opportunity."

"Whatever it is you've got to say, spit it out," said Falon, his men also stopping and closing in a circle around the two. Beyond Falon's men, Rudy saw Ernie and Orsen come riding up, ready for anything.

"All right, here it is," said Rudy. "There's some changes coming to Paradise and the rest of Wolf Valley. I want to start knowing ahead of time who'll be with me and who'll be against me."

"You're talking about taking over Paradise?" Falon asked, his voice going low, secretive.

"You heard me right," said Rudy, putting it all out front, seeing where Falon stood after watching his partner shot down in cold blood. "If you want a say in the way things are going to be, this is the time to tell me who you'll stand with: Jessup or me."

Listening, Kirby Falon cut in, saying, "You've got to be out of your damn mind, mister! Nobody has ever gotten the drop on Jessup and his men! They never will!"

"Hush up, Kirby," said Frank Falon. He looked at Rudy closely as he said to him, "My brother, Kirby, here speaks sometime when he should be listening. He's right though. Nobody ever has gotten the drop on Father Jessup. But that doesn't mean it *can't* happen."

"It is going to happen," said Rudy, taking out his flask of whiskey as he spoke and slipping it to Falon.

Falon looked at the whiskey flask in surprise, uncapped it and sniffed it as if to prove to himself that it really contained whiskey. "Damn," he said, "this doesn't even smell like Lexar's ol' snake-head brew! I believe this is sipping whiskey." He turned up a sizable drink, savored it, then swallowed it and let out a soft hiss.

Seeing the look of delight on his brother's face, Kirby asked Rudy, "It must be good stuff! Where did you get it?"

"Right under your noses, fellows," Rudy said, looking all around at Falon's men. "I just want to let everybody know that once I take over, there'll be plenty of whiskey—plenty of gaming, too."

"Damn, what about women?" Kirby asked, getting excited.

"Women, hell, yes," said Rudy, reaching out to take his flask back from Frank Falon. "I'd never live in a town that didn't have women ready to fall upon a man at the drop of hat. All these things are what the Lord intended for red-blooded men!" He nodded off toward Jessup at the head of the riders, leading Delphia on a horse behind him. "I notice that son of a bitch has women all around *himself,* but to hell with everybody else. I bet someplace he has a good bottle or two of whiskey as well. He's just keeping it all from the rest of yas!"

"Yeah, that son of a bitch!" said Kirby.

"Settle down, Kirby," said Frank Falon. To Rudy he said, "You're taking one hell of a chance, talking about something like this to us. How do you know we won't go straight to Jessup with it?"

"I've seen the way he treats you, Falon," said Rudy. "I've seen the way he treats all of yas. Don't tell me that this isn't something you haven't already been thinking about doing yourselves. I just happen to be the one who's going to go on with it."

"And you're wanting our help," said Falon.

"I could use your help, but it won't matter." Rudy shrugged. "I'm taking over either way. The main thing I want is for you to stay out of my way while I do." He lifted a quick sip of whiskey, then put the flask away, keeping an eye toward Jessup and his men. "I'll also want you to keep on running the trapping operation the way it's been going after I take things over."

"You're taking an awful big chance," Falon said again. "But if it works, why would we want to work for you?"

"Because I'll pay you more than Jessup pays you, and I'll treat you like men instead of like animals. How's that for starters?"

173

Falon looked at his brother, Kirby, then at the others, then back at Rudy Banatell. He spit and said, "Why not? What have we got to lose?"

"Now you're talking," said Rudy, wearing his sly grin. "Sit tight, Falon, and watch what happens next." He winked at Falon, turned his horse and rode away toward the front of the line.

Catching up to him, Orsen said, "You better hope you can trust these lousy hide trappers. I've never seen one that was worth a pound of his own shit."

"Have a little faith in your fellow man, Orsen." Rudy grinned. "Take a look at all these miserable wretches, the trappers, the station attendants. They've all been wronged and treated sorely by this stuffed-shirt preacher. If a man like Falon will kill for Jessup, the way he's been treated, imagine what he'll do for somebody like me, who treats him and his men like equals."

Orsen thought about Rudy's words for a moment and finally said, "Yeah, I have to admit you're on to something here, sure enough. But all this stuff is worrisome to me. I like robbing a bank and leaving town in a hurry—the way we've always done it before."

"Not this time, Orsen," said Rudy. "This time we're playing winner takes all. If this preacher can't run Paradise the way it should be run, I'm obliged to take it over and run it myself." He gigged his horse into a trot and rode toward the front of the riders, in eager anticipation of what awaited him once they arrived in Paradise.

PART III

Chapter 16

Upon arrival in Paradise, Rudy, Orsen and Ernie followed Reverend Jessup to the believers' meetinghouse, where they waited out front at the hitch rail while Jessup and his bodyguards walked inside and turned Delphia over to three of Jessup's other wives. "Look after her," he said. "Tonight we will all rejoice at having one of our own back among us." Turning to another of his followers who had stayed behind to watch Paradise, he said, "Now then, Brother Paul, what have you learned for me in my absence?"

"I have learned much, Father," the tall, gaunt man said, rolling down his shirtsleeves as he spoke.

"I can always count on you, beloved Brother Paul," Jessup beamed, laying a hand on the man's broad shoulder. The man bowed slightly, turned and walked to the rear door, with Jessup and his bodyguards right behind him.

"I would never let you down, Father," said Brother Paul, reaching out and opening the rear door for him and his bodyguards.

Out front Rudy leaned against the hitch rail with Orsen and Ernie, Jessup's men standing a few yards away. Beyond them Falon and his men stood in a small circle talking among themselves. Instinctively Rudy eyed the street in both directions, searching for anything out of the ordinary. Seeing nothing noteworthy, he relaxed a bit and said quietly to Orsen,

"I'm ready to make our move, just as soon as Jessup shows us another opening. Keep your eyes peeled and your gun hands ready."

Orsen smiled and replied without facing Rudy, "We're ready when you are, Rudy. I'm just wondering where Gun and Jim Heady are."

"The Gun will show up when he sees it's time," said Rudy. "I expect that he's got Heady on a short leash right about now, keeping him from doing something stupid."

Orsen started to say something else, but before he could, Jessup and his bodyguards came walking quickly toward them from the meetinghouse. As Jessup approached, the rest of his men fell in around the bodyguards and walked purposefully forward, causing Rudy a moment of concern.

"Something's up," Rudy whispered sidelong to Orsen.

"We're ready for it," said Orsen. He blew a chewed-up wooden match from his mouth and let his hand lie poised near his holstered Colt. Beside him, Ernie did the same, none of the three making any move that appeared defensive, yet each of them ready to draw their weapons and began a rain of gunfire with a second's notice.

But to their surprise, Jessup stopped a few feet away and said in a jovial tone, "Gentlemen, where are my manners?" He tossed his hands as if to chastise himself and said, "Come inside. Let's have some cool water and rest out of the sun."

Rudy breathed easier and asked coolly, "While we're drinking water, maybe you'll send Mr. Lexar over to the bank and get our money for us, Reverend."

"Oh, your money, of course," said Jessup as if the money had slipped his mind. He glanced at Lexar, who stood with the rest of Jessup's men. "Bother Lexar, go get the money and bring it to us inside the meetinghouse."

"Yes, Father," said Lexar. He bowed slightly and hurried away toward the bank across the street.

"Now then, gentlemen," said Jessup, sweeping a

hand toward the meetinghouse door, "if you'll join me, I have something to show you that I know you'll find most interesting." Seeing the slightest hesitancy on Rudy's part, Jessup added, "It concerns Mr. Sloane Mosely and his current standing in our Community of Believers."

Rudy, Orsen and Ernie started to step forward, but one of the bodyguards held up a hand stopping them, saying, "First, I'm afraid I have to ask you for your guns."

Rudy tensed, so did Orsen and Ernie, flanking him. "I'm getting real tired of handing over my firearm every time I turn a corner in this town," Rudy said firmly.

"It's the rule," said Searcy, also firmly. "No firearms inside the meetinghouse."

Before Rudy could respond, Jessup stepped forward, saying, "Come, come, Brother Searcy. It's all right this time. These men have trusted us with their railroad's money. Surely we can trust them to carry their guns in a civil manner. I only created that rule to ensure harmony in cases of solving disputes between some of the nonbeliever settlers when we first arrived here." He tossed his hands. "Now that there are no more nonbelievers settled in Wolf Valley, I believe we can forgo that ruling." He smiled amiably. "Wouldn't you agree, Mr. Able?"

"Completely, Reverend." Rudy relaxed, allowing his hand to come away from his gun butt. Jessup was making this easy for him, he thought, stepping forward, motioning for Orsen and Ernie to follow. "Come on, fellows. The good reverend is making an exception in our case. Now that's the kind of courtesy I could grow accustomed to. After you, Reverend."

The three fell in behind Jessup and followed him and his two bodyguards inside the meetinghouse. Once inside, Rudy looked around fondly at polished wooden chairs and pulpits glowing in soft candlelight from brass lanterns that lined walls adorned with religious paintings and tapestries of a quality fit for a royal castle. Hearing Rudy let out a short gasp of admiration, Jessup stopped for a moment, turned and said, "Gentlemen, let us stand here for a moment and drink in the beauty of this most holy place." He turned to the two bodyguards and said, "Brother Searcy, you and Brother Edmunds go to the bank and see what's taking Brother Lexar so long. He should have been back with the money by now."

"But, Father," Searcy said in a lowered voice, as if to keep his words hidden from Rudy and his men. He flicked his eyes toward Rudy, implying a concern for Jessup's safety.

"Nonsense, Brother Searcy," said Jessup. "I have nothing to fear from these good businessmen! Run along! Bring back the money. We'll wait here for you in this place of peace." He spread his hands to take in the inside of the meetinghouse.

Rudy gave Orsen and Ernie a sharp glance as soon as the two bodyguards closed the front door behind themselves. "Now's the time," Rudy whispered. "*Let's do it!*"

Jessup had turned to face a long altar, where candlelight glinted off ornate golden goblets and serving platters. But on hearing the slightest commotion behind him, he turned back toward the three and found himself looking down the barrel of Rudy's cocked Colt. Startled, Jessup looked all around as if it had suddenly dawned on him that he'd sent his bodyguards away and left himself vulnerable. "Oh my," he said calmly, raising his hands chest high, "I certainly walked blindly into this, didn't I?"

Rudy grinned cruelly. "Yeah, I would say so. But be too hard on yourself, Preacher. It happens to the best of us."

"You're not railroad men at all, are you?" Jessup asked.

"No, not at all," said Rudy. "We're thieves, plain and simple. We came here to rob Paradise."

"The bank?" Jessup stared at him.

"Of course, the bank," said Rudy.

"Yes, of course." Jessup sighed as if chastising himself for not knowing it all along. "And to think I trusted you ... took you in among my believers, rode with you on a matter most personal to me. All along this is what you came here to do."

"Robbing the bank was what we *came* here to do," said Rudy, "but things have changed. After seeing the way you're robbing this whole town on a day-to-day basis, I've decided I want more than just a few stolen dollars and a hard ride across Wolf Valley." His grinned widened. "Besides, you've already shown us that nobody is going to escape you here on your own ground. I have to say I'm obliged for you showing me that."

"If not the bank, what is it you want now?" Jessup asked, getting an even warier look on his face.

"I'm taking everything you've got going here, Jessup: your women, your money, your power. From now on, I'll be ruling Paradise."

Jessup shook his head slowly. My believers will never allow that, Mr. Able—if that's your real name."

"My real name is Banatell," said Rudy, "but don't waste your time trying to remember it. You're not going to be here long. As for your believers"—he shrugged—"they'll come around. I've already talked to your station attendants. They can't wait to hear I've put a bullet in your brain. The same goes with Falon and your trappers. You've treated everybody so bad for so long, I'm not going to have a bit of trouble taking this place over."

"And there isn't a thing I can do to save my own life?" Jessup asked.

"Not a thing I can think of, Jessup," said Rudy. "You gave me the opening, letting those bodyguards leave you here with me. There's nothing left for me to do but kill you." His eyes narrowed as he extended his arm, leveled the cocked Colt and aimed at Jessup's forehead from less than six feet away. "Adios, Preacher," Rudy growled under his breath, his fist tightening around the gun butt, his finger tightening on the trigger. On either side of him, Ernie and Orsen did the same.

Jessup didn't so much as flinch when all three hammers fell with nothing more than an impotent metal on metal click.

"*Gawddamn it!*" Rudy shouted, already realizing that something had gone wrong with his whole plan. Yet, even as his heart sank with the realization, he quickly thumbed back his hammer twice more, each time hearing it fall with the same result.

Staring at his Colt in wide-eyed disbelief, Ernie cried out in a shaky voice as his and Orsen's guns made the same dull clicking sounds. "It's a miracle! He really *is* God!"

"Shut up, you damn fool!" said Rudy. "We've been *had!*"

"Indeed, you have been," said Jessup, raising a hand and giving a signal. Doors and windows flew open; gun barrels pointed in at the three hapless gunmen from every direction. "Brothers Searcy and Edmunds, come in here quickly. Take their guns. I'm growing weary of this little charade."

"Damn, Rudy!" Orsen cried out. "What are we going to do?"

"I expect we're going to die, Orsen," Rudy replied, staring coldly into Jessup's eyes.

"That's the first time you've been right all day," Jessup said. Over his shoulder he said, "Falon, get in here. Let this fool see just how many of you he had on his side."

Frank Falon walked in through the rear door, stopped and looked Rudy in the eye. "He didn't have anybody on his side, Father," said Falon. To Rudy he said, "You thought Paradise was easy pickings. Now look at you. You don't look so proud and bold now, do you?"

"You son of a bitch," Rudy growled. "I'm still bolder and prouder than you! I might die trying to take over Paradise, but your sorry ass will always be enslaved here!" He spit in contempt at Falon's feet.

"Why did you play along with us, Jessup?" Orsen asked, watching Brother Edmunds take his Colt from his hand and shove it down into his belt. "Why didn't you just have it out with us to begin with? Why all this?"

"After you came here flashing all that so-called railroad money around," said Jessup, "I had to see if there was anything to it." He turned to Falon and said, "Good work, Frank. That will be all."

Frank Falon gave Rudy a sour smile, saying, "See you in hell," before he turned and left.

Rudy refused to acknowledge Falon with a second glance. "That money is all yours, Jessup," he said, making a weak move at saving his life. "All you have to do is let us ride out of here. Call this whole thing a bad dream. We'll never come back to Paradise. You've got my word on that."

"I think not," said Jessup, as if he had actually considered Rudy's proposition. "I won't need your word on it after you're dead. Besides, we've checked the money over good. It's all fake, every dollar of it."

Rudy didn't flinch. Instead he said, "I've still got my best gunman running loose out there. He won't take this sitting still. You kill us, he'll hound you till the day he dies."

"Oh, you must mean Shelby," said Jessup.

"That's right," said Rudy. "If you know anything about him, you'll know that he's a straight-up killer!"

"Yes, I'm sure he is." Jessup shrugged, unconcerned. "But tell me about Sloane Mosely."

"What about Sloane Mosely?" Rudy asked. "I don't know anything about the man. First time I laid eyes on him was when we rode to his house with you and your men."

"I saw the way you and he looked at one another," said Jessup. "I couldn't help but think the two of you had crossed trails before. If there's anything you can tell me about him, I suggest you do so now, before my patience with you wears thin."

"You mean, if I could tell you anything about Sloane Mosely, that would get us off this spot, save our lives?" Rudy asked, looking for a way to save himself and the others.

"No, I don't think it would save your lives," said Jessup. As he spoke, he walked past Rudy to the rear door and swung it open. "But there is something good to be said about dying *quickly*."

Rudy tried another weak threat as he followed Jessup out into a yard surrounded by high stone walls. "I'm not sure who'll be doing the dying here once the Gun hears what's going on. For all I know, he could be putting you in his rifle sights right now."

"I hardly think so," said Jessup, directing Rudy's and his men's attention toward the body of the Gun hanging from an iron rack with a long steel spike driven through his forehead.

"Good God!" said Rudy, stopping cold and swallowing hard at the gruesome sight. He noted that the Gun's fingers were missing from both hands and that his lips had been sliced away, leaving the corpse with a wide, sardonic grin. Most of the skin had been carved away from the Gun's chest. Short, bloody strips of viscera still hung limply down from the corpse's lower belly.

"As you can see, your friend the Gun was hard-headed to the end, and this is the end he chose for himself."

"Where's Heady?" Rudy asked

"Young Mr. Heady has seen the light since last we met," said Jessup. "Brother Paul tells me that the dear fellow has done a complete turnaround in his thinking and is at this very moment being administered religious instruction by some of my qualified believers at a quiet location. I can't wait to have him stand at my side."

"Jesus," Rudy whispered, shaking his head slowly at the prospect of Jim Heady standing by Jessup's side after what Jessup had done to him. "I've got to hand it to you, Preacher," he said. "You know how to bend and mold people into whatever shape you want them in."

"You made a common mistake," said Jessup, "thinking these folks wanted out from under my thumb. This is where they are secure. They feel safe with my whip always looming above their heads. If not for my stern discipline, Paradise would be no different than any other hell hole in this godforsaken wilderness."

"Give me five minutes and a bottle of whiskey and I can change Heady's mind all over again, Preacher, and I believe you know that."

"Yes, I do know that," said Jessup, "and that is all the more reason why a weak person like Heady needs someone like me to keep him beaten into submission." Jessup tossed the matter aside. "Be that as it may"—he looked at the face of each of the three men in turn—"I wonder if any of you will have the good sense to tell me about Sloane Mosely." He raised a hand toward the corpse of the Gun. "Or is this sort of harsh, terrible death more preferable to you?"

Seeing the look on Orsen's and Ernie's faces, Rudy said to Jessup, "Why are you so worried about Sloane Mosely."

"Because his gun skills are legendary," said Jessup. "I'm not ashamed to admit that I don't want to risk the lives of my followers against someone like Mosely."

"You got the drop on us without firing a shot, Preacher," said Rudy, "so I don't think you're too afraid of Mosely."

Before Jessup could reply, Searcy escorted Frank Falon back into the yard and walked him up close to Jessup's side. "Yes, what is it, Falon?" Jessup snapped.

Falon leaned closer and whispered between Jessup and himself. Jessup's expression changed as he nodded and considered Falon's words. "Well, then," Jessup said, "it appears I won't have to squeeze any secrets out of you three after all. Falon has just informed me that the man we've all thought is Sloane Mosely is actually a ne'er-do-well named CC Ellis."

"Falon's lying," said Rudy, doing what he could to protect Ellis.

Jessup gave Falon an expectant look.

"My brother, Kirby, and Willie Singer just told me. This is the man they had the shootout with along the creek. They both heard him say he's CC Ellis."

"CC Ellis, the *long rider,*" Jessup mused. "Now we're starting to get somewhere."

"You never heard it from me," Rudy cut in.

"No," said Jessup. "Yet the look on your face at this moment tells me Falon's information is correct." He paused, considering the information. "I'm beginning to understand. Sloane Mosely is not around. His young wife has been taken over by this man, who is impersonating her husband. That poor, dear woman. I'll have to make things right for her. I won't allow her to be used by some two-bit gunman."

"If you think Ellis is nothing but a *two-bit* gunman," said Rudy, "I'd give anything to be alive and see your face when he opens your belly with a fistful of bullets."

"But sadly for you, you won't be alive," said Jessup. From the open doorway, Brother Paul appeared with Jim Heady standing shakily beside him. Turning toward them, Jessup said, "Yes, Brother Paul?"

"I have our newest convert here, Father. He can't wait to tell you what he's already learned from our instruction session."

Jessup grinned at Rudy, then said to Brother Paul, "By all means, let's hear what our young convert has to say."

Brother Paul led Jim Heady forward. Heady deliberately kept his face turned downward and away from the Gun's tortured body. "There now, Brother Jim," said Brother Paul, "tell Father what you've learned already."

Jim Heady sank to his knees and said in a tight, fearful voice, "God is good! Father is good!"

"Eh?" said Jessup, cocking an ear toward the kneeling convert. "I didn't quite hear you. Speak up now."

"God is good. Father is good. God is good. Father is good!" Jim Heady said loudly.

Heady started to repeat himself, but Jessup laid a hand on his bare head, stopping him for a moment. "Brother Paul, I have to say, you are truly gifted when it comes to teaching the unbelievers."

Rudy had seen all he could take. "Get off your knees, Heady, you spineless son of a bitch!"

Hearing Rudy, Heady began chanting again, his voice growing louder as if to drown out Rudy's words. "God is good. Father is good! God is good. Father is good!"

"Come on, Preacher, you low snake!" Rudy shouted. "Let's get it over with. I'd rather die and go to hell than live on the same piece of earth you're on!"

Jessup gave him a flat, harsh grin, stroking Jim Heady's hair while Heady droned on repeatedly. "Then go to hell you shall, sir." He turned to Brothers Searcy and Edmunds. "Take them away. I'm done with them."

Hearing Jessup's words, Jim Heady wrapped his arms around the reverend's leg, pleading in fear, "Not me! Not me! Not me!"

"No, not you, child," said Jessup, again patting and stroking his head. "You just continue reciting for me. I love hearing you say those words."

Chapter 17

Two days passed before Randall Turner could maintain consciousness for any longer than a few drifting moments. The wound in his head was a graze, but it was a deep graze, one that shattered his skull bone severely. Callie had to prepare herself for seeing the terrible wound before she could clean and dress it without her hands shaking unsteadily. When Randall finally managed to stay conscious long enough to eat some warm broth, he looked at Callie, CC Ellis and Dillard standing over him and asked weakly, "Am I … able to ride yet?"

"Randall," said Ellis as gently as he could, "you're not even able to sit up yet without passing out. I know you want to go get your wife away from Jessup, and I don't blame you. But if you don't sit still long enough for your skull to mend, you'll die and Jessup will win, hands down. Do you understand me?"

Randall let out a breath, knowing Ellis was right. "I'm obliged … for all you folks … have done for me," he said haltingly. "I'll try to lay still … a while longer."

"Good," said Callie. "Now you two sit here quietly for a moment while I go get you some cool water to drink." She looked down at Dillard, saying, "Come along, Dillard. You can help me draw water."

Randall's blurry eyes followed her until she was out of

the room. Looking back at Ellis he said, "I think … I figured it out. You're here to keep … her and the boy from being swallowed up by Jessup … the same way he did Delphia and me."

"Yep, that's it," said Ellis. "Our plan was to slip away without Jessup noticing. But now that he's been here and we've come close to locking horns, it's not going to work the way I wanted it to."

"And I took your best horses," Randall commented. "So … now you can't even try to outrun him." He shook his bandaged head slightly. "I'm sorry. I never meant to cause you trouble."

"I know you didn't," said Ellis. "And if I was you, I would have done the same thing. So say no more about it. You've shown me that Jessup can't be outrun anyway. He's got too many followers for that to happen."

"What are you going to do?" Randall asked.

"It's a poker game for now," said Ellis. "I wait and see what Jessup puts on the table next, see how much he knows. I'm hoping I might still ease the woman and her son away from him some way. But for now I can only wait and see what his next move might be."

"Kill him," said Randall, a strength seeming to return to his voice for a moment. "That's all that can stop him. He talks about God … like the two of them are one and the same. But underneath the pretense, Jessup is nothing less than the devil from hell." Randall began to shake; his eyes took on a dark cast.

"Easy, Randall," said Ellis.

Behind him the door opened and Dillard ran in wide-eyed and excited, saying to Ellis, "Mother says hurry! Come quick! One of the Brothers is riding into the yard!"

"Here we go," Ellis said under his breath, his hand instinctively going to his holstered Colt.

"Help me up. I'm with you," Randall said, struggling to raise himself.

But Ellis pressed him back down to the bed. "No, stay put! If you want to help me, keep quiet in here! Let me get rid of him. If Jessup finds out you're here, he'll kill you."

Randall lay back and stopped struggling.

"Stay here with him, Dillard," said Ellis, heading out the door. He stepped out onto the porch at the same time as Callie came running up from the well.

"I'll get the shotgun!" she said, stopping only long enough to make sure Ellis saw the rider come around the turn in the trail and up toward the house.

Ellis caught her by the arm before she could get past him. "Get it, but stay inside with it," he said, his eyes on the rider, watching him come closer by the second.

"All right," said Callie. "I'll be at the window."

Letting her go, Ellis stepped over the front edge of the porch and stood with his feet shoulder width apart, his hand resting near his big Colt. When the rider stopped six yards back from the porch, Ellis called out, "What can I do for you, mister?"

"Mr. Mosely," said the rider, "I'm Brother Paul Chapin from the Community of Believers in Paradise. Father Jessup sent me to clear the air between you and our folks after what happened here the other night and bring you some good news."

"I didn't realize the air needed clearing," Ellis replied. "But if you've rode out here in peace, you'll leave here the same way."

"Much obliged, Mr. Mosely," said Brother Paul. "It might interest you to know that Father and his wife have been reunited, and the man who caused all the trouble is dead." Under his breath he added, "May God condemn his soul to everlasting hell."

"That's harsh," said Ellis, "but I'm glad everything is settled." He breathed a little, knowing that Jessup and his men thought Randall Turner was dead.

"Harsh, yet fair when seen through the eyes of God," said

Brother Paul.

Ellis wasn't going to debate the matter of what things looked like through the eyes of God. "Whatever you say, Brother Paul," he said. "Through *my eyes,* I came out of it losing a couple of horses I couldn't afford to lose. But I expect I'll recover from my loss sooner or later."

"That's the good news I bring to you," said Brother Paul, offering a stiff, unpleasant smile. "Father said to tell you we have your horses, and you are free to pick them up in Paradise any day of your choosing. As a token of friendship, he insists that there be no livery fee for feeding and boarding them until you come for them."

"I am most pleased to hear that, Brother Paul," said Ellis, "and most obliged to Father Jessup for his hospitality."

"Very well. When can I tell Father to expect you?" He stared at Ellis with the same unpleasant smile, awaiting an answer, as if knowing that he had just put the other man on a spot.

Staring back at him with poker eyes, Ellis said flatly, "I'll be there first thing in the morning. I wouldn't have my horses eating away at your generosity."

"Tomorrow morning," said Brother Paul, with deliberation. "He will be expecting you then."

"Tomorrow it is," said Ellis, seeing the man turn his horse to leave. "Feel free to water yourself and your horse before leaving."

"Thank you, but both my horse and myself are fine." Brother Paul touched the wide brim of his flat-crowned hat, turned and gigged his horse back toward the trail to Paradise.

Stepping out onto the porch before Brother Paul was out of sight, Callie moved in close beside Ellis and said, "Jessup knows, doesn't he?"

"I think so, Callie," said Ellis, "but I can't be sure of it. So I'm going in for the horses in the morning, just like I said I would."

"You can't take a chance like that, Ellis!" Callie said. "If he knows you're an impostor, you will never come back from Paradise!"

"If he *does* know, then we're already at his mercy anyway," said Ellis. "I can die here or I can die in Paradise. At least by going there for the horses, I have an outside chance that he doesn't even suspect I'm not your husband. If that's so, we get the horses back and can still try to slip out of here."

"But he knows you're *not* Sloane Mosely and he's just luring you into town, you're dead!" said Callie.

"If dying in Paradise keeps you or the boy from catching a bullet, then that in itself is worth something to me."

"And that might be exactly what Jessup is counting on you thinking," said Callie.

"If it is, then I salute him for it." Ellis stared off at the rise of dust left standing in the air by Brother Paul. "Maybe that's the way it should be. There's no point in you and the boy dying." He gave her a stern solemn look.

"How dare you?" Callie spat. "I'm not going to give myself over to that pig of a preacher! I've told you, I'll die first!"

"I know what you've told me, Callie," said Ellis. "But riding into Paradise is the best play in this game right now. You'll have to trust my judgment, if you can't see that yourself."

Callie settled down, looked out at the rise of dust, then said quietly, "All right, go to town. I'll take care of Randall. I'll wait for you. But if Jessup shows up instead of you, I want you to know here and now that I went down fighting."

Ellis thought about things for a moment, then said, "Callie, I've got to tell you some things—things I should have told you sooner, but I couldn't bring myself around to it."

She looked it him expectantly, but hesitated as she asked, "This is about Sloane, isn't it?"

"Yes, it is," said Ellis. "You see, I knew Sloane Mosely."

"*Knew?*" Callie said. "Then he is dead?"

Ellis nodded solemnly. "Yes, by now I expect he is."

"How did he die?" she asked, after a moment of sad contemplation.

"That's the part I've been having trouble figuring out how to tell you, Callie," Ellis said.

"How did my husband die?" she asked more firmly. "I need to know, in order to tell his son."

"You won't want to tell Dillard how his father died, Callie." Ellis took a deep breath and said, "Sloane Mosely hanged for the killing of a bank guard down in Texas."

"No!" Callie gasped, and staggered back a step before Ellis caught her by her arms and eased her down into a wooden chair.

Looking at the door and window to make sure Dillard wasn't in hearing range, he said quietly, "I know this isn't the right place or the right way to tell you about this, but I thought I better, before I ride into Paradise."

"And how is it you *knew* my husband?" she asked. "Did you actually know him, or did you just happen to know of his fate?" She stared at him as if dreading to hear his answer.

"We rode together some, Callie. Not all the time, but some. I'm not going to lie to you, I'm an outlaw. I believe you thought as much when you found me beside that creek and brought me here."

She didn't answer. Instead she said, "And those men you met in Paradise the other day? They also knew Sloane, didn't they?"

"Yes, they did," said Ellis. "Those men, your husband and I are all a part of the same gang. Sloane only took up with us the past couple of years. The rest of us have been robbing ever since the end of the war. The man you saw in Paradise, Rudy Banatell, recognized you from a picture Sloane carried in his pocket watch case."

Seeing no reason to doubt anything Ellis was telling her, Callie sighed. "That explains some things. There was a time just about a couple of years ago when my husband and I were struggling to get by. He'd lost his position with the Midwestern Detective Agency. Although he was little more than a hired gun for the agency, losing the income hurt us badly. But then he made a trip to Texas, to see about some money owed him from an old friend, supposedly. After that trip our financial worries were over."

The expression in Ellis's eyes confirmed for her that this would have been the time her husband joined up with Rudy and the gang.

Callie's expression seemed to sharpen as she looked into Ellis's eyes and recalled that time. "When he came back he had enough money to hold us over for a *long* time."

"I know," Ellis said softly.

Callie continued. "But before three weeks had passed, he had to make another trip, this time to look at some land in Missouri. I all but begged him to wait another week, but for some reason he had to get going. Now I realize he had to meet up with the rest of you, didn't he?"

Ellis only nodded, lowering his eyes a bit.

"I suppose I should have realized he was up to something," Callie said. "Perhaps I looked the other way, not wanting to admit to myself that my husband had gone afoul of the law."

"Callie, whatever your husband did, you can't blame yourself for it. I didn't know Sloane Mosely as well as I know the rest of the fellows, but I knew him well enough to know that he loved you very much. I expect at the end of every man's life, if we went looking for something bad in him, we'd find it most every time." As he spoke, he reached out a hand and brushed a strand of hair from her face. "All I can tell you is not to look for it."

Tears glistened in her eyes but did not fall. "Did you come here knowing I was his wife? Were you coming to tell me about him when you were ambushed alongside the creek? Did Sloane send you?"

"No," said Ellis, "I almost wish that was the case. Then I could have told you straight up what had happened to him and there would have been no secret to keep from you."

"You would have told me, then gone on your way?" Callie asked.

"I would have told you, Callie," Ellis replied. "As far as leaving, I can't say. There would have still been the problem with Jessup to deal with. I would have still seen your face in my dreams." He offered a trace of a smile. "Who can say how it might have gone? But since I wasn't here to bring you a message on Sloane's behalf, I couldn't bring myself to tell you what he'd done, or how he'd died. That would have been betraying one of my own."

"I can't say that I understand that sort of thinking," Callie said, "but it is the kind of alliance men seem to respect among themselves. It's what Sloane would have done, given the same situation, I'm certain."

Ellis hesitated for a moment before saying, "Callie, there's something else I want to tell you. Before his execution, Sloane Mosely insisted that Rudy and the rest of us come rob the bank in Paradise."

Callie shook her head slightly. "I don't understand."

"I believe Sloane Mosely wanted Rudy and the rest of us to come to Paradise, knowing that Jessup and his men would ride us down crossing Wolf Valley."

"You don't mean that Sloane wanted to get all of you killed, do you?" she asked in astonishment.

"No," said Ellis. "If you knew these men as well as I know them, as well as Sloane knew them, you'd realize that it wouldn't be us who died—it would be Jessup and his men."

"You mean …" Callie's words trailed as she pondered what he'd said.

"I believe that even though your husband knew he was going to die, he tried to see to it that you never fell under Jessup's rule."

195

"Yes," Callie said, "that *is* something Sloane would try to do. Whatever else he might have been, or whatever he might have done, he loved Dillard and me. I've never doubted that."

"That's why I want to get all this said. It might have been no more than simple fate that brought me to the creek-bank. It might have been nothing but circumstance that drew you and me together. But I like to think that maybe Sloane Mosely knew what might happen here if you were left alone, and maybe he would even approve of us being together. Anyway, this is what I wanted you to know before I ride out to meet Jessup."

"I'm glad you decided to tell me," said Callie. She squeezed his hand gently.

"I figured I had to," said Ellis, "as close as we've been, as much as you and the boy have come to mean to me. If something goes wrong in Paradise, I'd want you to know that I never intended to take advantage. I've been a long rider and a man of intemperateness most of my life. But I have never misused a woman. And I would especially never misuse someone as precious to me as you are."

"Ellis," she whispered, drawing him to her in an embrace.

"I had to get that said, Callie," he whispered in reply.

"Why does life always take the hardest path?" she asked in a hushed tone against his ear.

"I hope you don't want me to try answering that one," he said, clinging to her tightly, his eyes closed.

Chapter 18

Night shrouded the vast, rugged terrain when CC Ellis put the big silver stallion forward in the light of a half-moon, riding down the last stretch of sloping hillside into Wolf Valley where the trail turned toward Paradise. He had told Jessup through Brother Paul that he would be there first thing in the morning. But something told him it would be wise to try slipping into town under the cover of night.

If Rudy Banatell and his men were still in Paradise, and Ellis had no reason to think otherwise, they would be his ace in the hole. Should he find out his worst fears were true and that Jessup knew he was only impersonating Sloane Mosely, he would need all the help Rudy Banatell could throw his way. Out of habit Ellis hadn't mentioned to Callie that Rudy had talked about still making a run on Paradise, possibly something more than just robbing the bank. Ellis had never known the outlaw leader to make a claim without following through on it. But until he saw Rudy, he couldn't afford to leave anything to chance.

He rode on.

Another hour passed before the first dim golden glow of dawn wreathed the jagged hills on the far side of the valley. At a place where the trail widened into a cultivated dirt road leading into town, Ellis stopped the big stallion long enough to check his Colt and slip it back into his slim-jim belly holster.

Beneath him the big stallion shuffled its hooves restlessly and raised its nostrils to the night breeze, as if in anticipation of what lay ahead.

"Easy, big fellow," Ellis murmured, patting the stallion's neck. He smiled grimly to himself. This was not the first time Sloane Mosely's stallion had ridden in under a cloak of darkness, feeling the night breeze sweep through its mane. He tapped the stallion forward with his heels and kept it pinned to a quiet walk.

The last mile outside of Paradise, he studied the outline of the low hill, where the three crosses stood in dark silhouette against the sky. He'd seen the crosses on his last trip into Paradise, but this time there was a difference. It was a difference he at first sensed, and his senses warned him to move forward with caution.

Drawing nearer to the crest of the hill, he stared in stunned disbelief at three bodies hanging pale and naked in the grainy darkness.

"Oh my God!" he said aloud to himself, already having an idea who he would find hanging on the large rough-hewn crosses. Stopping the stallion, he looked up at the bodies, seeing their dead, sun-cooked faces staring blindly back at him, barely recognizing Orsen and Ernie Harpe. On the third cross hung the body of Forrest Beckman, the former bank manager.

Instinctively Ellis had drawn his Colt on the way up the low hillside. He let it drift back and forth as he made a swift searching glance around the area. To his left the land lay shadowed in silent darkness. But he snapped to his right at the sound of a raspy voice pleading faintly, "Water ... Please, water!"

The big stallion perked its ears toward the sound of the voice and nickered warily. Hearing the stallion, the voice asked weakly, "Who's there?"

Ellis's eyes and cocked Colt instantly fixed toward the

sound of the voice, and spotted a fourth wooden cross, this one lying flat on the ground. Staring at the cross, Ellis saw a head rise the slightest bit, then collapse under its own weight. It took Ellis only a second to decide who was lying there.

"Rudy? Old pard, is that you?" Ellis asked.

The voice had gone into a low, mindless babbling, but at the sound of his own name, Rudy Banatell fell quiet for a second and raised his head again. "CC? CC Ellis?" he groaned. "Is that you?"

"It's me, Rudy," Ellis replied, tapping the stallion forward, but still keeping an eye toward the darkness, least there be someone lying in wait.

"Come over here, Ellis. Let me take ... a look at you," Rudy said, his voice sounding raspy and spent.

"I'm coming, Rudy!" Ellis said, stopping the stallion and swinging down from his saddle. He snatched a canteen of tepid water from his saddle horn on his way. "Jesus, what has he done to you?" he asked, getting a better look at Banatell in the thin moonlight.

"He called it *redeeming* me, Ellis," Rudy gasped.

"Redeeming you from what?" Ellis asked, not expecting an answer, and not getting one. Rudy's only reply was a long moan of agony as Ellis stooped down and took a closer look at his twisted, bloodstained figure. "Oh, Rudy," Ellis sighed, seeing how brutally his old trail partner had been tortured.

Rudy Banatell's hands and feet had been nailed to the cross with long steel spikes. But ropes and steel wire also circled his arms tightly, the wire cutting into his flesh, holding him to the rough cross, making the nails nothing more than an additional element of cruelty. "Never thought I'd ... end up like this," Rudy said haltingly. "I'm in ... terrible shape."

Both of Rudy's eyes were bloody from the relentless pecking of birds; as were his ears, forearms and chest.

"I'm here now, Rudy," said Ellis. "I'll get you taken care of."

"I never told him nothing, CC," Rudy whispered through swollen, split lips.

"Lay still now, Rudy. Take it easy," said Ellis. He poured water from the canteen into his cupped hand, then let it trickle onto Rudy's lips. "I don't care what you told him. A man is apt to tell anything, under this kind of treatment."

"But I didn't tell him, CC," Rudy said, the water running down into his parched throat. "Neither did Orsen or Ernie, God love 'em." His bloody eyes turned up toward the other two men on the crosses, not seeing them but rather recalling where they were from earlier in his ordeal.

"Who's the other man?" Ellis asked, taking off his bandanna, soaking it and swabbing Rudy's cracked and blistered forehead.

"A banker ... can you imagine?" said Rudy. "Me dying beside a banker. I couldn't stand the thought of it. I wiggled this cross back and forth ... till it came down." He tried to offer a weak grin, his bloody eyes struggling to make out Ellis's face. "I was praying it was you coming, Ellis," he said. "Jessup would have liked that, me praying ... him being a religious man and all."

"This is not religion, Rudy," said Ellis. "This is nothing but craziness."

Rudy coughed and choked and said, his voice failing, "Ever notice how the crazier they are, the more God agrees with them on things?"

"God doesn't agree with them, Rudy," said Ellis, trickling more water onto Rudy's burned forehead.

"But he talks to them," said Rudy, grasping Ellis by his forearm. "He talks to Jessup all the time." His bloody eyes swam back and forth, unable to see Ellis clearly. "How come God never talked to me? I would have listened ... had he talked to me."

"I know you would, Rudy. Now lay still. I'll get something to pry these nails out. We'll get you fixed up someway." Even as Ellis spoke, he saw no way to pull out the nails without causing the man more pain.

"That ain't what I was praying for, Ellis," Rudy murmured, his bloody eyes steadying for a moment in the direction of Ellis's face. "I was praying you'd get here in time to do us all some good."

"Orsen and Ernie are both dead, Rudy," said Ellis.

"But I ain't," Rudy whispered. "You can do me some good."

"Rudy, I can't do that," Ellis said, knowing what was being asked of him. "But maybe I can save you. Just hang on."

"Ellis, I don't want ... to hang on," Rudy pleaded. "For God's sake, look at me."

Ellis did look at him, and he realized the dying outlaw was right. Standing up slowly, he drew his Colt again, cocking it as quietly as he could. "You want me to set this thing right with Jessup for you, Rudy?" he asked.

"Naw, that's not important to me, Ellis," Rudy whispered, his voice growing more faint with resolve. He tried to form a thin smile. "Of course if you come across him ... I'm obliged if you put a bullet in his head."

"You can count on it, Rudy," Ellis said. He held his Colt out at arm's length and started to squeeze the trigger; but the explosion he heard was not the sound of his Colt firing. It was the sound of an explosion inside his head as a rifle butt snapped forward from behind, smacked him soundly and sent him swirling to the ground, into a sea of black unconsciousness.

"That's that," said Arby Ryan, taking a deep breath, letting go of his tension. He stood over Ellis, relaxing his rifle but still prepared to deliver another blow if need be. Kicking Ellis's Colt aside, Arby called out to the others a few yards away on the other side of the low rising hill. "I got him, Frank! Hear me? I got him cold!"

On the ground, Rudy's eyes swam back and forth, trying to focus on blurred shadows. "Who's that? What's going on? Ellis? Ellis?"

"Quiet down, you blind, dying son of a bitch, you!" said Ryan. He gave Rudy a short kick in the side. Rudy grunted, but was already too far gone to feel any pain.

Frank Falon walked up over the hill leading his horse, the others right behind him. They circled close around Ellis, looking down at him. A trickle of blood ran on the side of Ellis's head. "You didn't kill him, did you?" Falon asked flatly.

"No, but I didn't take no chances either," said Ryan. He looked at the others in turn, his gaze stopping on Willie Singer. "I don't pussyfoot around like some."

"I hope you ain't talking to me and Kirby," said Singer, "because if you are, I'll be surely bound to stick that rifle up your stinking ass!"

"You might be surely bound to try," said Ryan, taking a step toward him.

"Get back, Arby. Shut up, Willie!" said Frank Falon. To Willie he added, "You best take some shorter steps for a while around me. You're damned lucky I haven't killed you for lying to me!"

Beside Willie Singer, Kirby shrank back a step. Seeing him, his brother, Frank, said, "That goes for you, too, you stupid little turd!"

Both men shrank back farther. "Frank, it was all a misunderstanding," Willie said weakly.

"I don't want to hear it, Willie!" Falon shouted. "You two get this man over a saddle, if you're not afraid he'll wake up and kill you!"

Willie looked down at Ellis warily. "I'd feel better if we put a bullet in his ear first."

"Or in his back?" said Ryan, with a cruel grin. "That's more to your taste."

"All of you shut up, gawdamn it!" Frank Falon shrieked, losing control for a moment. Settling himself, he said slowly with deliberation, "Jessup wants this man alive. That's how he'll get him. Now pull him up and get him on his horse."

On the ground near Frank Falon's feet, Rudy said in his failing voice, "Falon … shoot me, please.…"

"Huh? What's that?" Falon said in a mock tone. "Shoot you? A big, cocky gunman like yourself? You'd ask a lowly wolf trapper to shoot you? My, my, but ain't I honored!"

"Come on, Falon … don't leave me laying here like this," Rudy pleaded.

"Go to hell!" said Falon. "You should have had the good sense to stay up there with your friends, die and get it over with." As he spoke, he nodded up toward the bodies on the crosses. Then he looked back down in contempt at Rudy's cross lying on the ground. "You miserable bastard, you was going to do so much. You was going to take over Paradise. You was going to include me in things. All's I had to do was stay back out of the way and let you handle everything. Ha!" Falon laughed scornfully and spit on Rudy's bloody bare chest.

"At least … I tried …" Rudy's voice trailed off.

"Well, now that's just damn admirable, ain't it?" Falon said in a sarcastic tone. "You tried and this is what it got you. But look at me!" He spread his arms wide, gloating. "I'm still where I was, not nailed to a cross for buzzards to pick at my guts!"

"Come on, Falon … shoot me," Rudy begged.

Falon watched Kirby and Willie Singer raise Ellis up between them and carry him toward the stallion. "Tonight the coyotes and lizards will eat you apart little at a time," he said sidelong to Rudy on the ground. "Shoot you? Hell, you ain't worth a bullet." He kicked Rudy's ribs. Jaw Hughes and a couple of the others stared at him.

"You hate, don't you, Falon?" Rudy gasped. "You hate not being a man, not being able to stand up to the likes of Jessup. Not being able to—"

Rudy's words were cut short beneath two quick explosions from Falon's Colt. Rudy's body bucked twice with the impact, then relaxed limply on the wooden cross. Dark blood spread into a puddle on the ground beneath him.

"There, you sorry son of a bitch!" said Falon. "I hope that satisfies you!"

The silence seemed to answer for Rudy Banatell. Jaw Hughes wiped the splatter of Rudy's blood from his face and said in a surprised tone, "Damn, Frank! Warn a fellow sometime! Look what a mess I've got here."

"Shut up, Hughes, or I'll shoot you, too," Falon growled. The men looked at one another, then back at Falon as he turned and walked away.

"What about him, Frank?" asked Lewis Barr, looking down at the bullet holes in Rudy's lifeless bare chest. "Are we going to leave him lay here for the wolves and coyotes?"

"Hell, yes!" Falon called back over his shoulder. "We was leaving him here anyway. Let the coyotes have at him. He was nothing but bait for the trap. Jessup knew he'd shake that cross loose and make it fall. That was all to get CC Ellis's attention." He swung up on his saddle. "If you think the ones in town had it rough, wait until you see what Jessup ends up doing to this one if he don't get what he wants." He glanced toward Ellis and gave a dark chuckle. "I almost feel sorry for this poor son of a bitch."

Chapter 19

On the main street of Paradise, two of the Believers stood watching Frank Falon and his men ride in. Falon was leading CC Ellis on the silver stallion behind him. "More trouble coming, Brother Willem," one of the Believers whispered to the other, cupping a hand to this mouth as if someone watching might read his lips.

"Yes, Brother Ted, that would be my guess as well," Willem Burdock replied, not cupping his hand but rather ducking his head slightly as he spoke. "And if things aren't bad enough, I understand that Brother Forrest Beckman has been replaced at the Paradise bank."

"No!" said Brother Ted Noland, unable to conceal his surprise at such news. "Where is Brother Forrest? Who in the world will Father choose to replace him?"

Brother Willem said in a guarded tone, "We are not to call Forrest Beckman *Brother* anymore. As for a replacement, Father has already seated Brother Lexar into the position."

"Oh no," said Brother Ted. "I know we are not to speak ill of our brethren, but Lexar reminds me of something I wouldn't want to find crawling through my barn late at night."

"Then your barn is safe," said Burdock. "It's our money in the bank that draws my concern."

"Mine, too," said Noland. "I know we're not supposed to gossip about our Community of Believers, but I have to tell you things are not as they should be here. Father is too busy gathering himself wives and belongings, when he should be taking care of more important matters."

They stood for a silent moment, staring at Falon and his riders as they reined up out front of the meeting house. Ellis sat slumped in his saddle, bare-headed, his hand tied in front of him. "Many of our faithful are slipping away from Wolf Valley unnoticed while Father and his inner circle are off chasing people whose lives should not concern us."

The two men looked at one another closer. "For those wanting to leave here, there could be no better time," Burdock said.

"Yes, I believe you're right," Noland agreed. The two turned and walked purposefully toward their wagons sitting at a hitch rail.

Out front of the meetinghouse, Frank Falon and his men stepped down and stood beside their horses. Having seen the men ride in, one of the door guards rushed inside and told Jessup. Before Frank Falon had finished slapping dust from the front of his shirt, Jessup came walking out, dressed in a black suit over a crisp white shirt, with a black string tie tipped with two small golden crosses.

"Frank Falon, you have not failed me!" Jessup beamed, stepping in close and shaking Falon's sweaty hand. "This gains you a lot of favor in my eyes." He looked at Falon's men, then back at Falon, saying, "And it's about time you made such a showing for yourself."

"Obliged, Father," Falon said humbly, avoiding the looks from his men. "We always want to do a good job for you."

Without answering him, Jessup looked up at Ellis sitting half-conscious atop the silver stallion. "So like any good *trapper of wolves*, you set the trap and the trap worked!" Jessup said proudly.

"Yes, Father," said Falon. "He rode in, found one of his friends lying on the ground and, while he was attending to him, I slipped in and let him have it."

Hearing Frank's version of the story, his men turned a look toward Arby Ryan, who had actually been the one to slip in and capture Ellis. But Ryan only sat and stared grimly in silence, listening to Falon take credit for his actions.

"Well?" said Jessup, tossing his large hands as if in exasperation. "Are you going to bring this man down and take him inside for me, or must I do everything myself?"

"Beg your pardon, Father," said Falon, hurrying over to Ellis, giving him a shove from atop the stallion.

Ellis landed with a grunt, still half-dazed from the slam of the rifle butt. With his tied hands doing him little good, he struggled up to his knees and rocked there for a moment until Arby Ryan and Splint Mullins stepped down from their saddles and pulled him to his feet between them. At the rear of the riders, Lewis Barr said quietly to Quentin Fuller, "Now it looks like everybody wants Jessup to see what a good hand they are."

Fuller replied wryly, "Reckon you ought to get up there and show him something yourself?"

"He don't want to see what I'd show him," whispered Barr.

With Ellis pressed between them, Ryan and Mullins began half-leading, half-dragging him to the meetinghouse. Jessup started to turn and walk there himself, but upon seeing Falon try to walk along beside him, Jessup stopped abruptly and said, "Where do you think you're going, Frank?"

Surprised, Falon said awkwardly, "I thought— That is, the men and I need some drinking water to cut the dust, after sitting out there all night, waiting for him to show up."

"Because I allowed you to enter the meetinghouse once, Falon, doesn't mean you and your men have free rein to come and go as you please!" Jessup snapped.

"No, Father, of course not!" said Falon, backing off, looking embarrassed in front of his men.

Jessup faced the rest of the men, saying, "You are not Believers. No matter what good works you might do, you are still nothing but unclean sinners until you find a way to receive the Lord's mercy and acceptance." He raised a finger for emphasis, adding, "Never forget that ... and never forget yourselves in my presence."

Falon and his men stood staring in rejected silence until Ryan and Mullins turned Ellis over to two guards standing outside the meetinghouse doors. Behind the others, Lewis Barr said to Quentin Fuller, "The man on the cross might not have had such a bad idea, wanting to take this place over."

"Yeah, maybe," said Fuller, "but I damn sure don't want to trade places with him."

"What's that back there?" Frank Falon asked, giving the two a cold stare. "If anybody has something to say, step up here and say it. Don't stand back and cluck about it like a couple of old hens!"

"It weren't nothing, Frank," Fuller ventured.

"It better not be!" Falon bellowed at them, still stinging from Jessup's low treatment and wanting to take his anger out on someone. "Now all of you clear away from here! Let's go get some cold water to drink ... since that's all there is to drink here in wonderful Paradise!" He threw up his hands in frustration.

From a window in the Believers' meetinghouse, Jessup stood watching Falon and his men drift away. He stood smiling out at the street, his hands folded behind his back while Searcy and Edmunds set Ellis in a wooden chair, threw a dipper of cold water in his face and shook him by his wet hair.

"Can you hear me?" Searcy asked, still shaking roughly until Ellis finally acknowledged him with an upward stare.

"He's awake, Father," Brother Searcy said.

"Very well," said Jessup, turning from the window and facing Ellis from ten feet away, his hands still folded behind his back. For a moment he studied Ellis closely, his expression blank, forbidding. But with a sigh, he stepped closer, stooped slightly and said into Ellis's ear, "How long did you think you could get by with this charade of yours, CC Ellis?"

"For as long as it took, Jessup," Ellis said defiantly through his bruised and swollen jaw.

Searcy grabbed his hair again and shook him soundly. "When you address Father by name, you call him *Father* Jessup."

"I'm not one of your Believers," said Ellis. "Why do you want me calling him *Father?* I'm not his son."

"I'm afraid he's got you there, Brother Searcy." Jessup chuckled, interceding with a hand held out to keep Searcy from punching Ellis in his swollen jaw. As Searcy moved back, Jessup stepped closer again. "Let me set you straight on what I already know, so we won't be going over ground already tilled. I know you are CC Ellis, one of the so-called *long riders* that no one seems to be able to handle since the war ended." He gave a grimace of distaste. "I know that you, Rudolph Banatell and his cut-throats came here to sack Paradise, and do God only knows what all else."

"Rudy didn't tell you any of that, Jessup," said Ellis, trying to remain obstinate.

Hearing him address Jessup by name, Searcy started to draw back his fist. Again, Jessup gestured Searcy back.

"Oh?" Jessup cocked an eyebrow at Ellie. "And how can you be so sure he didn't?"

"Because he told me he didn't," said Ellis.

"And you believe a fellow *long rider,* an outlaw and social miscreant, before you believe a minister of God?"

"Any day of the week, I do in your case," said Ellis. "Had he gave me up, he would have told me so. I know what Rudy was … I doubt if anybody knows *what* you are."

"I see." Jessup's brow furrowed as if troubled by Ellis's words. "I bet you are one of those who have been terribly mistreated by a man of the cloth in the past. Since then you have been bitter and resentful of every servant of the Lord, blaming *all*, as it were, for the dark deed of that *one* bad individual. Isn't that correct?"

"I've seen who and what you are," said Ellis, ignoring the question. "I know what you want—you want the Mosely woman."

"Oh, that poor woman who is out there all alone? Who needs someone to look after her? Who owns that land and has no man to either till it or stock it for her?" He tilted his head sideways, and said, "Yes! Indeed yes! I *do* want that woman! I want to save and protect her, from the likes of you and those of your kind. What sort of monster would I be to ignore her, after all the lies and illusion you have filled her head with."

"Then what's keeping you from taking her?" Ellis asked flatly.

Jessup thought for a second, then said, "I want her to come to me. I am not a man who would force himself on anyone, especially a woman so vulnerable now that her husband is deceased." He paused and watched Ellis's reaction when he went on to ask, "Sloane Mosely *is deceased,* isn't he?"

So that was it, Ellis thought. Jessup was still afraid to make a move on Callie Mosely until he knew Sloane Mosely was dead. Ellis considered the situation, wanting to buy Callie as much time as he could, hoping she could find a way out of this for herself if he couldn't manage to get away. "No, he's alive and well," said Ellis, bluffing his way along. "What made you think otherwise?"

"I ask the questions here, CC Ellis," said Jessup. "You answer them."

Ellis looked around at the two bodyguards, noticing for the first time that, in one corner, sat Jim Heady, cowering like a whipped hound. Around his neck he wore a wide leather collar with a six foot leather leash hanging from it. "Fair enough," said Ellis. "You asked if Mosely is dead. He's not."

"Then what were you doing out there, living in sin with his wife?" Jessup asked.

"We weren't living *in sin*," said Ellis. "He asked me to stay with her until he returns from Texas, just so someone like you doesn't come along and try to take advantage."

"Do you think I believe for one moment that you weren't sleeping with that woman?" Jessup asked, his face reddening at the thought of the sin.

"Don't judge every man's action by what yours would be," said Ellis. "Sloane Mosely is my friend. I did his bidding. You can ask him yourself when he gets back here, *Jessup*."

Searcy bristled, clenched his teeth, but heeded Jessup's restraining gesture.

Jessup's cheeks stung from the sharpness of Ellis's words. But he managed to keep his anger in check by taking in a long breath and letting it out slowly. Stepping forward again, he bent slightly, grabbed Ellis's tied hands and looked them over closely. "The hands of a gunman," he mused. Then dropping Ellis's hands, he stepped back and said with a smile, "Just to keep our conversation from dragging on as a game of defiance, what say we lop off a finger or two? That tends to always make one sit up and show some respect."

"You don't want respect, Jessup. All you want is fear," said Ellis. "But whichever you want, you're getting neither from me."

"Don't speak so hastily, CC Ellis," said Jessup, his voice growing almost sympathetic. "It hurts something awful, losing a finger." He said to Edmunds, "Isn't that so, Brother Edmunds?"

Edmunds held up his left hand, showing two stubs where his ring and little fingers had been. "Ouch!" he said with a faint twisted smile, agreeing with Jessup.

"Cutting off my finger isn't going to get you what you want, Jessup. Sloane Mosely is alive. He won't stand for you taking his wife and child, the way some weaker men have done. He'll kill you. I think you already know that."

"I wasn't talking about *one* of your fingers, CC Ellis," said Jessup, offering his cruel grin. "Even Brother Edmunds lost two fingers, and you have to realize, he and I were already friends."

Ellis looked back and forth between Jessup, Edmunds and Searcy, trying to discern whether or not Jessup was only bluffing.

"Brother Searcy," Jessup said over his shoulder, "get the rope chopper out of the storage bench. Bring them over and remove CC Ellis's *little* finger ... to begin with."

In the corner where Jim Heady lay cowering and listening, Heady watched Brother Searcy lift the seat of a long wooden bench. Ellis watched closely as Searcy rummaged through its contents, even picking up a rifle before taking out a pair of rope choppers.

"God is good! Father is good!" Heady began to chant fearfully. Heady gasped at the sight of Searcy working the long rope chopper handles back and forth with a metallic snipping sound, and his voice grew louder and more urgent. "God is *good!* Father is *better!* Father is *better!* Father *is God!*"

Ellis threw a quick glance in Heady's direction, the sound of the man's near hysterical chanting unnerving him. He looked back over at Searcy coming toward him with the rope choppers. Letting out a breath, Ellis relented, saying, "All right, you win. I'll call you *Father*."

"That's courteous of you, CC Ellis," said Jessup. "But I'm afraid you should have done so earlier. Your little finger is coming off. There's nothing you can do to save it. The only question now is, how badly do you want to keep the other nine?"

"Father *is God!*" Jim Heady shrieked loudly, covering his ears with both hands. "*Father is God!*"

"Wait!" Ellis shouted, coming halfway out of his chair before Brother Edmunds shoved him back down and held him firmly in place.

"I'll take those, Brother Searcy," said Jessup, reaching out for the rope choppers. "I want CC Ellis to realize that this is about a matter *most personal* to me. I'll teach you that you can take my word, CC Ellis. I'll show you that you *must*."

Jessup worked the long handle back and forth the same way Searcy did when he took the tool from the bench. "Now let me explain, CC Ellis, that this is how I like to do things." As he spoke, he continued working the handles back and forth, the chopper blades opening and closing with a glint of sharp steel. "I like to see if a man has self-restraint. If we have to hold you down, we'll take off one, two fingers, maybe more!" His eyes glistened wide and wetly. "But if you can sit there calmly, and submit without putting us to a lot of trouble … well, we'll only remove half of your little finger to start with, just enough to see if it improves your attitude."

Ellis's breath pounded in and out of his lungs. But he could see that Jessup was serious. He forced himself to settle down and looked away from Jessup and the other two and out through the open window, where a warm breeze licked at the edge of the short curtains. "Chop away, Father Jessup!" he said, his voice filled with tension, humiliation, loathing. Steadying his hands he held them sidelong out toward the steel blades. "You'll get no resistance from me."

Chapter 20

Across the street from the meetinghouse, Falon and his men stopped on their way to the livery barn and stood with their horses' reins in their hands. They looked as one back toward the open window of the meetinghouse, hearing Ellis let out one short, restrained yelp of pain. In the silence that followed, Jaw Hughes winced and said, "Well, sounds like he made it past the worst part."

"How do you know what the worst part is, Hughes?" said Falon, stepping back and forth restlessly. "Damn, what are we going to do now that Lexar is running the bank? Who'll slip us some whiskey at times like this?"

"Give Jessup time," said Mullins. "He'll find himself somebody to sell us whiskey without him *knowing* about it." He winked at his joke. "He ain't going to miss a chance to make a few dollars off us."

"What about right now though," said Hughes. "I always do my drinking *today*, not tomorrow." He looked all around as if searching for something. "Somewhere in this town is some whiskey, and I know it!"

"You both talk too damn much," said Falon. "Don't forget what happened to Jim Heady. You want to end up like him?"

"I don't want to end up like nobody," said Hughes. "I just want a drink or two, to celebrate what we did out there this morning."

"What was that?" said Falon. "Shooting a man who's laying nailed to a cross? Is that what we ought to be celebrating?"

The men looked at one another. "Naw, Frank, that ain't what I meant at all."

"Stay back away from me, all of yas," said Falon. "I'm getting sick of looking at you!" He jerked his horse away from the others and walked on toward the livery barn.

"It's getting too damn hard to talk to anybody anymore," Hughes commented under his breath.

"Look at this!" said Splint Mullins, getting excited, pointing toward the bank, where Lexar stood in the open doorway waving them toward him, giving them a discreet hand signal of taking a drink.

"Oh, yeah!" said Willie Singer to Kirby Falon, poking him in his ribs. "Father Jessup is right! There must be a God after all!" The men hurried across the street, too excited to call out to Falon before he walked out of sight.

"Lord, boys!" said Hughes. "Let's get over there before Lexar changes his mind!" They all crossed the street, trying not to look anxious to any of the passing townsfolk.

At the door to the bank, Lexar fanned them all inside and closed the door behind them. "You must be a mind reader, Lexar!" said Kirby Falon.

"No, I'm just very attentive." Lexar grinned. "Mind reading is a sin."

Jaw Hughes and Splint Mullins already had their money out and in their hand. Lexar walked to the window and looked out toward the meetinghouse door, where Brother Paul was hurrying inside. "Let me see what's going on," he said, looking back and eyeing the money in their hands. "Then we'll get things going."

"Are you still going to be the one selling the whiskey here, Lexar?" Quentin Fuller asked.

"For now, I am," said Lexar, staring back at the meetinghouse, seeing Brother Paul come back out and walk to the hitch rail where he mounted a big sorrel mule and headed out of town on it. Lexar breathed a little easier. "All right now, where were we?"

"You know where we were!" Mullins laughed. "Get us some whiskey."

The rest of the men hooted and cheered. Lexar smiled and disappeared behind the bank counter toward the safe, saying back to them, "Hold your horses! I won't be but a moment."

Across the street, in the back room of the meetinghouse, Searcy and Edmunds shoved Ellis onto a hard bare cot and pitched some gauze wound dressing down beside him. Behind them, Jim Heady slinked into the room and went to a far corner, the leash still dangling from his collar. "Put plenty of salve on that stub," Edmunds said to Ellis with a detached tone. "That's what I did. It'll keep it from infecting." The two turned and looked at Heady before leaving. "Are you staying or going, Brother?" Edmunds asked.

"Sta-staying," Heady said in a shaky voice.

"All right men," said Edmunds, "but don't snag your leash on something and break your neck."

"Remember what Brother Paul taught you. Don't listen to any thing these non-Believers tell you."

"I—I won't," said Heady.

"And what are all these non-Believers?" Searcy asked, quizzing him.

"They're all lying, sinning dogs," said Heady, giving Ellis a cold distrusting stare.

"Yes, Brother is going to be all right." Searcy laughed, walking through the doorway behind Edmunds.

Long after the door closed, Ellis sat wrapping the gauze around the half finger, after smearing it with salve from a tin Jessup's men had left for him. Pain throbbed in his entire hand. Losing half of his finger, especially the way he had lost it, left a sick feeling in the pit of his stomach.

He didn't feel like speaking. But he forced himself to. As he wrapped the gauze he looked over at Jim Heady, kept his voice from shaking and said in a matter-of-fact manner, "You can stop the playacting now. I'm not going to tell Jessup anything you say."

"I'm not playacting," said Jim Heady, giving a worried glance at the closed door. "God is good. Father is good. God is good. Father is—"

"I know, *Father is good*. I heard you before, remember," said Ellis, cutting him off. He gently tucked the end of the gauze under itself, securing it. "But they are gone now. I don't believe you're as cowed down as they think you are."

"I am a Believer now," Heady said softly, his eyes appearing on the verge of tears. "I trust nobody but fellow Believers. I worship but one God, and that God is good. Father is good."

"You're Jim Heady. Jessup bullwhipped you in front of the whole town," said Ellis. "I didn't see it but I rode in right after it happened."

"Then how do you know it was me?" Heady asked, a curious look coming to his face.

"The other man who was there to be whipped that day— he told me."

Heady perked up. "You mean Randall? Randall Turner told you?"

"That's right. Randall told me," said Ellis. "But he never told me how you ran out of guts and knuckled under to Jessup and his followers."

"Is—is *he* alive?" Heady asked. "I heard he's dead." A noticeable difference had come over Heady.

"*He?* You mean Randall Turner?" Ellis thought for a moment, realizing if Heady knew that Randall was alive and he passed that information on to Jessup, there would be riders going to the Mosely house at a full run to kill the young man. Ellis wanted to keep Heady talking to see if his mind cleared

217

any. Without answering his question, Ellis said, "Before Falon and his wolf hunters caught up to him, Randall had them all beaten. He and his wife ran out of horses. That's what got them caught."

"And killed?" Heady pried. "Did *he* get killed?"

"You know how you won't trust anybody who's *not* a Believer?" Ellis asked. "Well, you see, Heady, I don't trust any of you who *are*." He cocked his head and gave Heady a curious look. "Why are you so concerned about Randall Turner? You won't even say his name!"

"We're forbidden to say his name in Paradise," said Heady.

"Then why are you even asking about him?" Ellis persisted.

"Randall—" Heady stopped and corrected himself. "That is, *he*, the man you're talking about, befriended me," said Heady. "Even though he had troubles of his own, he wet my back and helped me make it through those first hours after my whipping—the hours where a man can swallow his own tongue and die from the pain." His eyes grew distant and hollow. "He was my friend. I never had a friend. But he was one. And if he's alive I just want to know it, that's all."

"That's really touching," said Ellis, deliberately goading him, "but you don't deserve a friend like Randall. Look at you. You're licking the hands of the man who stole Randall's wife. Sent men out to track him down and kill him." Ellis shook his head slowly. "You call that being a friend?"

"You don't know nothing," said Heady.

Ellis saw that his words were getting to the young man, just what he'd hoped to do. Maybe if he could spark some kind of fire in Heady, he could make him snap out of the trance he seemed to be in.

"Maybe I know more than you think I know," said Ellis. "I know a low, sniveling coward when I see one!"

Heady's eyes grew fiery. He jumped up from the floor and

sprang over to the latched door. Shaking the door violently, he shouted through a small barred panel, "Brother Searcy! Brother Edmunds! Somebody, *please* let me out!"

Ellis watched coolly, in spite of the pain in his maimed hand. Heady continued shaking the door until Searcy walked up, looked through the barred panel and laughed, saying, "All right, Brother, settle down. I'll let you out." He held up the key to the door and said, "But first, what is it you want to tell me?"

Heady gave Ellis a cold stare and said to Searcy through the door, "God is good! *Father* is good! God is good! *Father* is good!"

Ellis stared coldly back at him, unyielding, seeing tears glisten in Heady's troubled eyes.

In the back room of the Mosely house, Randall Turner had tried to get up off the bed every hour on the hour for the past day. But he'd been too weak and unsteady to do so. Finally, with Callie's help, he'd stood up on wobbly legs and walked about the room with his arm looped over her shoulders. "I hope we're not doing something that's going to make you worse," Callie said, seeing the pallor of his face and his sunken eyes.

"I've got to get mended fast, ma'am," he replied. "My wife is waiting for me."

"I'm afraid your wife must think you're dead, Mr. Turner," Callie said as gently as she could.

"I know she does, ma'am. All the more reason for me to get to her, ma'am," Randall said with determination in his strained voice. "I've got to let her know otherwise. She needs me."

"But she needs you *alive,*" said Callie. "Don't overdo it." She walked him back to the bed and helped him sit down on the edge. He touched his fingertips carefully to the fresh bandage atop his head.

"Another day is all I can give it," Randall said. "I've got to be over my dizziness and able to ride by tomorrow morning. That's all there is to it."

Callie shook her head in exasperation and said, "I'll fix you a bowl of hot stew and some fresh bread. You lie down and take it easy. We'll see about tomorrow when it gets here."

"Yes, ma'am," Randall said, still sitting up limp and unsteady as she left the room.

In the other room, Callie wondered about CC Ellis as she dipped stew from an iron kettle hanging in the hearth. She filled a bowl for Randall and set it on a serving tray atop the table. She knew that Ellis should have been back by now if all had gone smoothly and Jessup had no tricks up his sleeve. With a long knife, she sliced bread from a fresh loaf she had baked earlier and laid a slice beside the bowl of stew. But for now there was nothing she could do besides wait and hope · that Ellis would show up before dark and tell her things were all right.

She had just picked up the tray and headed for the back room when Dillard burst into the house, saying, "Mother! One of Jessup's men is coming! He's almost here!"

"Oh no!" she said. "Dillard, quickly go tell Mr. Turner to stay in the room and keep quiet!"

She hurriedly set the tray back on the table, took the bowl and poured the stew back into the pot, laid the slice of bread back into the breadbox and put the serving tray out of sight.

No sooner had she cleared things away than she heard a voice call from the front yard, "Hello the house."

She smoothed her apron down in front and stepped into the open doorway. The big hound stepped in close beside her and growled low.

"Yes, can I help you?" she called out to Brother Paul, who sat looking all about the front yard.

"Good day to you, ma'am. I'm Brother Paul Chapin, from the Community of Believers." He raised his hat courteously and lowered it back into place. "Father Jessup scnt me to make sure all is well out here. We caught the man who has been imposing himself on you. Father said to let you know that you won't be bothered by him again."

"That man didn't impose himself here, Mr. Chapin," said Callie. "He is a family friend! A very good friend of my husband!"

As if he hadn't heard her, Brother Paul said, "It turns out the man's name is CC Ellis. He is one of those long riders we hear so much about these days." He swung down from his horse and took a grass sack from behind his saddle. "But you won't have to worry about me bothering you again, ma'am."

Callie looked at the bag in his hand, horrified at what might be inside it. "What—what's in that?" she asked, the expression on her face causing Brother Paul to wonder what terrible image she had conjured up in her mind.

"Why, it's supplies, ma'am," said Brother Paul, walking over to the porch, reaching up and setting the bag at her feet. "Father is concerned that you and the boy might be under a hardship out here, your husband being gone."

Callie had expected something gruesome to come rolling out of the sack at her feet. She almost sighed in relief when Brother Paul pulled open the sack and showed her a modest mound of dried beans, corn meal, coffee and sugar. "Thank your *Father* for me, but tell him my child and I are doing well on our own, and we need no help. My husband will return most any day now."

"If Father Jessup may say so, Mrs. Mosely," said Brother Paul, "he feels that your husband is dead. In which case, Father cannot bear to see you and the boy do without. Indeed, he shudders at the thought of the two of you being alone out here, and he wonders if you might both be better off in Paradise, where he and the rest of us Believers can see to your needs properly."

Callie said, "Let's get right down to some straight talk, Brother Paul. We both know what Malcom Jessup is after …

and *he's* not going to get it. I know all about his wives and how he got them. I think it's disgusting. I think he is disgusting! Now you can turn around, go back to Paradise and tell him I said so!"

But instead of Brother Paul backing off, he stepped up onto the porch, then walked past her and into the house. But he stopped inside the door, facing Tic who stood with his teeth bared and his eyes shining widely, ready to lunge. "Whoa now, big fellow," Brother Paul said, his hand going to the gun under his coat. The bristled-up hound stood with his front paws wide apart, bracing himself, a growl rolling up from deep inside him.

"Don't shoot my dog!" Dillard shouted, running in and throwing himself down beside Tic and looping his arms around the dog's neck, making it impossible for Brother Paul to shoot the animal without hitting the boy. "Get out of here!" Dillard screamed at him.

"Yes, do get out of here!" Callie joined in. "How dare you come into my home without being invited!"

"I'm supposed to check this place out good for Father Jessup, ma'am," Brother Paul said.

"Get out," shouted Callie, "before we turn this dog loose on you!" She spoke loud enough for Randall Turner to hear her from the other room; but she prayed he would not think things were out of control and try to come in. The shape he was in, Brother Paul could easily kill him.

Brother Paul only hesitated for a second. "All right then. Everything seems to be in order in here." He backed away and out the door. Once he was on the porch, Tic settled down and stopped growling. "I still have to check the barn, ma'am," Brother Paul said.

"Check the barn for what?" Callie asked, outraged. "I don't want you here! Please leave!"

"I have to check it, ma'am, for your own safety and the boy's." He stepped down from the porch, up into his saddle and set his horse trotting quickly over to the barn.

Callie hurried along to catch up to him, but he was off his horse and inside the barn before she could make it to the front door.

"Unlatch this door!" she cried out, pounding the door with her fists, Brother Paul having laid the big timber latch in place from inside.

"I'll only be a minute, Mrs. Mosely," said Brother Paul. "Just long enough to check this horse."

"Stay away from that horse. He doesn't need checking," Callie screamed. "He's fine!"

"Uh-oh, just as I thought," said Brother Paul. "His leg is broken."

"What? You're crazy! You're lying!" Callie shouted, still pounding heavily on the big wooden door. "There's nothing wrong with that horse's—"

A single shot from Brother Paul's gun silenced her. The weight of the horse falling caused the ground to jar slightly. Callie clenched her fists and shouted, "Damn you!" In her rage she turned and ran to the house for the shotgun.

But before she could get back outside with the loaded shotgun, she heard Brother Paul call out from outside the barn, "If that's all I can do for you, I'll take leave now. No need thanking me for taking care of the horse for you. I trust you had no plans for going anywhere, did you?"

Callie ran out on the porch for a shot at him, but only managed to get the shotgun up for an aim when she saw Brother Paul disappear out of sight around the barn. "There went our last horse," she said aloud to herself, slumping down to the ground.

"Don't worry, ma'am," said Randall, walking up behind her, using a fireplace poker for a cane. "I'll bring you back some horses once I finish with Jessup and get Delphia back from him. Jessup knew what he was doing, sending that man out here. He's starting to put pressure on you. He wants to make sure you know you're trapped with no way to leave."

Callie looked at Randall Turner, his face ashen, his lips trembling from being on his feet too long. "How on earth will you even get to Paradise without a horse under you?"

"I'll be walking, ma'am," Randall said with unwavering determination, "first thing come morning."

"Walking to Paradise ..." Callie felt tears fall from her eyes as hopelessness fell upon her shoulders like a heavy shroud. "I hope to God you get her back, Randall," she sobbed. "And I hope to God she realizes what a good man she has in you."

"I'm nothing, ma'am," Randall said humbly. "But my Delphia is everything. I've got to get her back." He turned and hobbled unsteadily back to the house.

From the woods along the creek-bank, Brother Paul sat watching from his saddle. He smiled to himself, seeing the large bandage covering most of Randall Turner's head, and the effort it took for him to make it up the three wooden steps and into the house.

Brother Paul waited a moment longer, deciding how to best deal with the woman's shotgun. Then he drew the big pistol from under his coat and nudged his horse forward.

Chapter 21

Callie stood stunned for a moment when she first heard the sound of rapid hoofbeats racing across the front yard. Randall had gone on into the back room only moments earlier, and she had no doubt that by now he was asleep, the excitement having worn him down in his weakened condition. Snatching the shotgun up once again, she called out to Dillard, "Keep Tic in there with you, Dillard! Don't come out!"

Hearing the horse's hooves pound around the corner of the house as if circling it, Callie ran out the front door with the shotgun up in front of her.

"I'll take that, ma'am!" Brother Paul said, stepping out from beside the front door, where he'd stood flat against the front of the house. He grabbed the shotgun from her hands with ease and pulled her against his chest. "Now kindly tell your son that if he lets that hound loose on me, I will kill it."

"What do you want?" Callie asked, trembling in fear, but hoping to dissuade the man from coming in and killing poor Randall in his sleep.

"You know what I want!" said Brother Paul. "I saw him. Now I'm going to finish the job for Father."

Callie cried out, "Randall, look out!" But Brother Paul's big hand clasped over her mouth, muffling her words and the scream that followed. He shoved his way inside the front door, hearing the big hound barking fiercely beyond a closed door.

He shoved Callie away from him, saying, "Remember what I said. Keep that dog away from me!"

Holding on to her shotgun, Brother Paul went to the door to Randall's room and kicked it open, his pistol out at arm's length, ready for the kill. But when his eyes fell upon the empty bed, then the open window, he smiled, turned and hurried back toward the front door. Running out the front door, he called back to Callie almost in glee, "He won't get away! Not in the shape he's in."

Callie saw him stop abruptly just outside the doorway. He rocked back and forth on his heels making a strange gurgling sound from deep in his chest. She saw his pistol and her shotgun both fall to the porch as his big hands collapsed down to his sides.

"Oh my God!" Callie gasped, seeing him turn around toward her, with the blade of a scythe buried deep in his throat just below his Adam's apple. Blood sprayed from around the curved blade. Brother Paul stood rigid for a moment longer, a look of shock and disbelief in his wide eyes. Then he fell facedown, his weight shoving the tip of the blade out the back of his neck.

In Brother Paul's place stood Randall, looking unsteady, but with his arms poised, his fists clenched. Breathing hard, he looked down at the dead man. Behind him, in the yard, Brother Paul's horse had made a complete circle around the house and come to halt at the hitch rail. Randall looked at the horse, then back at Callie.

"There's a horse," Randall said in a labored voice. "You and the boy take it and get as far from here as you can."

Callie came forward, stepped over the body in the doorway and helped Randall down into a wooden porch chair. Behind her, Dillard and Tic ventured out from the other room, Dillard clutching the hound by its leather collar. The two stared at the dead man on the floor in a widening puddle of blood.

"We're not taking the horse, Mr. Turner," Callie said,

looking closely at the bandage on Randall's head to make sure the wound had not started bleeding.

"You've got to, ma'am," Randall said, his voice sounding exhausted.

"No, I don't have to," said Callie. "We'll use the horse to drag his body away. But then you're taking the horse. Otherwise you'll never make it to Paradise."

Randall nodded, grateful that Callie had made the decision for him. "We'll come back for you, ma'am. Delphia and me won't forget about you."

"I know you won't, Mr. Turner," Callie said softly.

In Reverend Jessup's large family house, Delphia Turner stood naked in the bathing room, washing herself with a soft cloth. She had spent the night with Jessup and it seemed that no amount of soap and water could cleanse him from her skin. She stared grimly at the suds on her inner forearm, down to her wrist, and at the pale blue veins carrying her lifeblood just beneath her skin. Her thoughts frightened her, yet they offered her peace. She remained engrossed in her thoughts until behind her a kindly voice said, "There you are, Delphia."

Turning, she saw two other wives step into the bathing room with her. They slipped off their gingham dresses and joined her. "Here, Delphia, let us help you," said one, pulling a wooden stool from the wall, centering it beneath the water stem, where a pull chain hung down from a large copper holding tank.

"Thank you, Anne," Delphia replied. She sat down and cradled the beginnings of a rounding belly in her hands. "Do you suppose he will soon leave me alone, once I've grown large with child?"

The two women gave one another a look. "With my first child, Father stopped calling on me of a night when I reached the fourth month," said Anne, the younger of the two. She gathered Delphia's hair atop her head and pinned it in place.

"But I was fourteen then." She reflected for a moment. "With my other five children, I believe he continued laying with me a little longer. But since then the Lord has had him take on more wives." She passed a faint smile to the other woman. "I get more time to myself. What about you, Lydia?"

The other woman took a thick bar of soap and the cloth from Delphia's hand. She dipped them into a pail of warm water and began gently washing Delphia's shoulders and back. "Father seldom pesters me anymore." She shrugged. "I turned thirty. That is much too old for Father Jessup's tastes." Having spoke, she glanced around as if to make sure no one had heard her.

"I can't bear the thought of giving birth to his child," said Delphia.

"You'll be all right, dear Delphia," said Anne, also picking up a cloth and lathering it with a bar of soap. "You've been through a lot. But time is the healer of all wounds. You'll soon overcome the past. Your future will be busy with your children, with joining the rest of us in making a good home for Father and all our offspring."

Delphia felt tears well up at the thought. "I'm afraid of what I might do to myself and this baby when I'm alone," she confessed.

"Come now. You mustn't talk like that," Anne coaxed, washing her breasts gently, raising her arms and washing under them. "Life will get better for you here. You have to be willing to *let* it." Her hands caressed and soothed and cleansed in rhythm to her consoling voice.

While Anne attended to the front of her, Lydia hummed soft and soothingly as she washed Delphia's back, her shoulders, her neck, in the same slow rhythm. "Yes, you must let things take their course," Lydia said, ceasing her humming long enough to speak. "Soon Father will tire of you in *this* regard ... the way he has the rest of us."

"We all learn to care for one another, like sisters," said

Anne, making everything sound tolerable.

But the tears still welled up in Delphia's eyes. She shut them and thought about her husband, and how he had died trying to save her.

Shouldn't she demand the same of herself? She opened her eyes and looked over at Lydia's dress hanging from a line of pegs along the wall. She saw the thin wooden scissor handles sticking up from the flat dress pocket. She decided then and there that somehow when she left the bathing room, those scissors would be hers.

"Oh, did you hear the news, Anne?" Lydia asked, lowering her voice secretively. "The wolf trappers brought in the last of the men who came here to rob the bank! He is the one who killed two of the trappers along the creek back before the big rain!"

Delphia's senses perked. She listened intently.

"Shhh," said Anne. "Let's not upset Delphia by talking about any of that right now."

"No," said Delphia, "I want to hear about it. I believe that is the man who took Randall and me in and tried to hide us from Jessup. They have him prisoner here?"

"Yes, they do!" said Lydia. "Father called him a long rider. The other men he rode with have been severely punished and banished from Paradise. They found him posing as Sloane Mosely, living with Mrs. Mosely. I have a feeling Father will do more than just punish this man. I wouldn't be surprised if we don't have a public hanging!"

Delphia listened while Lydia continued to talk, but once again her eyes went to the scissor handles in the dress pocket.

Across town Father Jessup paced back and forth in the meetinghouse, now and then going to the window and looking in the direction of Wolf Valley. "Brother Paul should have made it back here last night," he said to Searcy and Edmunds, who stood on either side of the room observing his every move. "I sense there has been trouble out there."

"There's no one at the Mosely place except the woman and her son, Father," Searcy said.

"Brother Paul doesn't like traveling at night, Father," said Edmunds. "Perhaps he made a camp along the trail last evening."

"Perhaps," Jessup agreed, yet the suggestion didn't feel right to him. None of his followers would linger overnight, knowing he awaited their arrival.

Jessup's thoughts were suddenly interrupted by the sound of a gunshot coming from the direction of the livery barn. The three men froze for a moment as if listening for more. When another shot came, Jessup said, "All right, Brothers, let's see what this is about!"

They hurried from the meetinghouse to the livery barn, with the eyes of curious townsfolk on them their entire way. Jessup called out to the townsfolk in a reassuring voice, "Nothing to worry about, my children. Go on about your business. The Brothers and I will attend to this."

At the livery barn, Jessup and his bodyguards stopped and stared at Kirby Falon lying unconscious on the ground, a bloody welt on his forehead. Kirby's pistol lay near his side, smoke still curling from its barrel. At his other side was a corked whiskey bottle. Fifteen feet away, Willie Singer groaned in the dirt, clutching his bloody shoulder. Between the two stood Frank Falon, still wielding the heavy oaken bucket he had just used like a club on Kirby's forehead.

Jessup's eyes swept across all the men, seeing their drunken state. "What is going on here?" he demanded, fixing a cold stare on Frank Falon.

Falon dropped the wooden bucket, seeing the wary look on the two bodyguards' faces. "Nothing, Father," Falon said, talking quickly. "My brother, Kirby, and Willie Singer had some harsh words that went too far. I broke things up. No harm done, as you can see."

Jessup ignored Falon, walked over to the whiskey bottle and nudged it away with the toe of his boot. "No harm done?" He faced Falon again, his expression growing more harsh. "I've shown you and your men that drinking in Paradise will not be tolerated!" He pointed to Willie Singer and Kirby Falon and said to Searcy and Edmunds. "Get them up! Drag them to the meetinghouse!"

"Please, Father," said Frank Falon. "Kirby's my kid brother. Let me handle him … Willie, too. These are all my men. I take responsibility for them."

"Oh, do you?" Jessup stepped forward while Searcy and Edmunds raised Willie to his feet. Willie wobbled in place, his eyes whiskey-lit and blurry. "Then do you propose I punish you instead of them, Falon?"

"That's not what I meant, Father," said Falon, his face taking on a tight nervousness.

"Of course it isn't!" said Jessup. "So stand there and keep your mouth shut! These are your men, but you're no longer capable of controlling them, it appears!"

The rest of the trappers inched slowly around to Frank Falon's side. They were all clearly drunk.

Looking at them in disgust, Jessup demanded, "Where did they get this whiskey?"

Frank Falon hesitated, knowing full well that Jessup knew where the whiskey came from.

"Well, speak up!" Jessup demanded. "Somebody knows who sells this poison! Must I bullwhip the truth out of every one of you fools?"

Falon's men stood firm, none of them saying anything. Searcy and Edmunds saw that they might have their hands full at any second. Searcy ventured forward a step, making sure he kept the half-conscious Kirby in front of him. "Come on, Father," he said quietly to Jessup. "Let's get these two off the street."

Jessup caught the warning quality in Searcy's tone of

voice. He stepped back a step, saying, "I believe you're right, Brother. First things first."

"We ain't taking no more beatings from you, Preacher!" said Jaw Hughes, before Jessup and his two men could back away with Kirby and Singer.

"What did you call him?" Edmunds said, stepping forward, his hand clamping around his gun butt.

"You heard me," said Hughes, not giving an inch.

"Come on, Brother Edmunds," said Searcy, sternly. "Do like I said!"

Brother Edmunds backed away reluctantly, keeping a close eye on the enraged drunken trappers.

Chapter 22

Across the street in the meetinghouse, Ellis rested his gauze-wrapped left hand in the palm of his right. He stood at a small barred window, staring out at Jessup and his bodyguards, watching Searcy use Kirby Falon as a shield. "Come take a look, Heady," said Ellis. "Before the day is out, we're probably going to see a man whipped within an inch of his life, the way you were." He looked Heady up and down. "I wonder if he'll fold and start chanting Jessup's praises the way you did."

"You don't know *nothing* about me, mister," said Heady, getting more and more angry and ashamed.

"I know if there's ever a chance for you to make things right for yourself, it's coming now," said Ellis. "Falon and his men are about to turn on Jessup and his followers."

Heady eased forward and looked out the window himself. But only for a second. "No, they're not," he said. "If you think it, you'll be making the same mistake your friend made."

"You mean Rudy Banatell?" Ellis asked.

"That's right," said Heady. "He thought Falon would turn on Jessup, but thinking it got him killed. Hell, Falon wouldn't lift a finger to help me, and I was one of his men. Nobody here will turn on Jessup. He has them all under a spell. To them I reckon he *is* God."

"But not to you?" Ellis asked, noting the difference in Heady now that he had got him started talking.

"I'm not trusting anybody else," said Heady.

"You don't want out of here?" asked Ellis.

"No, not if it means ending up like all the others," said Heady. "I saw what they did to the Gun. They made me watch. Seeing it turned me into Jessup's lapdog." He shook the leash attached to his leather collar. "He might even know that I'm not really converted. But if he does, he must also know that I ain't sticking my neck out ever again." He gave Ellis a blank stare and said mechanically, "God is *good*. Father is *good*. God is *good*. Father is *good*."

Ellis stared at him for a moment, and decided there was no use trying to get his help. "I understand," he said, turning away and staring back out the window.

"I don't know what you're worried about anyway," Heady said behind him. "Jessup wants to keep you alive, at least for the time being. He wants to use you to get to that Mosely woman."

"I figured as much," said Ellis, watching Jessup and the bodyguards lead Kirby Falon toward the meetinghouse. "But I'm not allowing that to happen." He looked up and around the large room, searching for a way out.

Heady chuckled and said, "Getting out is no problem. But once you're out, it's getting away that's impossible. There's no way out of Paradise and across Wolf Valley."

"I'm not leaving Paradise, or Wolf Valley," said Ellis. He gripped the bars over the window and tested their strength, finding them to be strong, but mostly for show. "Not until I know there's nobody hounding my trail."

Across the street, Jessup looked back at Falon and his men, and said to Searcy and Edmunds, "You two take Kirby to the meetinghouse. I'm going to my family quarters to give Frank Falon and his men time to cool down."

"We need to stay with you, Father," said Searcy. "It's too dangerous right now."

"No," said Jessup, "I'll be all right in my quarters. I know Falon and his men. They'll drink their whiskey and blow off steam." He offered his two men a wry smile. "That's why I allow whiskey to be sold behind my back. Once they settle down, we'll turn Kirby loose with a couple of lashes and a warning. Everything will be fine. Now go on to the meetinghouse and wait for me there. We have plenty of other Brothers to help us if things get out of hand." He swept a hand along the street, at the faces of other Believers along the boardwalk and storefronts.

Searcy and Edmunds followed his orders and turned toward the meetinghouse, dragging Kirby Falon along between them. Jessup hurried on to a one-horse buggy sitting at a hitch rail. Climbing into the buggy, he turned it, slapped the reins to the horse's back and sent the small rig quickly to the far end of the street, where his private family quarters stood behind a tall ornate iron fence. At the entrance, a guard came forward and opened the gates.

"Is everything all right, Father?" the guard asked, giving a glance in the direction of Falon's men on the far end of the street.

"Yes, Brother Oscar," said Jessup, "all is well. But be alert as usual. I have many demons gathering behind me this day." He smiled and reined the buggy horse forward. Behind him, Brother Oscar closed and locked the iron gates, and hurried to a small building surrounded with flowers and stone angels. Inside the small, pleasant building, he took down a double-barreled ten-gauge shotgun from a gun rack, checked the weapon and cradled it in his right arm.

At the meetinghouse, Searcy and Edmunds shoved Kirby into the barred room. "Sleep it off, Kirby," Edmunds said. Searcy started to close the door behind him. But upon seeing Jim Heady cringing in the corner with a frightened look on his face, Brother Searcy stepped inside, saying, "Hey, Brother, what's got you so spooked?"

Heady didn't answer. Instead he flashed his eyes toward the rear window with its bars pried loose and pushed out on one side.

"Brother Edmunds, get around back!" Searcy cried out. "The long rider has escaped!" He turned and hurried out through the door, leaving it open behind him. Kirby lay in a drunken stupor on the floor. Jim Heady remained in his corner, listening to the sound of Searcy's and Edmunds's boots pound along the boardwalk and around the front corner of the meetinghouse. But there was no look of fear on Heady's face, only a cautious expression as he stared toward the open doorway.

"It's all right now," Heady whispered as if to himself. But across the room, Ellis slid out from under the bed and stepped quietly over Kirby Falon. "Obliged," he said quietly to Heady before stepping through the open door.

In the other room, Ellis went straight to the storage bench, where he'd seen the rope choppers and, more important, the rifle. Flipping the seat of the bench up he saw not only the rifle he'd seen earlier, but there were also three pistols, two rifles and a short-barreled shotgun. Ellis laid the rifle aside. But he checked all three pistols, found them loaded and shoved them down into his waistband. He scooped up extra bullets and filled his trouser pockets. He picked up the shotgun and scooped up a handful of loads that lay beside it. Breaking the shotgun open, he saw that both barrels were loaded.

"Amen," he said, snapping the shotgun shut with finality, no longer feeling the pain in his injured hand.

Frank Falon and his men had moved their angry gathering from the livery barn to the edge of the street. They stood between the meetinghouse, where Ellis and Heady were, and Jessup's family quarters at the far end of the street. Frank, being the only sober one, was the first to see Ellis walking with determination down the middle of the street toward them.

Along the boardwalk men and women quickly understood what was about to happen. They hurriedly ducked inside shops and businesses and peeped out through the glass.

"You're the first person I want, Falon!" Ellis shouted, keeping the shotgun in his injured left hand, his first finger over the trigger, his little finger stub sticking out bluntly, wrapped in gauze, red-tipped with blood. His eyes went to the belly holster Falon wore. "I'm taking my gun back."

"Like hell you are," Falon replied. He gave his men a look that told them to spread out. "As for nailing your friends up and all, I was just doing my job!" He planted his feet shoulder width apart, his hand already poised near the belly holster he'd taken off while Ellis lay knocked out on the ground beside Rudy Banatell.

"I'm just doing mine," said Ellis, coming steadily closer, but still too far away, Falon thought, waiting for him to get deeper into firing range. Knowing that Jaw Hughes was the only one of his men carrying a rifle right then, Falon said, "Jaw, level down. Put one in his eye."

"You've got it, Frank," said Hughes.

Hoping to distract Ellis, Falon saw the big heavy Walker Colt sticking up from his waistband and said, grinning, "Are you really going to try to draw that big chunk of iron?"

Jaw Hughes jerked the rifle butt to his shoulder. Ellis saw it. His right hand streaked to the Walker and brought it up with startling speed. Before Falon could believe it was happening, Ellis had fired, putting a bullet squarely in Jaw Hughes's chest.

"God almighty!" Falon shrieked, seeing Hughes turn with a stunned look on his face, a trickle of blood running down his lower lip, a large circle of blood spreading on his shattered chest.

"Kill him!" shouted Falon, already leaping for cover among a stack of wooden cargo crates stacked along the boardwalk.

Seeing that Ellis wasn't going to be satisfied with just

shooting Jaw Hughes, Falon's men all made their move at once, but in hasty disarray. Pistols roared. Shots sliced the air in Ellis' direction, all of them too high because Ellis dropped low on one knee. Taking good aim, he put a bullet through Splint Mullins's head, and another in Quentin Fuller's belly. Then he sprang to his feet, raced five yards to his right, stopped suddenly and shot Willie Singer in the chest. Before anyone could aim, he changed position again.

From a block away, searching for Ellis, Searcy and Edmunds heard the heavy gunfire erupt. They looked at each other, realizing that somehow they had been tricked, and raced toward the street, their guns drawn and ready.

"Don't shoot us!" shouted Arby Ryan. Lewis Barr, Frank Falon and he were the only ones left standing. But as Ellis dropped flat to the ground, shots from Searcy's and Edmunds's Colts forced Ryan and Barr to leap for the same cover Falon had taken.

Searcy and Edmunds ran at Ellis, firing, their aim much better than that of Falon's men. A shot grazed Ellis along his left forearm; another shot sliced into his side along his hip bone. Needing a quick hit, Ellis swung the shotgun into play. The first shot hit Edmunds in his crotch, the force of it driving his legs back and out from under him. He hit the ground face first, a bloody, smoky mist still lingering in the air. Edmunds screamed and rolled back and forth, both hands clutching a large bloody emptiness.

Searcy veered away, abandoning his charge at the sight of Edmunds writhing in pain. He made it behind a water trough as water and bits of wood exploded above him from the next shotgun blast.

From the front room of his family quarters, Jessup heard the gunfire and ran out to the gates, where Brother Oscar stood with his shotgun ready. In the middle of the street, beneath a rising cloud of burned powder, Jessup saw Ellis stand up from a crouch, run a few yards, turn and fire. "Whatever it takes,

Brother Oscar, you must stop that man from getting in here!"

"Who is he, Father?" Brother Oscar asked.

"He's one of those long riders who came here to destroy Paradise. You must stop him! Do you understand?"

"Yes. Don't worry, Father. He won't get past me," said Brother Oscar.

Slipping into Paradise from the other end of town, Randall Turner had heard the gunfire and stopped only for a second, long enough to determine where it was coming from. He had no idea the fighting was among Ellis, Falon's men and Jessup's Believers. He only knew that this might provide him the opportunity he needed to sneak into Jessup's family quarters, get Delphia and escape while everyone's attention was toward the street.

He rode Brother Paul's horse all the way to the iron fence behind the large house, stepped up onto the saddle, pitched Callie's shotgun onto the plush green lawn and, using all of his strength, pulled himself over, giving no regard to the mending head wound or the terrible feeling inside his temples when he landed with a jar on the ground.

He collected himself, picked up the shotgun and raced toward the house in a low crouch. Seeing Jessup run back to the house from the front gate, Randall whispered to himself, "I'm coming, Delphia," and hurried on toward the rear door.

Inside the house, Lydia, Anne and Delphia stood with frightened looks on their faces, watching Jessup come through the door, close it soundly behind himself and lock it. "Father, what is it?" Lydia asked.

"It's nothing, wives," said Jessup, brushing the matter aside. "A minor disturbance, nothing more." He looked all around and asked, "Where are the other wives and the children?"

"They are all upstairs in the special rooms, Father," Anne said. "They know not to come out until the gunfire stops and someone says all is clear."

"Good," said Jessup, not really concerned with anything but his own well-being. "You two join them," he said to Lydia and Anne.

"But, Father, what about you and Delphia?" Lydia asked.

"We'll be in my private study until this blows over. I know that by now every believer in Wolf Valley is rushing toward the sound of that gunfire even as we're talking." He offered a thin nervous smile. "Now please, both of you, do as you've been told."

Inside the rear door, Randall stood listening to the sound of Jessup's voice, followed by footsteps coming down a hall in his direction. He raised the shotgun and waited in silence in the darkened day kitchen.

"Hurry, my dear," Jessup said to Delphia. "We mustn't have our unborn child in harm's way." Delphia followed along behind him. Before reaching the day kitchen, Jessup led her into his private study—a candlelit room furnished expensively with polished oak furniture and wide leather sofas. On one wall a large golden cross hung above an extra wide bed whose ornate cover bore an elaborate initial J in the center of flying angels and cherubs.

"I say it's an ill wind that blows no good, eh?" Jessup said, loosening his tie, smiling at Delphia as he led her toward the bed. "Call me lustful, but the sound of violence close at hand always arouses me."

"No, please!" said Delphia, hesitating, as if she thought doing so might help. Down the street, muffled gunfire still roared.

"Come, come, darling," Jessup cooed. "Slip out of your dress and accommodate your loving husband."

She heard the urgency in his voice and knew she could not put him off. She slipped her dress up over her head. She wore nothing beneath it, as all Jessup's wives were instructed to do. Her face flushed in shame, she held her dress in front of herself, partially hiding her nakedness.

"Oh my!" Jessup said, his eyes going over her clear young flesh in the glow of candlelight. "I can't tell you what seeing you this way does to me!" He stepped forward, reaching out a hand toward the wadded-up dress. "No, let's do away with this, shall we?"

"No, don't," Delphia said, pulling back from him, knowing and dreading what would come next.

"Don't tell me *no!*" Jessup shouted. Again he reached for the dress, this time aggressively.

On the other side of the locked door, Randall had heard Delphia's voice almost pleading with Jessup. He could stand it no longer. He lunged with his shoulder against the heavy oaken door, forcing it to give, but not all the way.

"What was that?" Jessup said, startled, half turning toward the noise at the door. Delphia's dress hung loosely from his hand. Delphia stood naked, one hand covering the lower front of herself, the other hand behind her back. She didn't answer, but her eyes were riveted to the door as if intuition revealed who was there.

"Randall?" she gasped, hoping against hope, calling his name the way one called out the names of the dead.

"I'm coming, Delph!" Randall bellowed, his shoulder pounding the door again, this time causing a long split to form along the doorframe.

"Oh my God! Randall! You're alive! Alive!" Delphia sobbed and screamed in joyful hysteria at the sound of her husband's voice.

"Gawdamn it!" Jessup cursed loudly, seeing the rend in the doorframe, knowing that at any second the man would be upon him. "You won't be for long!" He rushed to a nightstand beside the bed, threw open a drawer and rummaged madly for the small gun he kept there. Another heavy thump from the door sounded as Jessup's hand closed around the small revolver. "There I have it!" he said. But as he turned, he felt scissors sink deep into his shoulder just below his collarbone.

As he screamed in pain and tried to raise the pistol to Delphia's face, the door burst open and Randall quickly aimed the shotgun at him, saying, "Drop the gun, Jessup, or you're dead!"

Jessup lowered the gun and let it drop to the floor. At the same time he grabbed Delphia by her forearm, keeping her close, too close for Randall to risk firing a blast from the shotgun. "Use your head, wolfer!" Jessup said, taking command. "Do you want to come this far, do this much, only to kill this poor, lovely woman?"

"The only person I want to kill is you, Jessup," Randall said with quiet resolve. He stepped forward, keeping the cocked shotgun to his shoulder with one hand, picking up the dress with his other. "Here, Delph! Put this on," he said.

Delphia reached out with Jessup holding her by her other arm, took the dress and held it up in front of her. "I—I thought you were dead, Randall," she said, her voice too emotional to be more than a breathless whisper.

"I know, Delph," Randall said. "I'm sorry you had to think that. I would have been dead if it wasn't for CC Ellis and the Mosely woman. My head is shot up pretty bad, but I'm going to be all right." He managed a faint smile. "Now that I see your face."

"Oh, Randall." She sobbed.

"Maybe you're forgetting, Wolfer," said Jessup. "I've got a whole townful of believers out there. Do you think they are going to just let you pass, especially after you've killed their leader?" He nodded toward the scissors sticking out of his shoulder.

"Jessup, I don't know what's going on out there, but it doesn't sound like too many of your believers are getting involved," said Randall.

"Not yet maybe," said Jessup, "but wait till they see what's been done to me. If I die, they'll rip you both apart like wild beasts! You and that long rider out there!"

"Ellis is out there?" Randall looked concerned.

"Not for long he won't be," said Jessup. "He'll soon be dead. So will you if you kill me."

Randall sighed, lowering the shotgun an inch. "Jessup, I came here to kill you, but the fact is, I can't."

Jessup looked surprised. "Oh … really?"

"All I want is what I've wanted all along: my beloved wife, Delph," Randall said. "I just want to take her away from here and forget this ever happened. He turned his eyes to Delphia. "I can't kill the man who fathered a child with my wife. I can't kill you and face my wife's child the rest of my life. Do you understand that, Delph?"

Delphia tugged her arm free from Jessup, who remained close to her anyway, half-hidden by her. "Yes, husband," she replied to Randall. "I don't know why God put this on us, but if I bring a child into this world, I don't want this snake's death hanging over any of our lives."

Jessup listened with a stunned expression. But then he cut in, seizing an opportunity for himself. "If you don't mind me saying so, that's the right way to feel about this. God would want you to treat this—"

"Shut up, Jessup!" said Randall, turning the shotgun back toward him. Jessup cowered back, raising his hand over his face. "You don't know nothing about God! All you know is how to use his word to get what you want for yourself!"

"You're right. That's true. God forgive me," Jessup said quickly. Outside the sounds of gunfire had lessened, but hadn't stopped altogether. "Don't listen to me! Do what God wants you to do!"

"We're going out there, Jessup, you and me," said Randall. "I want you to call your men off Ellis and let him ride away. I want you to let all of us leave without any bloodshed."

Jessup looked at him with a sincere expression and said, "I see no problem with doing that at all."

Randall gave Jessup a look of disgust and said, "Hand me

that necktie." He gestured toward the necktie Jessup had taken off moments earlier.

"Why?" Jessup asked, looking concerned.

"Just hand it to me," Randall demanded. He turned to Delphia and asked, "Darling, is there anything you need to take with you from here?"

"No," Delphia said firmly. "I want nothing from here but the dress I'm wearing. I'm burning it as soon as I get another."

Randall touched his fingertips to his bandaged head, feeling moist, fresh blood, which had seeped through the gauze. "All right, then." He looped the necktie over Jessup and held on to one end of it, jerking Jessup over in front of the shotgun barrel. "Let's take it real easy." He gestured Jessup toward the door.

Chapter 23

Amid the gunfire, Ellis managed to make his way to the bank, slip inside and close the thick door behind himself. Three bullets hit the door as soon as he'd done so. Across the counter, Lexar stood staring wide-eyed at the cocked Walker Colt in Ellis's hand, the tip of it aimed at his face. "Don't shoot!" Lexar pleaded, his hands held high and trembling. "Here, look! It's all yours! Take it and go. But don't shoot me!"

Ellis looked at the open carpetbag sitting on the counter in front of Lexar, and at the four bottles of whiskey standing beside it. "You're some piece of work, mister," Ellis said, dropping the latch on the door. Walking over to the counter, he took the shotgun from under his arm, laid it on the counter, picked up one of the bottles and pulled the cork with his teeth. He held the bottle out for Lexar to take a drink.

"Me?" said Lexar, looking surprised.

"Yeah," said Ellis, "you first."

"Oh, I see," said Lexar, sipping as Ellis held the bottle to his lips. "Nothing wrong with this whiskey." Lexar grinned nervously. Outside, the firing stopped for a moment Ellis raised the bottle to his lips and took a long swig. Lexar saw the blood on Ellis's hand around the bottle and said, "You've been shot, long rider!"

"I know it," said Ellis. "Am I going to find Jessup in that

big house up the street? I want to end this thing for once and for all."

"I don't know," said Lexar. "As you see, I was just about to leave Paradise myself."

"Yeah, I see," said Ellis, "with all the bank's money."

"Well ..." Lexar smiled. "You of all people ought to understand how money just has a way of making you want to steal it."

Ellis stared at the other man, not returning Lexar's wide ugly smile. He shoved the big Walker barrel closer to his frightened face. "Jessup!" he said flatly.

"Okay, all right!" said Lexar. "Yes, I would guess he's in his family quarters, got his head stuck up one of his wife's dresses. That's usually where he goes when something like this happens! Like I said, though, I'm leaving here. Far as I'm concerned, I'll split this money with you if you kill him and get us both across Wolf Valley."

"I'm going to turn away from you and look back around in a minute," said Ellis, picking up the shotgun and swinging it back up under his arm. "If I see you, I'm going to figure you're too damn stupid to live."

"I'm gone already," said Lexar. He snatched up the bottles, jammed them down into the carpetbag atop the stacks of money and ran to the rear door before Ellis had completely turned away from him.

As Ellis walked to the front window, he heard Lexar slam the back door. Looking out on the street, Ellis saw that Falon and his two remaining men had joined forces with Searcy, all four of them hunkering down among the fright boxes. Ellis looked both ways along the street, but to his surprise he saw that no more Believers had joined in the fight. "Maybe Paradise has grown as sick of you as I have, Jessup," he murmured to himself. Checking the shotgun and reloading the big Walker, he stepped over to the door, took a deep breath to brace himself and clear his mind, and said, "Here goes."

"Get him!" shouted Frank Falon, seeing the door to the bank swing open and Ellis come charging out, the Walker blazing in his right hand.

Arby Ryan jumped out from behind the freight boxes, taking aim; but before his shot exploded, a bullet from the Walker slammed into his chest and sent him crashing backward into Lewis Barr, his blood splattering all over Barr's face. Falon ducked down in time to miss a bullet that whistled past his head. But Searcy was not as lucky. He'd seen his chance to get Ellis while Ellis nailed Ryan. Rising for a quick shot, Searcy caught the full impact of the shotgun blast as Ellis swung the shotgun up with his injured left hand and pulled the trigger.

Ellis crouched, ready to take out the next man to show his face. But before that happened he heard Jessup's voice call out from up the street, "Cease firing, men! I've a gun to my head! I repeat, cease firing!"

Ellis remained poised, ready for anything. Behind the freight crates, Falon stood up slowly; so did Barr. Searcy lay against the front of a building, his lifeblood spilling from the large shotgun blast to his chest.

"Randall?" Ellis said, barely believing his own eyes, seeing the bandaged head close behind Jessup.

"It's me and Delph, Ellis!" said Randall. "Here's Jessup. We can all ride out of here. We've won!"

Ellis stepped over close enough to a buckboard wagon to take cover behind it if he had to. "Not as long as he's alive, Randall!" said Ellis. "Step away from him. I'll finish it!"

"No, Ellis," said Randall. "Delph and I talked it over. We can't abide that. We just want to leave here and go live in peace. We're not killers."

"I am," said Ellis. "Step away."

"No!" said Randall, adamantly. "There's been too much killing already!"

"Randall, this man holds all the high cards when it comes

to Wolf Valley," said Ellis. He'll have his men ride us down. He might be telling you he won't, but don't trust him, not for a minute!"

"We'll take all the horses from the livery barn. We'll lead them away from Paradise and turn them all loose outside the valley," said Randall. "That way we won't be followed."

"Randall, it's a mistake leaving him alive," said Ellis. "I'm putting a bullet in his head."

"I can't let you do that, Ellis," said Randall. "I told him no harm is coming to him. I've got to stick to my word."

"No, you don't, Randall," said Ellis, "not after all this bastard has done to you! Don't be crazy! We've got to kill him!"

"The Lord teaches us to forgive our enemies, Ellis," said Randall. "I've got to go the Lord's way with it."

"Look at us, Randall," said Ellis. "We're arguing over the son of a bitch who stole your wife! The Lord doesn't mean for you to forgive something like Jessup!"

"Then you tell me, Ellis. Who does the Lord mean for me to forgive, if not my enemy, Jessup? He's the only *enemy* I've got."

"Hell, I don't know, Randall." Ellis slumped, but kept the Walker pointed in Falon's direction. "You better hope you're right. I'm taking Callie Mosely and her son and making a run out of here. I don't want him and these Believers on my trail. I'll hold you responsible."

"All right, Ellis," said Randall, "I take full respons—" His words were cut short as Jessup spun, knocked the shotgun away from him and plunged the scissors into his chest.

Ellis could not fire for fear of hitting Randall or the woman. He ran forward but couldn't get there before Randall stumbled backward and fell to the ground, Jessup snatching the shotgun from his hands. "No!" Delphia screamed, lunging at Jessup, who moved quick, knocked her aside and aimed the shotgun at Randall's face from less than a foot away and squeezed the trigger. The shotgun exploded, but in the final second as Jessup fired, a rifle bullet knocked the back of his skull high into the air in a shower of blood and brain matter.

At the same time the ground beside Randall's head turned into a hole dug by the shotgun's blast. Randall rolled away yelling, clasping his ear, but otherwise unharmed. Ellis arrived next to him in time to drag him toward cover as the street began to explode once again in gunfire. In front of the meetinghouse, Jim Heady raised a rifle in the air and let out a loud war whoop, shouting, "Jessup is *dead!* Jessup is *dead!* That rotten bastard can burn in hell!"

Falon shouted, "Father, no!" and ran into the street, firing at Jim Heady. "Not Father!" But a bullet from the Walker lifted him backward and sent him rolling in the dirt. When he stopped rolling, his dead eyes stared blankly upward at the sky.

Ellis spun quickly toward Barr, who had stood up looking toward the boardwalk for help of any kind. Seeing no one come forward, Barr let his pistol roll off his fingertips to the ground. He backed away a few steps, then turned and disappeared into an alley. Ellis spun toward the boardwalk, hoping that letting Barr go wasn't a mistake he'd later regret.

A ringing silence set in. Ellis looked from door to door, window to window. When the door to a barber shop creaked open, he raised the Walker and aimed it, cocked and ready. "Don't shoot!" said a gruff but shaky voice. "You'll have no trouble with me!"

Another door creaked open; Ellis spun toward it. "Me neither," said a timid voice.

Slowly, one and two at a time, doors opened and people appeared along the boardwalk. The silence lasted a moment longer, Ellis staring tensely, the Walker still ready. He spun toward a sharp sound only to see an old man begin clapping his hands together. Ellis let out a breath as he realized that what he heard was the beginning of applause.

"I'll be damned," he said quietly, with a bemused look. He looked off in the direction of the crosses, as if wishing that Rudy Banatell and the others could hear it, too. Then he managed to smile as the applause built along the boardwalk and sounded all along the street. He thought of Callie, and smiled to himself, thinking how good life would be with her, now that all this was behind them.

Outside the livery barn, Ellis sat atop his big bay and held a lead rope to the big silver stallion behind him. He looked down at Randall and Delphia Turner and said, "I wouldn't stay too much longer if I were you. These people have a lot to go through, getting out from under Jessup and getting back on their own feet. Things could still be tricky here for a while."

"What?" Randall asked, unable to hear anything in his left ear.

Ellis started to repeat himself, but Delphia said, "He can't hear you, Ellis. But don't worry. We're getting away from here before dark ourselves. I want nothing more to do with this place."

"I understand," said Ellis. He looked once again at Randall and said to Delphia, "I know you two are going to take good care of one another."

"Yes, we will," said Delphia, "and we'll never forget how you helped us." She gazed off toward the end of town and said with a wary look, "I'd feel better if Barr wasn't out there somewhere. Randall said he is as sneaky as they come."

"I'll keep an eye peeled," said Ellis. He looked away at Jim Heady and said, "Much obliged for your help, Heady."

Heady only smiled, looking a bit embarrassed, and waved Ellis away. Putting the bay forward, Ellis did not look back on Paradise. He rode across the edge of Wolf Valley in the direction of the Mosely place until his trail led him upward into a stretch of rocky hills. As darkness drew around him in long shadows of rock and scrub juniper he twice thought he heard the sound of quiet hooves on the trail behind him. When he stopped and clearly made them out, he thought of Delphia's warning about Lewis Barr, and he pulled up into the cover of rock above the trail.

"I never should have let him go," he whispered to the big bay. A full five minutes passed before he saw the single rider move forward with caution on the trail beneath him. The dark figure lay low in his saddle, as if to stay bowed and out of sight. Ellis eased the bay and the silver down at an angle until he stepped the horses right out onto the trail, facing the man from less man fifteen feet away. He held his gun cocked and pointed, having taken the gun and his holster rig off Falon's body.

"You were too busy slipping up behind me," Ellis said. "You should have been looking up."

"What the …?" The rider jerked a tired-looking dun to a halt and sat limp, staring at Ellis in the grainy darkness.

Ellis looked at the rider close enough to know that this wasn't Lewis Barr. After a pause, Ellis said aloud, "Oh no," as recognition set in.

"CC? Is that you?" said a strained voice.

"Yep, it's me," Ellis replied. "Sloane?"

"Yeah," the voice replied, "but keep my name to yourself for awhile."

"We all thought you hanged," said Ellis. As he spoke, he felt his plans for Callie Mosely and himself coming apart.

"I almost did," said Sloane Mosely. "Hadn't been for the best damn attorney in Texas I would have."

"You mean Snake Warley got you off from that murder charge?" Ellis asked.

"Get me off? Hell no!" said Mosely. "What he got me was a *gun!* And he paid some whore to slip it to me. Said she was my sister come to see me one last time. Ellis, I'm hot off a jailbreak. I took a bullet in my right forearm. I can barely lift it, let alone draw my gun. Lucky for me it's you, and not some bounty hunter."

"Can't even lift your gun hand, huh?" Ellis asked, letting the thought run through his mind. "Well, at least you're alive. I'm getting over some wounds myself."

"Yeah?" Mosely stepped his horse closer and asked, "What are you doing out here anyway?"

"We came to take that bank you told us about," said Ellis.

"In Paradise?" Mosely didn't seem to recall ever mentioning it.

"Yes, and it all went to hell on us," said Ellis. "Rudy, Orsen, Ernie and the Gun are all dead."

"Damn, I'm sorry to hear it," said Mosely. "How bad are you wounded?"

"I'll be all right," said Ellis. "I got wounded on the way here." He paused for a moment, wondering how much he should tell. Finally he said, "Hadn't been for your wife and son, I wouldn't be alive right now. They took me in, nursed me along."

"Callie did that?" Mosely asked.

"She did," said Ellis, "and I'm forever obliged."

After a silence, Mosely asked in a flat tone, "Ellis, is there anything you want to tell me?"

"No," Ellis said. "Is there anything you want to ask?"

"I don't like the idea of you being there, with me off waiting to be hanged. It sets up a bad possibility." He recognized his silver stallion and said, "Hey, that's my stallion! What are you doing with him?"

"You did everything you could to get Rudy to come rob this bank, Sloane, so don't point a finger of blame at me." He moved closer and handed Mosely the lead rope to the stallion. "I was bringing him home to Callie. Now I reckon I don't have to."

"I was worried about that damned preacher in Paradise," Mosely said, taking the lead rope and looking the stallion over. "I was afraid he might take over my family."

"Well, stop worrying. He's dead," said Ellis.

"You killed him?" asked Mosely.

"No, but he's dead," Ellis said, feeling worse by the minute now that all was said and done. "That's what you wanted, wasn't it?"

"I can't say I'm sorry he's dead," said Mosely. "I want you to look at this from where I saw it. I was looking out for Callie. Can you blame me?"

"No, I can't blame you, Sloane. She's a good woman," Ellis said, hoping Mosely didn't notice the wistfulness in his voice.

"Then everything is all right?" Mosely asked.

"As far as I'm concerned, it is," said Ellis. "I might have done something I shouldn't though. I told her about what we do for a living."

"Damn it," said Mosely, "that's no way to treat a pard, Ellis."

"You should have told her before, Sloane. You knew she'd find out someday."

"Are you sure nothing happened between my wife and you?" Mosely asked more pointedly.

"Are you sure you want to ask?" said Ellis, not backing down an inch.

Another pause. Then Mosely said, "Forget it. I'm going to lay low for a while. What are you going to do now that Rudy and the others are dead? Are you still in the business?"

Ellis sighed, and tapped his bay forward. "I'm still in the business, Mosely. Come find me after you're rested up. I bet you owe Warley enough to keep you busy for the rest of your life."

"Ha! You can believe that." Sloane Mosely watched the bay pull away slowly along the trail, headed out of Wolf Valley. "*Long riders*, huh?" he called out to CC Ellis.

Without looking back, Ellis smiled wryly to himself, nodding, and said, "Yeah, *long riders*."

Chapter 1

Black Mesa

Here are preview chapters from Ralph Cotton's **Black Mesa***, the 14th book in the popular Arizona* **Ranger Sam Burrack** *series. Available soon in paperback and ebook editions.*

"I'm taking him back," Ranger Sam Burrack said with firm resolve.

"Huh-uh. You ain't taking him nowhere, Ranger," said Alvin Krey. "You made a bad mistake tracking him here. You're a long ways off your graze," he added, his big Remington pistol already out of its holster and cocked in his hand. "Hell, I've got as much authority here as *you* do." A dark grin formed in the corner of his mouth. "*More*, come to think of it." He jiggled the Remington slightly for emphasis.

The ranger looked calmly from face to face at the three men formed in a half-circle behind Krey in the small sod and pine plank saloon. Outside, the hooves of the saloon owner's horse fell away into the distance. Sam had wondered riding in why anyone would open a saloon on such a remote spot. Perhaps the owner had suddenly asked himself that same question, Sam had thought when he stepped inside, saw the owner's eyes widen at the sight of his badge, then saw him turn and dive out a rear window.

"Authority is only what we make of it," Sam replied quietly to Alvin Krey. His Colt had also slipped its holster earlier. The big gun stood poised, cocked and ready in his gloved right hand.

"You might scare barkeeps out the back window, but you ain't taking one of our friends no-damn-where," said Krey. "That's what *I* make of it."

"Clear me a way, all of you!" Sam called out in a strong tone, ignoring Krey and talking directly to the other three men. In his left hand, Sam held Toby Burns by his shirt collar. Burns lay slumped on the dirt floor at Sam's feet, a long red welt already swelling along the side of his head where the ranger's gun barrel had struck him moments earlier.

Sensing that the men standing behind him might give in to the ranger's demand, Krey said, "Stay where you are, boys. Let one lawdog have his way, it won't be long this whole Cimarron Desert will be crawling with them." His dark grin widened and he gave Sam a cold, determined stare. "Maybe you can't count, Ranger. You've got four guns staring at you. You best turn him loose and crawl your ass out of here."

On the floor, Toby Burns moaned and shook his head slowly to clear it. *Good timing*, Sam thought, knowing how difficult it would have been to drag the knocked-out Burns across the floor and out to the hitch rail. Behind the half-circle of gunmen, sunlight rose and fell quietly as the dusty blanket hanging in the front doorway did the same.

"Are you ready to go, Sam?" his partner, Maria, asked in a level tone, stepping inside the saloon and then taking two more steps to the right of Alvin Krey, getting herself out of Sam's line of fire.

The men half turned toward the front doorway, but Krey kept his eyes riveted on the ranger, even when he heard the sound of Maria's shotgun cocking behind him. "It makes no difference who's there, Ranger," he said. "You're still outnumbered—that's a fact."

"We're through talking, Krey," Sam warned, knowing that Maria had surprised them and thrown them off for a moment; but now a move had to be made before the gunmen recovered and started listening to Krey. "Lower your gun and step aside."

"Maybe you're through, Ranger," Krey said, still defiant, still ready for a bloody ending. His hand started to raise the big Remington. "But I've still got plenty to sa—"

His words stopped short. The ranger's bullet punched through his heart and sent shreds of it splattering on the sod wall in a wide spray of blood and bone fragments.

"Jesus!" a voice called out among the men. "You killed him!"

Maria swung the shotgun toward the other men, seeing that Sam's action had left them stunned for a second, their hands poised in reflex near their holsters. Any second she knew they would grab for their guns. "Hands up, quick!" she shouted, not wanting to give them time to think or consider anything other than what she demanded.

Hands went up chest high, then higher, seeing both the big sawed-off shotgun and the ranger's smoking Colt pointed at them in the small, confined space. "Everybody listen up," Sam said, letting the men know that the shooting had ended unless somebody else made a move to restart it. "None of you are under arrest. We're leaving here with Toby and we're taking your horses. You'll find them waiting for you a couple of miles down the trail."

"H-hold on, Ranger," said a tall, young gunman with a deep scar across the bridge of his crooked nose. "I-I'm not a part of this bunch!" His eyes flashed around at the other faces. "For God sakes, somebody tell him! I'm just an out-of-work stage driver, stopped in for some drinks. To tell the truth I was getting worried, wondering how I was going to pull away from this bunch and get out of here."

Stepping over to him, Sam eased the young man's pistol

up from his holster and pitched it over into a corner on the dirt floor. "Take it easy," Sam said to him. "You'll soon be on your way."

"You said none of us are under arrest?" an older man asked, his stubby hands raised high.

"That's right," Sam replied, "not if you do as you're told. We came here for Toby Burns. Once we're out of here, you're all free to go your own way. Just don't try to stop us." He eyed the old man closely. "You look familiar, mister. What's your name?"

"Arlo Heath," the old man said quickly. "You recognized me all right. A few years back you caught me and some others rustling goats outside of Cottonwood. Remember it?"

"Yep, I do," said Sam. "You and Gator Sal and a fellow called Frenchy. All three of you attempted to rustle an old woman's milk goats."

"That's right, but our intent was never proved beyond a reasonable doubt," said Heath, unashamed.

"You had one goat slaughtered, cooked and half eaten," Sam reminded him.

Heath shrugged, conceding, "Okay, that would have been one point in the law's favor."

"Are you some sort of an attorney now?" Sam asked, knowing better.

"No, but out here a man makes do for himself," Heath said with a crafty smile. "But the point is, you had your hands full at the time, hunting Montana Red Hollis. You let us all three go, warned us to get out of the territory and stay out." Heath's smile widened, revealing a wide part in his front teeth. "So that's what I did. I ain't been back there yet, not even for visiting kin at Christmas. You've had no trouble out of me ever since."

"Good," said the ranger, looking him up and down. "Let's try to keep it that way."

The old man cocked a skeptical eye. "Do I understand

you're saying that none of us are going to Judge Issac's court?" He sounded relieved but still unconvinced.

"We only want Toby Burns," the ranger repeated, reassuring him. He watched Maria step forward and lift the older gunman's Colt from his holster and pitch it over into the corner.

"Damn, that takes a terrible load off my mind," said the old man. He gave the others a look, saying, "This is that ranger who run me out of Arizona Territory, the one who killed Montana Red Hollis deader than hell . . . who killed Bent Jackson and took his black-eyed barb!"

The other two men milled, not knowing how to respond to Heath's information. "What about me, Ranger?" the one with the scarred nose asked.

Arlo Heath jerked his head toward the younger man while Maria stepped over to the next man and disarmed him. "He's telling you the truth. He ain't nobody. Like as not one of us would have cracked his skull open before this day's over, or worse." He scowled at the young man.

"See there, Ranger?" the young man with the scarred nose asked. "Can I go now? I swear I've got nothing to do with any of this. I never should have come here."

Sam looked closer at the younger man, seeing him stare back with a blank expression. "What's your name, mister?" he asked.

"Colbert," the young man replied quickly, "Tom Jefferson Colbert."

Sam only nodded, then turned to the others in time to see Maria disarm the last man and toss his pistol over with the rest. The last young man wore a buckskin shirt and a battered silk top hat. He stared straight ahead, sullen, trying to draw no undue attention to himself. "What's your name, mister?" Sam asked.

"What's it to you?" the man replied sharply. "You said you ain't arresting us. So keep my name out of your mouth. A man's name is his own business."

Sam stared at him for a moment until behind him the old man asked, "Well, ain't you going to let this innocent bystander leave? I already *verified on his behalf* that he ain't one of us." His voice quickly took on a semiofficial-sounding tone, but then changed back as he added, "We'll end up hurting him sure enough if you leave him here."

Sam gave the old man a look, saying, "In a minute." Turning back to the man in the silk top hat he said, "Your name is your own business . . . unless I match it to your face at the bottom of a pile of wanted posters."

"Like Krey said, you're too far off your graze to be making threats, Ranger," the young man sneered.

"Take the attitude Krey took," Sam replied, "it'll likely lead you to the same place." On the sod wall, Alvin Krey's blood ran down in long strings as the dry dirt soaked it in.

The man grew even more sullen and tight-lipped. Seeing the deadlock, Heath cut in saying, "Aw hell! His name is Bill Jones. Ain't no use in jawing back and forth about it all day."

"Keep your damn mouth shut, Heath," said the surly gunman. "Maybe you want to glad-hand this lawdog and talk like you're a big drop in the bucket, but I don't."

"All he asked was your name, fool," said Heath. "It ain't worth arguing about!"

"I said shut up, Heath!" the younger man shouted. Turning his eyes to Sam, he added in a surly tone, "Anyway, I'm clean. So go back to your own damn territory, crawl back under your rock."

Sam ignored the man's belligerent attitude. To Maria he said, "All right, let's march them outside."

Maria gave the man in the top hat a harsh glare, then motioned all the men toward the doorway, saying, "*Sí*, let's go. Everybody outside, pronto!"

Outside on the narrow dirt street, Maria kept the three men standing in front of her shotgun until Sam had Toby

Burns sitting slumped, handcuffed and bleary-eyed atop a big paint horse. "Where we headed next?" Burns asked with a thick tongue, still half dazed.

"All the way back to where you broke jail, Toby," the ranger said. Leaving the paint horse hitched to the rail, Sam stepped over beside Maria and said to the young man with the crooked nose, "All right, Colbert, you can go."

"Obliged, Ranger," the young man said. He stepped forward with a look of satisfaction on his face. "My gun?" He nodded toward the blanketed doorway of the saloon.

"Pick it up your next trip through here," Sam said firmly.

"I'm never coming back here," Colbert said. "Besides, one of these snakes will have stolen it before I'm a mile down the trail. Can't I just run in there, get it and—"

"You can either get on your horse and ride," Sam said, cutting him off sharply, "or you get back in line with these other two."

Without another word on the matter, Colbert turned and hurried to the hitch rail. In a moment he'd mounted, turned his horse and left a cloud of dust looming in his wake.

Stepping over beside Sam, Maria whispered just between the two of them, "You did not believe a word he said, did you?"

"Nope, not a word," said Sam.

Maria nodded, then asked, "How much head start do you want to give him?"

"Just until he's out of sight," Sam whispered in reply. "I'd rather have him in front than behind us going down this high trail."

"*Sí*," Maria agreed, "that is what I thought."

Chapter 2

Black Mesa

No sooner had the ranger and Maria led their prisoner and the other horses around the side of the sloping land near the bottom of the tall mesa, than they caught sight of Tom Jefferson Colbert riding three hundred feet beneath them at a hard clip out onto the flatlands. "He's in a hurry to meet somebody," Sam said, scanning a few miles farther out along a meandering trail, where he spotted five riders rise up into sight, "and I expect this is them."

Maria gazed out with him, judging to herself how long it would take for Colbert and the riders to meet on the desert floor. "If they follow us, we have a half hour head start at the most," she summarized, "provided we leave quickly."

"We will," Sam reassured her. With his naked eye he still managed to see that the riders wore blue, dust-streaked army uniforms. They rode single file, but loosely, and had no military bearing about them. "This is interesting," he said.

"*Sí*, it is," said Maria, also staring intently at the riders on the desert floor.

Sam stepped down from his barb and led the prisoner and the horses to the side of the trail. He hitched the prisoner's horse to a rock crevice, pulled him down from the saddle and handcuffed him to a stirrup. Then he took out a dusty field lens from his saddlebags and wiped it off with his gloved hand.

262

"My head's killing me," Toby Burns said, his voice sounding better but still a hit groggy. "My whole right shoulder hurts like hell."

"It'll wear off soon. Stay here and don't cause us any trouble," Sam responded, ignoring Burns' aches and pains. Stepping back over to the spot that allowed a good view of the flatlands, Sam lay down on his stomach at the edge of the trail and gazed closer at the riders coming into sight. Maria had kept an eye on the desert floor. Now that Sam had returned, she stepped down from her saddle and led her horse over beside the ranger's. She came back in a crouch, slipping down beside Sam. "Do you recognize any of them?" she asked.

"Yep," said Sam, staring intently through the field lens, "the one in front wearing a lieutenant uniform is Freeman Turnbaugh." Eyeing the heavily loaded saddlebags the first two riders carried behind their saddles, he added, "Looks like they've been busy somewhere along the way."

"*Sí*, playing soldiers," said Maria.

They watched Tom Jefferson Colbert race his horse across the flatlands toward the distant riders. Studying the faces of the riders as they grew larger, he said, "I recognize these others from some Texas wanted posters that made it into the territory. The one beside Free Turnbaugh is Max Krey, Alvin Krey's brother. He likes being called Killer Krey."

"Killer Krey." Maria's hand tightened instinctively on the small of her rifle stock. "And now that you have shot his brother, he will want revenge."

"I expect he will." Sam nodded, still studying the riders, their faces, their expressions, the condition of their horses, their armament. "The two behind Turnbaugh and Krey are the New York brothers, the ones with no names."

"The ones known as the Dead Rabbits Gang?" Maria asked, all business, studying the riders as closely as she could with her naked eye.

"Yep," said Sam, "they used to belong to the Dead Rabbits

Gang." He lowered the lens, saying, "These two Dead Rabbits have made fools out of all the railroad detectives for the past year."

"And now we have stumbled upon them," Maria said, squinting slightly against the harsh glare of sunlight. "But are there any charges against any of them in our territory?"

"None that I can think of," said Sam, staring through the lens. "But charges won't make any difference once Max Krey learns that I killed his brother." He paused, and looked over toward Colbert, still a good twenty-five minutes away from the riders, but pushing his horse hard.

"How have these men moved around so freely with so many bounty hunters and detectives ready to take off their heads?" Maria asked. "This man Turnbaugh is either very brazen or completely crazy."

"Turnbaugh's not crazy. Maybe he enjoys the thrill of it," Sam commented in speculation. "He's known to live fast and loose. Maybe he likes feeling like he can move around under everybody's noses and get by with it."

"*Sí*," Maria said, contemplating along with him. "Where did they get those uniforms?" she asked a moment later.

"Off dead soldiers would be my guess." Sam studied the riders. "I saw a washed-out bullet hole on the chest of one of them. It's Harvey Fanin, I believe." He turned, silent in thought for a moment, then added, "I heard about an army payroll detail getting ambushed along the border back in June."

"Let me see," said Maria.

Sam handed her the lens, rubbed his eye and watched her study the riders for a moment. "See any more bullet holes?" he asked.

"No. Wait! Yes," Maria said. "On the trouser leg of one of the Dead Rabbits. There is a bloodstain, barely visible. They did a good job patching and washing the uniforms."

"Yep," said Sam. As he spoke he reached back inside his

memory and said, "So that ambush wasn't the Apache after all."

"You never thought it was for a moment, did you?" Maria said.

"Nope, not for a minute," said Sam. "Apache have no use for money—not in that sense. And they wouldn't have shot so many horses. Those army horses would have taken them deep into Mexico. The blanket Apache are much smarter than that." He pondered something, then added quietly, "Even the *Comadrehas* wouldn't have killed the horses."

Maria lowered the lens and gave him a pointed look. "Would not those same horses have served these just as well?"

Sam took the lens as she passed it to him. But instead of looking through it, he gazed out with his naked eyes and said, "You would think so. But Free Turnbaugh and his men must have felt cocksure of themselves. They weren't worried about having to run to Mexico if something went wrong."

"Because nothing could go wrong," Maria interjected as if completing his thought for him. "They had no need for extra horses."

"That's right," said Sam, scooting back from the edge and standing, slapping dust from his chest. "We better have a little talk with Toby Burns while we're moving along, see what he can tell us about this bunch before they get too hot on our trail."

"Good idea," said Maria, also dusting herself.

But before she and the ranger could turn toward Toby Burns, Maria saw Sam stop dusting himself and look back down onto the flatlands, where a two-horse buggy raced into sight from behind a short, stubby mesa less than a hundred yards from the riders and sped toward them. "Hold on. What do we have here?" Sam asked, pondering the big buggy as it bounced and rocked back and forth along the rough, flat trail.

Maria turned the lens back to the flatlands, studying the buggy and its driver briefly. "It is a woman, Sam," she said, sounding only a bit surprised, lowering the lens and holding it out to the ranger.

Sam took the lens, raised it to his eye for a moment, then with a stark look of surprise lowered it and said, "It's Ella Lang."

"Ella Lang?" said Maria. "*The* Ella Lang? The one who has become so popular?"

"Yep, that's her," Sam said, his voice taking on a different, softer tone. "*Lovely* Ella Lang." Sam lowered the lens for a second. "That's what the newspapers and periodicals have called her," he said tactfully, raising the lens back to his eye and adjusting it toward the buggy.

"Oh?" said Maria, coolly. "Is she indeed lovely?"

Instead of a definite answer, Sam said, "She sells lots of newspapers." He lowered the lens and handed it back to Maria. "Like you said, she's very popular."

"I see," Maria said coyly, looking back through the lens, her eyes going from the riders to the fancy two-horse rig. "She is Freeman Turnbaugh's woman?"

"I wouldn't be surprised," Sam replied. "She's known to consort with outlaws."

"Oh?" Maria caught something in Sam's voice that caused her to lower the lens an inch and give him an inquisitive look.

"Or so I've heard," Sam said. He seemed to stall for a moment, then said, "But I doubt if a woman like Ella Lang belongs to any man." He continued gazing down at the buggy as it stopped amid the riders. "I figure she's just one more member of the gang. Whatever she does, she's doing to her own advantage, like anyone else who lives that kind of life."

"Sam," said Maria, not understanding the look she saw in his eyes or the expression on his face, "you seem to know a great deal about this woman."

"I'm a lawman, Maria. I make it a point to know what I can about anybody who walks on the other side of the law," Sam replied. He added in dismissal, "Come on, we best get as far ahead of them as we can. We've done what we came here to do. So long as this bunch is in Indian Territory they belong to Judge Parker and his deputies."

"*Sí*," said Maria, studying him closely, still uncertain of what she saw in his eyes or read in his expression. "Let's get going." She gave a curious look back down toward the flatlands floor, then turned and walked with the ranger to the horses. Whatever questions she had would have to wait for now.

On the basin floor, Ella Lang let out a short squeal of laughter, with one hand holding her hat in place, as Freeman Turnbaugh's horse spun in one last quick circle and came to a sharp halt. She kissed Turnbaugh on his dusty cheek, then spit and ran a hand across her lips. "Agh! You filthy man! Put me down!" she called out playfully.

Turnbaugh squeezed her around her waist and whispered close to her ear, "God, Ella, I have missed you something awful."

"Well, you can just stop missing me right now, Free," she whispered in reply. "I'm right here." But then she pushed him back from her with a hand and said, "Now put me down this instant. How much money did we make?"

Turnbaugh chuckled. "I never like to stop and count with *federales* shooting at us."

"That's all right," said Ella. "Max will know." She turned to Max Krey, who had stepped down from his saddle and stood holding the buggy reins.

"Then let's just ask him," said Turnbaugh. Letting Ella slip from his arm to the ground, Turnbaugh called out, "Max! Here she comes. You better tell her how much we made."

Krey gazed down, then out across the rugged terrain as if not noticing the way the two had kissed deeply upon Ella's arrival. Hearing Turnbaugh call out to him, he looked around in time to catch Ella Lang in his arms as she ran to him.

Turnbaugh and the others looked on as the two kissed.

"This is the part I could do without," Harvey Fanin said sidelong and secretively to the two Dead Rabbits gunmen, who had reined their horses up beside him. He turned his eyes away from Ella and Krey.

The Dead Rabbits grinned and passed each other a glance. "Would it be a wee bit of jealousy I hear speaking?" said one to the other.

"Aye, I believe it 'tis," the other replied, neither of them looking at Fanin.

"Aw hell," Fanin growled, jerking his horse away from them, "what do you know about anything?" He gigged the horse over alongside the buggy and stopped. Peeling off his sweat-streaked wool army shirt and flinging it to the ground, he leaned low in his saddle and jerked a clean but faded plaid shirt from the pile of clothes lying behind the driver's seat.

Answering Ella, Max said, just between the two of them, "I figure it to be thirty thousand, give or take." He held Ella around her thin waist, her hands clasped behind his dusty neck. "Damn you smell good," he said.

"Pesos or greenbacks?" Ella asked, swinging herself gently back and forth in his arms.

"Both," said Max, swaying with her. "What's the difference? They both spend the same around here." He nodded toward the bulging saddlebags. "There's also plenty of Mexican gold coins . . . if you're drawn more to beauty than you are performance." His eyes made a quick dart toward Turnbaugh, then came back to hers.

"I can enjoy both, can't I?" Ella said, smiling.

"You know you can," said Max. He squeezed her. "God, Ella, it's all I can do to keep from raising this skirt over your head and falling to the ground right here and now."

"But it will be much better tonight," she said, leaning in close to his ear, "after a hot bath, a good meal, some whiskey." She nipped firmly but gently on his earlobe.

While the two whispered quietly to each other, Turnbaugh and the Dead Rabbits rode up beside the buggy, stepped down and began pulling fresh clothes from behind the driver's seat. "All right, you two," Turnbaugh said to Ella and Krey, "keep it decent. Let's get changed and count out the money. I'm tired of sleeping outdoors."

"Go on without us," said Krey, only half joking. "We'll catch up later. You can have our share."

"Huh-uh!" said Ella, giving him a shove, coming out of his loose embrace. "All this attention feels real good, but you've been gone over a month. I'm running out of *God's own medicine.*[1] Let's go."

Turnbaugh caught her by the forearm as she tried to step back up into the buggy. "How bad is it?" he asked pointedly.

"It's under control," Ella said, resisting his hold on her arm. "I haven't tried to hide it from you."

"I know you haven't, Ella," Turnbaugh said, unbuttoning the cuff of her long blouse sleeve. "But let's just take a look."

Ella sighed, and watched him shove her sleeve up her forearm until a snaking trail of needle marks appeared raw along the faint blue vein. "See, I told you I've got it under control," she said coolly. She cupped herself low on her belly. "Want to see up here too?"

"Yes, later," Turnbaugh said seriously.

Ella's mood changed quickly. "Go to hell if you don't believe me," she spat at him. "The morphine is part of the deal," she said. "If you don't want it around, you don't want me around either."

"Keep pumping it this hard and you won't be around," Turnbaugh warned. "You'll be dead."

She gave Turnbaugh an obscene gesture with her hand and jerked herself away from him. But Max Krey caught her, saying, "Easy, Ella! Free is only looking out for your best interests. He's worried about you. So am I."

---

1   *A common term in the mid-1800s for morphine.*

Ella settled, let out a breath and said, "All right, I know he is. I know you both are. But when I say I have it under control, I mean it. And I don't like being looked on and doubted by my two best friends." She glared back and forth between Krey and Turnbaugh. "Do we all understand one another?"

Freeman Turnbaugh only nodded and stepped away, saying to the other men, "All right, get a move on."

Max Krey turned a harsh glare to the Dead Rabbits and Harvey Fanin, and seeing them staring curiously, he growled, "What the hell's everybody gawking at? You heard the man. Get busy!"

As the men continued changing their clothes, Harvey Fanin looked out across the desert floor and saw the rise of dust behind the tiny spec of a rider headed toward them. "Rider coming, Free!" he said.

"Damn it," Freeman Turnbaugh said, turning his gaze in the direction of the rise of dust, "I smell trouble." As he spoke, he stepped over to his horse and drew his rifle from its saddle boot.

Chapter 3

Black Mesa

Tom Jefferson Colbert reined his tired horse to a halt and jerked it sideways to Freeman Turnbaugh and his men on the Cimarron Desert floor. "Damn, Cut-nose!" Max Krey said, stepping up and grabbing the worn horse by its froth-covered bridle. "You just about rode this poor sumbitch to death!"

"I know," Colbert said, panting, his face covered with a layer of red-gray dust. "I had no choice."

"This better be good, Colbert," Freeman Turnbaugh called out, riding his horse forward, staring at the worn horse and rider. "I told everybody to stay put up there."

"Unless we had trouble," Colbert reminded him, taking a half-full canteen from his saddle horn as he spoke, "which we do." He uncapped the canteen, took a mouthful of warm water, swished it around and spit it out in a long brownish stream. "I had to come tell you," he said, gasping, running a hand across his wet lips. "A lawdog rode in on us, took us by surprise and dragged Toby Burns out by the scruff of his neck!"

The men stared at him with cold expressions. "Dragged him out to where?" Turnbaugh asked coldly.

"Dragged him out and horsed him!" said Colbert. "I expect they're riding down the trail right now. That's why I got a head start and hurried down to tell you."

"You fools let one of Parker's deputies ride in and catch all of you by surprise?" said Turnbaugh.

"This ain't one of Parker's boys," said Colbert. "This one is a ranger—an Arizona ranger at that."

"What the hell is an Arizona ranger doing in Indian Nations?" Max Krey asked, still holding Colbert's horse by its bridle.

Standing beside her buggy, Ella Lang had watched and listened with detached interest. But now, before Colbert could offer an answer, she stepped forward and asked with a sense of urgency, "An Arizona ranger? What's he look like? What's his name?"

"I don't recall he said his name," Colbert replied. "But he travels with a Spanish woman. Arlo said he's the one who killed Montana Red Hollis and ole Bent Jackson. He never denied it."

"Sam," Ella said in almost a whisper.

"What?" Turnbaugh said, giving her a look. "Do you know this ranger?"

Ella corrected herself quickly, "Sam Burrack. Yes, I know him, or I know of him, I should say."

"You won't be knowing of him long," said Turnbaugh, giving a glance toward the distant mesas strung out across the wide desert floor. "We've got enough lawmen on our backs. We're not letting some damned Arizona ranger ride into our territory and take a man from under our noses."

Max Krey cut in, saying, "What was my brother doing all this time? He's got himself some tall explaining to do, letting this lawman—"

"Alvin's dead, Max," Colbert said, cutting him off before he chastised his brother too harshly.

"Dead?" Max Krey stared blankly at him. "What the hell are you saying, Cut-nose?"

"He's dead, Max," Colbert repeated. "The ranger shot his heart out. It was a terrible thing to see."

Max Krey stood in stunned silence for a moment, then said in a tone of controlled rage, "My brother, Alvin, is dead, and none of you sumbitches killed the lousy lawman who shot him?"

"There was nothing we could do!" Colbert said, his voice taking on a plea. "This ranger came in drawn and cocked. He had that woman behind us with a scattergun! We couldn't make a move—I swear it!"

Linston McGinty, one of the Dead Rabbit boys, whispered to his brother, Michael, standing beside him, "Step away with me, Michael *b'hoy*. There's a killing coming here."

But even as the Dead Rabbits stepped back out of the way and both Krey and Colbert closed their gun hands around their pistol butts, Turnbaugh called out, "Stand down, damn it, both of yas!"

"I come all the way down here to warn you, Free, not to get into a gunfight!" Colbert said, keeping his hand tight around his gun butt and his eyes on Krey.

"Max!" Turnbaugh shouted. "This ain't the place to do any shooting, not unless you want to warn that ranger where we are and what we're doing!"

"My brother is dead, Free, Gawddamn it! Somebody's going to pay!" Krey bellowed.

"You're right," said Turnbaugh. "This ranger is going to pay. We're going to ambush him when he comes down onto the trail. Now get your hand off that gun!"

Krey obeyed Turnbaugh's order, but he did so reluctantly, his cold stare still fixed on Colbert until he stepped back and saw Colbert remove his hand as well. "Don't think it's over between you and me, Cut-nose," he said to Colbert in a lowered, more controlled voice. "I ain't forgetting this."

Colbert didn't answer. Instead he cut his gaze back to Turnbaugh, saying, "I convinced him that I'm an out-of-work stage driver who had nothing to do with Burns or Alvin or anybody else." Offering a trace of a wry smile, Colbert continued. "He believed every word of it."

"Yeah, every word?" said Turnbaugh, cocking a brow slightly.

Colbert shrugged. "He must have. He cut me loose." His trace of a smile widened. "I can be pretty convincing, if I do say so myself."

"Are you sure he didn't cut you loose just so he could follow you?" asked Turnbaugh, his eyes cutting back across the flatlands and up the side of the mesa.

"Naw, he didn't suspect I was lying to him. Arlo vouched for me, said if the ranger left me there with them I might get hurt."

Turnbaugh considered everything for a moment, then said to everyone, "All right, all of yas finish dressing. Get those uniforms into the buggy. We've got some ground to cover before nightfall."

"Wait a minute," said Max Krey, sensing that Turnbaugh had changed his mind about ambushing the ranger. "What about my brother?"

"Not now, Max," said Turnbaugh. "He's laying in wait up there—you can bet on it." He turned to Ella Lang. "What do you say, Ella? You know that ranger. Did he fall for Colbert's story?"

Ella shook her head slowly. "Not a way in the world. If I know Sam Burrack, he's piecing together a big Swiss rifle right now. There's not a switchback in the mesa trail I'd want to ride right now."

"But my poor brother, Alvin!" said Max. "I want this ranger dead! I want him choking on his own blood for what he's done!"

"He'll have to keep, Max," Turnbaugh said in a stronger tone. "We know his name. We know where to find him. We're not going to play into his hand. Is that clear enough for you?"

Max Krey forced himself to settle down, seeing in Turnbaugh's eyes that there would no more discussion of the matter. "If you say so," he grumbled. He turned and stomped over to the buggy, where he threw in his army tunic, then stomped over to his horse, shoving his clean shirt into his trousers.

Standing close beside Turnbaugh, Ella Lang asked him in private, "Is he going to listen to you?"

"He better," Turnbaugh replied, a bit of a warning in his voice. "We're going to swing wide and go around to the other side of the mesa before we trail up. Even if that ranger is tracking Colbert he won't expect us to duck around him." He turned enough to look Ella up and down, and asked, "Will he?"

Ella sighed, considering it seriously. "I don't know. He might. He's a hard man to figure out."

"How well *do* you know him, Ella? And don't tell me you only know of him. I saw right through that one."

Ella stared at him. "You didn't see anything that surprised you, did you?"

"No surprise," said Turnbaugh. "Just that along with every other son of a bitch between here and Chicago, now I find out you've bedded down with a damned lawman."

"Go to hell, Free," Ella hissed. She turned to walk away, but Turnbaugh caught her by her arm and swung her back around, facing him.

"Listen to me, Gawddamn it!" said Turnbaugh. "He's slipped into the mesa and killed one of my top gunmen before anybody could put up a fight! I want to know who he is, and what I'm up against!"

Ella settled down and stared at Turnbaugh's hand on her forearm until he took the hint and loosened his grip. "Some folks in the badlands say he's half crazy. They say he's seen too much blood and it's left him as bloodthirsty as the ones he's hunting."

Studying her eyes, Turnbaugh saw that she didn't agree with those people. "But what do you think?"

"Crazy? I don't know. He never waits for a man to make the first move. He carries a list of men he's hunting, and when he catches up to them, they end up dead." She stared at him, took a breath and let it out slowly. "He's tough, Free. For my money we're better off staying away from him."

"And you and him . . . ?" Turnbaugh let his question trail.

"Yes, I bedded with him," Ella said, unashamed. She gazed off across endless mesas and rolling flatlands full of brush and barrel cactus. "The truth is, there's nights when I can still feel his arms around me . . . if I let myself."

"Oh, I see," said Turnbaugh.

She saw a spark of jealousy in his eyes. "You asked," she said, "so I told you. You did expect the truth, didn't you?" Her voice hardened as she continued. "From a woman who's bedded down with every son of a bitch between here and Chicago?"

"Damn it, Ella, that was just temper talking. You know I meant nothing by that little remark," said Turnbaugh.

Ella felt a familiar aching deep down in her stomach. She thought about the small leather bag waiting for her under the buggy seat, and raising a hand to Turnbaugh's cheek, she offered a tired smile and said, "I know, Free. Forget it ever happened."

Freeman Turnbaugh nodded and gestured his eyes toward Max, who had stepped up into his saddle along with the rest of the men. "Keep a close eye on him tonight, Ella," he said quietly. "I don't want him flaring up and doing something stupid."

"Don't worry," Ella said in a suggestive tone, turning and walking to the buggy. "I'll see to it he doesn't want to slip away in the night."

The group rode on toward the land sloping upward at the foot of the mesa. But instead of turning onto the steep trail Colbert had taken down to the flatlands, Turnbaugh led them onto another trail that swung around the belly of the mesa in an upward-reaching series of rocky switchback paths.

When the fading sunlight grew too dim to allow safe travel in the rugged land, Turnbaugh directed the riders off the trail to a secluded flat spot beneath a cliff overhang. Stepping down from their saddles, Turnbaugh said to the Dead Rabbit brothers, "Linston, you and your brother take down the buggy and roll it all the way back in there." He gestured toward the blackness beneath the overhang. "We'll leave it stashed here. Come morning, Ella will ride one of the buggy horses."

In the buggy, Ella quickly shoved the small leather bag inside her blouse and stepped down, turning the buggy over to the brothers. "M'lady," said Michael McGinty, giving her an assisting hand.

"I'm glad to see we've taken in some real gentlemen," Ella said, giving the younger of the two a smile in the grainy darkness.

"Anytime I can be of service, ma'am," Michael replied, sweeping his billed wool cap from his head.

As Ella walked away toward Max Krey, Linston McGinty said to his brother in a guarded tone, "Easy does it, *b'hoy*. All good things come to he who waits."

"Aye," said Michael, "I see how this works. I'm just letting her know I'm here." The two watched Ella and Max Krey walk away in the darkness, Max leading his horse, carrying a blanket over his shoulder.

"You know I can't stand still for this, Ella," Max said quietly as the two stepped into the deeper darkness beneath the cliff overhang. He handed Ella the blanket and she spread it on the ground while he dropped the saddle from his horse and laid the heavily loaded saddlebags beside the blanket.

"I know it's your brother, and I know how you feel," said Ella, lying down and stretching out on the blanket. "But Free is right—killing the ranger has to keep for now. We've got too much at stake."

"You know I'm going, though, don't you?" Max said, lying down beside her.

277

"You're putting me in a bad spot, Max," Ella whispered, her fingers reaching his shirt buttons. "I'm supposed to keep an eye on you."

"I'm making it right with you," said Max. He reached up and put a thick roll of folded dollars into her hand.

"Oh my, that feels big," Ella whispered.

As he spoke, his hand drew her riding skirt up and felt her warm skin. "All you have to do is say you had no idea what I was up to. I'll disappear in the night, kill that ranger and be back up in the mesa before midnight tomorrow." He kissed her.

But Ella cut the kiss short and said into his seeking lips, "Max, this ranger is no easy piece of work."

"I hope he's not," said Max, trying to continue the kiss as Ella pressed him back. "I want to kill him slow, him and the woman too."

"All right, Max, I've warned you," Ella said, lying back, giving in to him. "If you're not here in the morning, I didn't know a thing about it." As she unbuttoned her blouse and spread it open, she took the roll of money and the small leather bag and laid them both under the corner of the blanket.

Other Books by Ralph Cotton

The Gun Culture Series

1. Friend of a Friend   *2015*
2. Season of the Wind
...More to Come...

Western Classics

The Life and Times of Jeston Nash

1. While Angels Dance*   *1994*

2. Powder River   *1995*

3. Price of a Horse   *1996*

4. Cost of a Killing   *1996*

5. Killers of Man   *1997*

6. Trick of the Trade   *1997*

** **While Angels Dance** was a candidate for the **Pulitzer Prize** in fiction in 1994. This entire **Western Classic** series has been released and is available from Amazon.com and other retailers, as well as Kindle and other ebook formats.*

Dead or Alive Trilogy

1. Hangman's Choice   *2000*

2. Devil's Due   *2001*

3. Blood Money   *2002*

*The **Dead or Alive Trilogy** is available from Amazon.com and other retailers, as well as Kindle and other ebook formats, as part of **Ralph Cotton's Western Classics.***

Other Books by Ralph Cotton

Danny Duggin (Written for the Estate of Ralph Compton)

1. The Shadow of a Noose	2000
2. Riders of Judgement	2001
3. Death Along the Cimarron	2003

Gunman's Reputation (Lawrence Shaw)

1. Gunman's Song	2004
2. Between Hell and Texas	2004
3. The Law in Somos Santos	2005
4. Bad Day at Willow Creek	2006
5. Fast Guns Out of Texas	2007
6. Gunmen of the Desert Sands	2008
7. Ride to Hell's Gate	2008
8. Crossing Fire River	2009
9. Escape From Fire River	2009
10. Gun Country	2010
11. City of Bad Men	2011

Spin-Off Novels

1. Webb's Posse	2003
2. Fighting Men (Sherman Dahl)	2010
3. Gun Law (Sherman Dahl)	2011
4. Summer's Horses (Will Summers)	2011
5. Incident at Gunn Point (Will Summers)	2012
6. Midnight Rider (Will Summers)	2012

Other Books by Ralph Cotton

Other Books by Ralph Cotton

28. *Valley of the Gun*	*2012*
29. *High Wild Desert*	*2013*
30. *Red Moon*	*2013*
31. *Lawless Trail*	*2013*
32. *Twisted Hills*	*2014*
33. *Shadow River*	*2014*
34. *Golden Riders*	*2014*
35. *Mesa Grande*	*2015*
36. *Scalpers*	*2015*
37. *Showdown at Gun Hill*	*2015*

Stand Alone Novels

1. *Jackpot Ridge*	*2003*
2. *Wolf Valley*	*2004*
3. *Blood Lands*	*2006*
4. *Midnight Rider*	*2012*

Author
Ralph
Cotton

Ralph Cotton is a *Best Selling Author* with over *Seventy* books to his credit and millions of books in print. Ralph's books are top sellers in the Western and Civil War/Western genres, and in 2015 he debuted his new **Gun Culture** series with **Friend of a Friend**. Known for fast-paced narrative and wry dark humor, Ralph's introduction to the Florida crime fiction genre has been well received

Wolf Valley is a stand alone western novel written in 2004 and reissued in 2016 in Ralph's Western Classics group of books, as well as an ebook. It was formerly titled, *"Guns of Wolf Valley."*

Ralph lives on the Florida coast with his wife Mary Lynn. He writes prodigiously, but also enjoys painting, photography, sailing and playing guitar.

44914121R00175

Made in the USA
San Bernardino, CA
26 January 2017

Made in the USA
San Bernardino, CA
26 December 2013